CW01638705

Bundle!

Mark Fieldsend

Life is like a bundle. It's great unless you're one of the people at the bottom.

Published in 2014 by FeedARead.com Publishing

A CIP catalogue record for this title is available from the British Library.

Cover design by Luke Westwood.

Disclaimer

This is a work of fiction about events that didn't happen. References made to real persons, living or dead, are made in tribute to those who encapsulated an era and the author apologises for any offence caused.

For Monger, Horse, Rita and the Iron to commemorate a long summer spent at The Abingdon Arms.

Prologue

Statistically Safer Than Driving

Gary watched forlornly as the luggage filed past in an endless procession of boxes and suitcases, none of which belonged to him. It was probably a good thing they didn't, since he found himself standing too far back in the crowd to make a grab for any of his possessions should they ever tumble down the chute and onto the conveyor belt. As he stood there, sweating amid the hordes of impatient, agitated travellers, Gary concluded that the traumas of baggage reclaim were enough to put a dampener on even the most wonderful of holidays. No level of relaxation or pampering could adequately prepare the traveller for the stress of this penultimate leg of the homeward journey.

The money he had spent unwinding and rejuvenating was inevitably flushed down the pan the minute he took his place in the luggage queue. The feeling was analogous to being stuck in traffic on a sweltering day. Except worse. Here he was without the protective cage of the car, forced instead to stand toe to toe with the most repellent of people. And the enforced physical closeness magnified their faults to the extreme; the most minor of eccentricities sparking feelings of genuine hatred. Bad posture, whistling, the cut of a pair of trousers, the occasional sniff, a nonconformist haircut, the wearing of sunglasses, a clearing of the throat, an 'amusing' t-shirt slogan; these trivial traits all became unbearable under the circumstances, and Gary found himself plotting homicide on a sweeping scale.

But it hadn't always been like this. There was a time when he wouldn't have had to lift a finger, when somebody would have collected the many suitcases on his behalf while a team of security officers ensured he always had a sufficient level of personal space. Of all the things he craved from his former lifestyle, these services appeared towards the top of his 2003 wish list.

The man in front heaved a gigantic bag from the passing polyester stream, swinging it through the air like a makeshift club.

Such was its immense weight that he lost control of it mid-flight and it came hurtling down to earth, coming to rest sharply and painfully on Gary's right foot. Still doggedly clutching the handle, the man almost lost his balance, only the sheer density of the crowd keeping him upright.

'Jesus! Shit!' he yelled at Gary. 'Give me some room, will ya...? Hey, aren't you...?'

Gary nodded sheepishly, trying to smile despite the wincing pain that was quickly spreading across his foot.

'You are, aren't you?!' cackled the man. 'Wait 'til I tell Vicky.'

He reached excitedly into the crowd and grabbed hold of a young girl, unceremoniously hauling her through a forest of suitcases, trolleys and legs.

'Hey, Vicky! Look who it is! It's the bloke from that band.'

'Where, Daddy?' she asked innocently.

'Oh, you're probably too young to remember. He used to be...'

'Excuse me, sir,' said Gary. 'I think I've just spotted my bag.'

This wasn't actually a lie; it was more of a lucky coincidence. He stepped past the man and his daughter before plucking his suitcase from the conveyor belt. Even though he was a hundred percent certain it was his, he proceeded to examine it, carefully checking the make, the markings and the luggage tag in the hope that the man would lose patience and walk away. The last thing Gary wanted was to be recognised and have to make polite small talk with an obnoxious prick who had nearly broken his foot. Any other time he wouldn't have minded too much, but right now all he wanted was to get out of the airport and make his way home.

As he turned back towards the huddle, he was relieved to see that the man had indeed gone. Letting out a thankful sigh, he hustled his way through the crowd, keeping his head low to avoid drawing any further attention to himself. He limped uneasily towards the passageway marked out for those who had nothing to declare, grateful for the wheeled suitcase, which allowed him to maintain a brisk pace without any additional pain. So it didn't appear as though he was in too much of a hurry, he slowed as soon as he entered the tunnel, doing his best to avoid eye contact with the uniformed guards who manned the inspection tables to his left. This was a deceptively difficult thing to do without making it obvious that he was doing it on purpose. He found himself scanning the surrounding area for objects he could justifiably be interested in, peering with an exaggerated, puzzled expression at various mundane signs and other passengers.

'Excuse me, sir.'

Gary suspected the voice was aimed at him, but he ignored it, praying its owner would cut his losses and allow him to be the one that got away.

'Sir?'

The voice was more assertive this time and there was no doubt that it called for his attention. Gary quickened his pace. He could see the light at the end of the tunnel, the sanctuary of the arrivals lounge only metres away. If he could just...

'Sir!'

A wrinkled hand on Gary's shoulder stopped him in his tracks. He felt his cheeks redden as he turned to face his stalker.

'I'm sorry, I had no idea you were talking to me,' he lied unconvincingly.

'That's ok, sir. Now, if you could follow me this way, please.'

Gary reluctantly followed the old man to one of the many tables he had passed mere moments before, all the while sensing the smirks and the relief of the other passengers as they filed through uninterrupted.

'In a bit of hurry were we, sir?'

'Not really. Well, in a way, I suppose. You know how it is when you're...'

He stopped mid-sentence as he realised the luggage inspector was only making conversation and had absolutely no interest whatsoever in his answer.

'I see, I see,' said the inspector, as if to confirm this belief. 'Could I see your ticket, please?'

'Yeah, I think I've still... Here you go.'

'Thank you.' The inspector squinted at the ticket over the rim of his glasses. 'Hmm, interesting. I'd always imagined you pop stars travelled first class. Or are you *keeping it real*?'

'You could say that,' mumbled Gary.

He always found it mildly embarrassing to hear youth speak dribbling from the mouths of the elderly.

'Do you have a key for this, sir?' asked the man, gesturing towards Gary's suitcase.

'Oh yeah, sure. Sorry.'

He fumbled around in his pockets for the key to the padlock that held the two zip fasteners together. They were always miniscule and it took him some time to locate it among the tissues, earplugs, notepad, headphones and whatever else he had pilfered from the aeroplane. Despite Gary's clumsy floundering, the inspector showed no signs of impatience; after all, he had all day.

'Thank you, sir,' said the inspector upon receiving the key.

He wasted no time in opening the suitcase and began to sift through its contents without any particular thoroughness or purpose. Gary winced as his careful folding work was destroyed before his eyes. And he didn't like the way the inspector's hands seemed to linger a fraction too long on some of his more intimate garments, either. Or maybe that was just his imagination. Either way, it would all need to be washed when he got home, just to be on the safe side.

'Everything appears to be in order, sir,' announced the inspector.

Gary felt almost annoyed that his belongings warranted such a paltry search, but this irritation was far outweighed by the knowledge that he was free to continue on his way. He gave the inspector a nod of acknowledgement and then turned to leave.

'One more thing, sir.'

Gary's heart sank. What could he possibly want now? He turned back to the guard, who was clutching a piece of paper and a pen.

‘Could you possibly sign this for me?’ he said, thrusting the pen into Gary’s hand.

‘It’s for my wife,’ he quickly added. ‘She’s a big fan.’

Gary glanced at the inspector’s left hand. He wasn’t wearing any rings.

‘Sure,’ smiled Gary. ‘What’s her name?’

‘Who?’

‘Your wife. So I can write a message to her.’

‘Oh, er, don’t worry about that. Just signing *your* name will do.’

Gary scribbled his name on the piece of paper, wondering whether he genuinely looked suspicious enough to merit having his luggage searched or whether the whole thing was a ploy on the inspector’s part to get him on his own. He didn’t know which was worse.

‘Thank you, sir. That’s very kind. Have a safe journey home.’

‘Thanks,’ replied Gary, half expecting to be called back for a photograph.

But this didn’t happen, and before he knew it he was on the home straight, emerging from the claustrophobia of the tunnel into the bustle of the arrivals hall. He trod forward wearily, readying himself for any unsolicited approaches from devoted fans, celebrity junkies or people showing off to their mates. It required mental preparation to appear friendly all the time. And as was often the case, he was likely to receive a few shout outs, or even a couple of screams if he was lucky.

Somewhat disappointingly, though, the end of the fenced area was swiftly approaching and there hadn’t been so much as a whisper of recognition. Gary was starting to allow himself to relax when he detected some unusual movement in his peripheral vision. Somebody had jumped over the barrier! Experience told him that the best thing to do in a situation like this was to carry on as if nothing was out of the ordinary. For all he knew, the fence hurdler might be here to meet a loved one and couldn’t bear to spend one further moment apart. But no, the figure was heading his way, and the unidentified person was *running*, getting closer by the second!

Gary felt his heartbeat quicken. What if it was one of those crazy stalker people he had read about in the newspapers? What if he or she had been tracking his movements, waiting for an opportunity to get close to him to do who *knows* what? Gary clenched his spare hand into a tight fist and slowed slightly so that he would be ready when the stranger arrived. But the person had slowed to a far less intimidating pace by the time he or she was alongside him. Even so, Gary shot the stranger a glance to see what he was dealing with.

It wasn't a typical fan – not the young, female variety Gary was used to – but a trendy-looking man in his mid-twenties. This in itself wasn't cause for alarm, since Gary knew the group had always had a large gay following. And the man *seemed* friendly enough. He was probably after an autograph like the baggage inspector. Gary didn't particularly want to put pen to paper and spark what could be an autograph-hunting frenzy, but he figured it would be rude not to, and he could probably get away with just the one. Yet the man didn't appear to be carrying anything with him. He seemed content for the time being to walk along beside him, almost as if he were thinking up something to say. He kept opening his mouth to speak and then closing it at the last second before any sound was omitted. Then, just as Gary started to entertain the idea that the man might be mute, he plucked up the courage to say something.

'Er, hi. *Gary* isn't it?'

'Yes.'

'Hi, my name's Big D. Pleased to meet you.'

The man offered his hand for Gary to shake.

'Pleased to meet you, too.'

Gary took the man's hand, and before he knew it he was flat on his back on the cold airport floor, utterly dazed. How he had ended up there was a mystery to him as it had happened so fast. Worse still, the man was trying to clamber on top of him, stretching himself out across his midriff in some bizarre attempt to pin him down. But the worst was yet to come. With a banshee-like wail, the man let out a shout of such ferocity that Gary felt it vibrate through the very depths of his bowels.

'BUUUNDLE!!!'

'What the hell are you do—?'

There was an excited commotion to his right and Gary turned his head towards the sound, just in time to see three more men leap over the barrier.

Don't forget to double lock the front door and make sure the curtains are drawn.

Dad

We're out of milk again!

Curse of the Working Classes

If we're going to go about this in the proper fashion, I suppose I ought to start by introducing myself. Although you probably already know me anyway, or know *of* me at least. You bloody well should do. Unless, that is, you've been so absorbed by your own self-importance for the last six months you've become blind to what's going on in the big wide world around you. If that's the case then it's time for a reality check; a big one at that. Because the thing is, most people seem to know me these days. For the life of me, I can't fucking help it.

It's like, normally, when you roll into a place, people try and suss you out, form that all-important first impression. But for me it's different. They don't need to form an impression, because they already have one. They've already made up their minds.

I guess that's one of the problems with being famous.

But still, I feel I ought to introduce myself anyway, for the sake of formality if nothing else. My name's Dom Carter. Big D to my friends. *Big D*. It's a funny nickname, to tell you the truth, because I'm really not that Big, being neither tall nor fat. I'm not *Big* in the other respect either (although I often tell the ladies that therein lies the source of my title). And I'm certainly not feeling too Big right now while I'm lying here telling you all this. But Big D is what they choose to call me, and I don't find the designation disagreeable enough to tell them to do otherwise. Maybe it's because, in some ways, I'm a leader. Not in the sense that I'm some kind of dictator or that my mates hold me in particularly high regard, but in the sense that I'm an ideas man. You see, when we get up to all kinds of weird shit, I'm usually at the bottom of it.

Me and my fucking ideas.

They say every story has to have a beginning, a middle and an end, and mine has a definite starting point. It all began about nine months ago – that hot, hot summer of 2003 – with me and the Yeti sitting in our local as we do most Friday nights; the only other companions at our table a pint of bitter for me and a bottle of lager for him. Yeti isn't much of a conversationalist, more of a silent prop, so I'm pleased when Gaz rocks up to turn the company into a crowd. Gaz has a habit of arriving around half an hour late, because there's usually something on TV he just absolutely *has* to watch, like his life won't be worth living if he doesn't.

At the moment it's *Big Brother 4*, and he proceeds to tell us who's been evicted and how this isn't the outcome that has generally been anticipated by the viewing public. Like we give a shit. I don't know why he can't use a fucking video recorder like any normal person would. But at least he's here. I just received a text from Bertie saying he's got to work late and he probably won't make it. This is typical of Bertie, who has a twisted way of prioritising things. I mean, who works on a Friday night, for fuck's sake?

Despite Gaz being late, his timing is actually pretty spot on, because I'm getting to the bottom of my pint and I quite fancy another. He moans a bit that he always has to get the first full round in, tight-fisted bastard that he is, but me and Yeti say that it serves him right for always being so fucking late.

'Same again. And don't forget the pork scrotums,' we instruct him as he mopes off to the bar while we finish our drinks. He's bound to take his time getting served like he always does, being as he is, so goddamn polite. A real British queuer is Gaz.

Beyond commenting on his lateness, me and Yeti don't say much while we wait for Gaz to return. You may wonder why we bother coming out if we're not going to speak to one another, but our friendship is such that we don't always feel the need to talk. You know how it is, some people you just feel comfortable to be around, whether they say anything or not. Plus I'm convinced that one day Yeti will open his mouth and come out with something truly astonishing, and I want to be there when he does. I'm not talking about a baffling statistic or a hilarious anecdote, either. I'm talking about a scientific breakthrough on the scale of space travel, or hard evidence for the existence of God.

This aside, our early arrival allows us to put in the groundwork for the session and, more importantly, gives us the chance to nab a decent table. If available, we always grab the one near the jukebox, given that it provides the best view of the pub and we can keep a close watch on all the T&A on show. And there's usually plenty. I promise you, most Fridays you can't move for fanny in this place. The table also gives rise to the opportunity for some convenient flirting as the totty come to choose their tunes. Gloria Gaynor and Sister Sledge. Women are so fucking predictable when it comes to music.

'Here you go, boys,' says Gaz as he slides the drinks onto the table. He appears to have forgotten the scratchings, but this may be for the best, so neither of us mentions it.

Judging by the spillage gap at the top of my pint, you would think he'd had to negotiate a *Crystal Maze* physical challenge to carry it here. Gaz hasn't got great balance; it has something to do with the accident he had a few years back when he lost his left ear. He wears a prosthetic one now. Luckily for him, it's pretty convincing, and his indie-kid hairstyle serves well to conceal it. However, he finds being the world's most drunk-looking sober man more difficult to hide.

'Where's Bertie?' queries Gaz, wiping the froth from his upper lip with his sleeve.

'He says he might not make it,' I reply.

'Jesus,' mutters Gaz, shaking his head like he's just been told his house has been burgled. I don't know why he's acting so surprised; we've come to expect this from Bertie of late.

'What about Volkan?' asks Gaz.

Man, you'd think our company wasn't good enough for him, he seems so goddamn eager for others to arrive.

'Dunno,' I answer, 'he never said he wasn't coming.'

'Here he comes now,' Yeti pipes up, and nods his matted locks in the direction of the bar.

Sure enough, Volk is strutting his way through the bar like he's some sort of celebrity, your archetypal man's man, feet pointed slightly outwards as though the toes of his trainers contain repellent magnets that prevent them from moving too close together. He's a cocky lad is Volk, especially after he's been playing football, which on this occasion I believe he has.

'Evenin' fellas,' he says, briskly rubbing his hands together, like he's psyching himself up for the commencement of some kind of strenuous task. 'Where's the Bertmeister?'

'Working late,' me and Gaz reply in unison.

'Fuckin' typical,' curses Volk. 'You guys sorted for drinks?'

We all nod. I've barely touched my second pint. Volk disappears as quickly as he arrived, wasting no time in getting to the bar. And it's just the three of us again. The three amigos. The three musketeers. Ours is the group within the group, mainly because we all work together at the local Italian restaurant. You'd think we'd be sick of each other's company by now, but it doesn't ever seem to get that way.

'Ah, shit! I forgot the pig foreskins,' curses Gaz, the heavy change in his pocket suddenly revealing his mistake to him.

He starts to get up, but we tell him it doesn't matter.

'How's things with Michelle?' I ask Volk when he returns.

'Not too bad,' he replies with a total lack of conviction. 'She keeps hinting we should move in together, though.'

The rest of us exchange glances, knowing Volk's days of freedom are numbered. Despite his cocksure attitude, he has this total inability to say no to people. Here's the man who ducked into a travel agent's to shelter from the rain and emerged with a trip for two to the Pyrenees.

'Did you net today?' I ask him, changing the subject to one he's more comfortable with.

'Yeah, I notched a brace in a 2-0 victory. One was a penalty.'

'Good stuff, Volk. How many's that for the season?'

'Twenty-six.'

'Fuckin' hell,' exclaims Gaz. 'It's not even halfway through yet.'

'Yeah,' says Volk bashfully, 'it's been a potent couple of months.'

'You asked that barmaid out yet, Gaz?' I change the focus of the conversation once more, in case Volk starts boasting. Not that he would, but better safe than sorry.

'Not yet,' Gaz replies, clearly embarrassed.

His answer comes as no surprise. He's fancied her for weeks, but we all know he doesn't have the guts to do it. He claims to be waiting for the right moment, but I hate to think what this would constitute. He's probably holding out for the day when he can approach her to the gentle throngs of a string quartet while rose petals float down from the sky, forming the shape of a heart on the warm, white sand beneath their feet. Once upon a time he would've just gone up and done it, but his confidence has taken a bit of a bashing since the ear thing. You see, most of his recent forays into the world of women ended somewhat abruptly once the lady in question discovers he's missing a shell. It's pretty shallow on their part really, but I guess it must come as quite a shock when your partner places an ear on the bedside table before hitting the sack.

'You'd better not wait *too* long, 'cause girls like that don't stay single for long,' I tell him.

Like he doesn't already know.

'Do you honestly expect me to stroll up and ask her at the bar? She'll think I'm a drunken tosser,' argues Gaz.

He's probably right. Barmaids must get asked out all the time. Especially ones of the blonde hair and big boobs variety, of which she's a prime example. From what I've seen, she's never more than a couple of weeks without a boyfriend, that girl. She's one of those birds that *needs* to be in a relationship. I'd be tempted to label her a slag if it wasn't for the fact that Gaz likes to think of her as his future wife. Instead, we've come to a mutual understanding she's 'open-minded' when it comes to choosing potential partners, but also quick to recognise when she isn't dating Mr Right. And anyway, apparently she's too good looking to be a slag.

However, 'slag' is a description befitting a number of the women in this place tonight, which I'm not ashamed to admit is part of the reason we always come here. It certainly isn't for the décor, which looks like it's been thrown together by a GCSE woodwork class. Dawn, sitting at the table to our left, is a classic example. This is a girl who, according to Volk, has accommodated the penises of more than half the local football team at one time or another. And then some. If she's trying to work her way through the town's male population, she's doing a commendable job. In fact, Dawn is a bit like a sexual Wheel of Fortune: round and round she goes, where she'll stop, nobody knows. And by the sounds of it she's a firm believer in killing two birds with one stone, if you know what I mean.

It would probably be possible to get away with this level of promiscuity if you lived in a large, anonymous city like London, but word gets around quickly in a place like this. Not that it should bother her in the slightest, as I'm sure her reputation works in her favour; the end more than justifying the means. Besides, while none of us would actively pursue her, I think I'm safe in saying that no-one sitting at our table would turn her down given the option. Except maybe Yeti, who we suspect may be gay. And Gaz always tries to gain the moral high ground by saying he wouldn't touch her for shit, but we all know this is pure bravado, and if it came down to it his pants would be around his ankles as quickly as they would for the rest of us.

You see, back at school, Dawn was a bit of a stunner, and while I wouldn't try to claim that time has been kind, she hasn't completely let herself go either. I guess you could say she's filled out a bit, but her newly developed curvaceous physique fits well with her general image. And there is definitely something to be said for her tight black top, which exposes a cleavage that would require crampons and ropes to safely negotiate; the hooped earrings, which are so big budgies could perch from their lower rim; and a belt of such girth that she must have stolen it from "Macho Man" Randy Savage. Believe me, it doesn't matter who you are, when you're in a certain frame of mind there's no substitute for a filthy-mouthed rude-girl in fuck-me boots.

She's ripe for a one-night stand is Dawn; the kind of girl young boys dream of losing their virginity to. Me, I'm not asking for much, a mere ten minutes with those breasts and I'd be happy. But all this chat and fantasising is inconsequential. To Dawn we're invisible, part of the furniture. We certainly don't fit the bad boy image she tends to go for. You see, girls like her aren't impressed by style or wit, they just want some charmless, would-be gangsta to drive them about in a customised Golf, buy them a couple of Bacardi Breezers and give them a good seeing to come the end of the night.

'What you up to this weekend, Dom?' asks Volk.

'You know, the same old shit,' I reply, "the same old shit" meaning nothing in this case.

I never really made time in the week to plan this weekend, which means I'll probably be sitting around the house for most of it and back in here tomorrow night for more of the same. I suppose we could all go into Oxford for a change of scenery, but I'm feeling a bit skint and don't know whether I can be bothered to make the extra effort.

'What about you?' I ask half-heartedly.

'Oh, you know,' smiles Volk, 'same old shit.'

I could go around the rest of them and ask the same question, but I'd only get two more identical answers. It makes me laugh in a way. None of us have progressed very far down the path to independence and maturity in the three years since graduation. Perhaps that's one of the reasons we get on so well. Out of the group, the absent Bertie is the only one who's not living with his parents. And Bertie is the only one in a job he'd still be happy to be doing in a couple of years. The rest of us are just kind of drifting along, waiting for somebody to sort our lives out. I can't really imagine who's going to stop by and point me in the right direction, though – I'm relying on the existence of a local good Samaritan. I accept that such a person is unlikely to be found at the pub.

The glass collector is doing her rounds and we fall silent as she plucks the empties from the table. She's a beauty, no doubt about it. Better still, when she bends over you can catch a glimpse of her thong poking out the top of her jeans and we all take a good, long look at the closest thing to a bare arse any of us will see tonight. We're a sad bunch, I won't try and fool you into thinking otherwise. Volk is the odd one out in that he's actually got a girlfriend, although most of the time he probably wishes he hadn't. I can't tell you how much *I* could do with a girlfriend right now to help pass away these endless summer months.

I glance over in Dawn's direction and she happens to be looking right back. Eye contact: the first sign of attraction. I don't read anything into this, mind you. If you stare at someone for long enough, they're bound to look back eventually; to see what the hell you're gawping at if nothing else.

The girl picks up the last of the glasses and drifts away. We continue to sit in silence, our heads filled with carnal thoughts rather than ideas for conversation. I'd like to think I could pull her if I tried. I concede that she's way out of my league in the looks department, but she's a glass collector for fuck's sake. By comparison, my waiting job working for the greasy Italians is a highly skilled vocation. *And* I've got a degree, which some might argue makes me her intellectual superior. In that respect, I'd be a good catch from her point of view. But there's always the chance she's only doing the job to pay her way through university, meaning she's intelligent and self-motivated as well as fit.

Plus, more importantly, it would be a significant blow to my ego to be turned down. It's a common male fallacy to think you're more desirable to the opposite sex than you are in reality. Deep down, most blokes know this to be true, which is why it takes us so fucking long to ask a woman out. You see, a bloke always thinks he's in with a chance, right up until the point when a move is made. At this point he either scores or it's crash and burn time, and believe me when I say that the latter is a belittling experience quite unlike any other. Hence there is considerable comfort in admiring from afar, in sitting back and thinking: 'I could have her if I *really* wanted to'. This way, the opportunity eternally exists, because she hasn't actually turned you down yet. It's kind of like that Schrödinger's cat stuff. She simultaneously fancies you and doesn't fancy you, but it isn't until you open the box that you find out which it is, at which point the other reality is destroyed and there's no chance of ever getting it back. And when it comes to asking a girl out, I would generally put my money on the pussy being dead.

But anyway, all this philosophising is inconsequential, because I'm not going to ask her out. I'm just chatting bare breeze.

'She is *well* slick,' swoons Volk. Dirty minds think alike.

'You can't say that!' protests Gaz. 'You're virtually married!'

'Married? We're not even living together yet.' *Yet.* 'Besides, you're allowed to look.'

'I'm sure Michelle does,' I quip.

'What's that supposed to mean?' demands Volk.

'Come on, mate. Do you honestly think that because she's going out with *you* she's immune to the charms of the rest of the male population?'

Volk doesn't answer, and I can tell by his face he doesn't like what I'm saying, so I make moves to save his ego.

'Everybody looks, it's human nature. Just as long as they don't touch.'

'Well, *she* certainly doesn't,' Volk affirms. 'And neither do I.'

'Oooh, defensive,' mocks Gaz. 'Is there something you should be telling us?'

'The only thing I'm going to tell you is to FUCK OFF,' grins Volk. 'Why can't one of you lot get a love life? Then you wouldn't have to take the piss out of mine all the time.'

It's a fair question.

'I think it's better this way, mate,' I say, patting his back in a condescending manner.

'Wankers,' he mutters, chuckling to himself as he takes a swig of his pint.

'How was work today, Volk?' Gaz puts an end to the piss-taking by throwing in a serious question.

'Not too bad. Except that I got a bit of a bollocking from my boss.'

'What for?' I ask.

Volk is such a butt-kisser when it comes to work, I can't imagine him ever getting a dressing down. Unless they got sick of his tongue poking around their arses all the time.

'Pissing on the floor,' he announces, and I almost choke on my pint.

'Pissing on the floor?!' Gaz is laughing so much he can barely speak. 'What, you got your knob out and took a piss on the office carpet?'

'No,' chuckles Volk, 'as if I'd do that! No, it was in the toilets, but I kind of missed the bowl.'

'Missed the bowl!?'

We scrunch our eyebrows in bewilderment. Poor aim is something most people have overcome by the time they leave infant school.

'But how the hell did they ever know it was you?' I question. 'I mean, it's not the kind of thing you normally bring up in office conversation. "Hey, guess what guys? I just pissed all over the floor."'

'The manager used the toilet after me. He said, "Look's like we've got a leak," so I said, "Actually, that was me." Cue bollocking. Well, more of a stern lecture.'

Gaz shakes his head.

'You twat.'

'Like it's never happened to you before!'

'Not recently, no! I mean, what the fuck were you doing? Didn't you bother holding on or something? Were you seeing what would happen if you left it to its own devices?'

'You know how it is,' Volk argues. 'Like in the morning sometimes when it comes out at a funny angle.'

'Or twin jets,' adds Yeti, who suddenly wakes up from his hibernation.

'What the fuck causes twin jets, anyway?' I ask. 'A random blockage in the jap's eye?'

'Dunno,' Volk replies, 'but it was that kind of problem at work.'

'You should've adopted the superman position,' I tell him, extending a clenched fist and pretending to lean against an imaginary wall.

'It's all very well with hindsight,' says Volk.

'Faced with that situation I'd usually take a seat,' I advise him further.

Listen to me, an authority on pissing. It's funny how you suddenly become a pseudo-intellectual the minute you set foot in a pub, thinking you can speak intelligently and credibly on any given subject, be it sporting injuries, the political situation in Zimbabwe or the problems associated with urinating.

Further means of remedying an erratic flow are nipped in the bud when a large hand is placed on Volk's shoulder. We all turn around to see who it is and are greeted by a familiar face, a real blast from the past. It's Bummole.

'Alright lads?' he says, delivering a quick glance around the group to acknowledge us.

'Alright Bummole?' comes our staggered reply.

He obviously wants to chat, but none of us have anything we particularly want to say to him. When you haven't spoken to somebody for about eight years, you're virtually demoted to stranger status again; strangers that recognise each other, which is pretty much the worst thing you can be. Sometimes it's easier to just walk on by, but evidently Bummole doesn't agree. Luckily for the rest of us, though, he chooses Volk as his main victim. I think they used to play football together, so I guess he knows him a bit better. They quickly dive into the subject of the beautiful game, asking each other if they still play and so on. From what I can gather, Bummole *doesn't* play anymore. To be fair, I could've guessed this from a brief assessment of his physique, which is far from what you would call athletic. And with no new sporting triumphs to speak of, he opts to reminisce about the glory days, back when he and Volk were about fifteen and playing in the same team. Every sentence starts with: 'Do you remember the time when…?' or 'What about the match when…?' Volk looks bored within about two minutes, but Bummole's had a few and he isn't going to stop in a hurry. I turn back to the rest of the group.

'Remind me why he's called Bummole again?' queries Gaz softly.

'Not really sure,' I reply in similarly hushed tones. 'He's always been called that. Apparently even his mum calls him it. The only explanation for its origin I've ever heard is that his face looks like a bum hole.'

Gaz laughs while Yeti grins from ear to ear, revealing a set of faultless teeth. This is the only aspect of Yeti's physical appearance you could describe as faultless. And I don't mean that in a bad way. You see, like a lot of people these days, his general style is one of deliberate scruffiness, but he just happens to be in possession of a pearly set of chompers that would be the envy of Hollywood's finest.

'He'll forever be known as Bummole,' I continue. 'When he gets married, the vicar will say: "Do you, Bummole, take this lady to be your lawfully wedded wife?" And when he dies, the name "Bummole" will probably be on the headstone. Otherwise, nobody would know who the fuck the grave belonged to.'

'What actually *is* his name?' asks Gaz.

'Bummole,' I reply.

'Ha ha. No, what's his *real* name?'

'Bummole.'

'What was he christened?' Yeti butts in. 'Pedantic fucker.'

'Don't know,' I admit. 'I've always known him as Bummole. I'll find out.'

I turn to ask the man himself, but he looks to be in full flow, so I decide against it. Instead, I listen to what he's saying, wondering what the hell he's spouting on about that's so important it requires an intense stare and lots of pointing.

'Do you remember the penalty I scored in the 2-1 victory over Flackwell Heath?'

'No, that one also seems to have slipped my mind,' sighs Volk.

'It was one-all with only three minutes to go and Ryan was brought down in the area. I took on the responsibility, having already netted early in the first half. It was a textbook penalty. I saw the keeper move to the left, so I placed it calmly to the right. Goal. Never a doubt in anyone's mind. And what about that volley I got against Bourne End?'

I glance over at Volk to gauge his reaction. His expression is a mixture of extreme boredom and utter contempt. And by the way he's handling his pint, I'm concerned he might glass him at any moment. He doesn't say much, just nods every now and then or utters the occasional word.

'No, I don't remember that one, but I'd really love to hear about it.'

To me the sarcasm is clear, but it's lost on Bummole, who describes the goal in vivid detail, right down to the fact that he struggled to turn in the mud due to a missing stud on his left boot. It's amazing the things people remember sometimes. When I turn back to the other two, I see that they too are listening, each wearing an expression of entertained bemusement.

It's a good fifteen minutes or so before Volk rejoins the group, and he looks like he's lost the will to live.

'I thought he'd never fucking leave,' he moans. 'He talked me through his whole fucking goal-scoring career.'

‘Weird bloke,’ comments Gaz, a succinctly accurate description if ever there was one.

‘You don’t say! I mean, he was a good player, but the way he was talking you’d think he was a pro!’

‘What’s he doing now?’ I ask with genuine curiosity.

I’m always interested to hear what other people are up to in the hope that their embattled lives make me feel better about my own mediocre existence. I can’t help but feel I’ve underachieved up to this point in time. The one saving grace is that there’s plenty of it left.

‘No idea. He walked off after he’d recounted his last goal for the under-16s. Fucking twat. Warn me if he comes back so I can hide in the toilet or something.’

‘Will do. Were *any* of his stories interesting? One of them must’ve been, you were talking to him long enough.’

‘Er, maybe a couple. I wouldn’t have talked to him for so long, but it’s quite hard to end a conversation without being rude.’

‘Why should you care?’ Gaz has a point.

‘I don’t dislike the guy, he’s just a bit dull.’ Typical Volk, the eternal Mr Nice Guy when it comes to people he doesn’t know very well. ‘I don’t particularly want to offend him to spare five minutes of my time.’

‘Fifteen minutes,’ Yeti corrects him.

‘Whatever. Anyway, he reminded me of this time when he got injured from being bundled after he scored a goal. I’d forgotten about that, and looking back it was fucking hilarious.’

Bundle. Now there’s a word you don’t hear used very often these days, at least not in *this* context. It’s one of those things from your childhood you take for granted at the time, but then completely forget about until it’s randomly brought up again during your adult years. Stuff like *Fingermouse*, British bulldog, *Garbage Pail Kids* and those ice creams where you get a couple of gobstoppers at the bottom of the plastic cone. Back in the days of primary school innocence, not a break time would pass without at least one unfortunate person being pinned to the tarmac by a mound of bodies, the victim's laughter turning to screams as what started off as a bit of fun grew more and more painful with each extra body that jumped onto the heap. But now, aside from the occasional half-hearted effort you see on the football field, the act (or should that be *art*) of bundling is something that is rarely seen.

It's a tragedy in a way, because the bundle was a wonderful thing. What better way to bring a person down to size than to throw them on the ground, lie on top of them and openly invite others to do the same? What better image can you think of to symbolise a victory for the masses against a dominant individual? Such a simple concept, yet so flawlessly effective. Once underneath a couple of bodies, the person at the bottom is helpless and has to lie back and take what's coming to them. And due to its improbable form – like a gigantic Alsatian has swallowed a bunch of people whole and then taken a crap – the bundle also brings amusement to the casual onlooker. Basically, you can't beat a good bundle.

'It's time to resurrect the bundle,' I announce.

The others stare at me blankly, and I realise this statement sounds like madness when spoken in isolation. I'm going to need to take a slightly more persuasive route if I'm to successfully convert the masses.

'Tell me, Gaz, when was the last time you bundled someone?'

'Don't know, I can't re–'

'Volk?'

'Ages ago. Probably not since secondary sch–'

'How about you, Yeti?'

'No idea, mate.'

'I thought as much. Ok, think back to the last time you *were* involved in a bundle. Tell me, was it not fucking superb?'

Again I'm faced by perplexed looks, all three expressing bafflement in their own familiar way. Gaz cocks his head at a funny angle, Yeti looks for the answer in the wet patch beneath his pint glass and Volk peers down his nose at me like I'm some sort of cunt.

'Well, as far as I remember – and I don't think I'm picturing it to be better than it was just because it's in the past – bundling was quality.'

A smile edges its way across Gaz's lips and I'm relieved that at least *he* has seen the light, even if the other two remain unconvinced. But a single believer is no good to me, as bundling requires weight of numbers. I continue with a specific example to jog their memories.

'Remember that time we got put in detention for bundling that bloke Monger while we were waiting to get into the science block?'

'Oh yeah,' grins Yeti. 'I remember that. Monger had to go home to change because his Capri-Sun exploded over his shirt under the weight. That was well funny.'

'*Finally* you see what I'm talking about.'

That's two out of three. Well, two out of four really, but since Bertie isn't here I'll have to tell him about it another time. Only Volk remains and he's usually the hardest to convince to do stuff like this because he's forever trying to maintain his fly image. The amount of stuff he refuses to do in case it damages his man-about-town reputation is unreal, and it's made all the more frustrating by the fact that he doesn't actually have one.

'And *who* exactly do you propose that we bundle?' he asks.

Typical Volk, always worried over trivialities. He can be so fucking anal at times.

'I don't know! Do you expect me to have drawn up a list already?'

'Just asking. There was me thinking you might've thought this one through properly for a change.'

His attitude riles me, especially since he's dismissed my idea before I've even had the chance to build up a head of steam. I need to respond quickly to save face, and my mind races for possible targets as I glance around the room for inspiration. A red-top in the newspaper rack comes to my aid and I read out the first word of today's front page headline.

'Celebrities.'

A dramatic pause follows that couldn't have worked better if I'd planned it.

'Celebrities,' repeats Volk, just to confirm he heard correctly.

'Celebrities,' I say again, just to confirm he *has* heard correctly.

'You're proposing that we bundle celebrities.' He delivers the words as a statement rather than a question.

'That is *exactly* what I'm proposing. You're *real* quick today, Volk.'

'You're insane, Big D. Of all the ridiculous ideas you've ever come up with, *that* is the most ridiculous so far. *By far* the most ridiculous, in fact. Even the sponsored cowpat sit made more sense than this.'

'What you talking about? It makes perfect sense,' I argue.

'Well I'm sorry to put a dampener on your great plan,' he takes an exaggerated look around the room and then holds his hands out with open palms, 'but I don't see any celebrities in here tonight.'

'Don't be so fucking short-sighted. Imagine if the person who invented autograph hunting had thrown out the idea because of a lack of celebrities in the immediate vicinity!'

The other two lean back in their chairs and assume the role of spectators as me and Volk set to engage in a battle of wills that neither of us is prepared to lose. Many an argument boils down to me and Volk at loggerheads, mainly because he can be so goddamn opinionated. If Dirty Bertie were here he probably would've joined in as well – whether he felt strongly about the subject or not – but Gaz and Yeti tend to sit back and watch in these situations.

'Getting someone to sign a piece of paper and throwing them to the ground before lying on top of them are hardly the same thing, Dom.'

'What difference does it make? If you're close enough to hand them pen and paper, you're close enough to bundle them.'

'Ok, ok. But how the hell do you suggest we track down these *celebrities*?'

'I admit that I haven't really thought that far ahead yet. But how hard can it be?'

'Pretty fucking hard. If there was a way of easily locating celebrities, don't you think you'd already be doing it? I mean, you for one would've found a way to meet Britney Spears a long time ago.'

Too fucking right I would. Britney is a goddess without peer, the world's most precious diamond. Absolutely no doubt about it. I hear people bandy about names like Lopez or Minogue, but they don't even come close. They're not even in the same *league* as the pop princess. To meet the exquisite Miss Spears would be to fulfil the first of only two genuine ambitions. The achievement of the second is closely related, but it would require her to accept my hand in marriage, and is therefore even more farfetched than the first.

'Britney, will you marry me?'

'Yes! Nothing in the world would make me happier! When I broke up with Justin, it was because I knew there was somebody out there like you. Now let's go to my hotel room and you can show me why they call you Big D…'

Let's face it – it's not going to happen.

'Not *specific* celebrities. Like I said before, it will be like autograph hunting. We'll be opportunists.'

'Opportunists?'

'Yeah, opportunists!' What started off as a bit of a joke is actually beginning to make sense to me, and I find myself getting excited at the prospect of putting the plan into action. 'For example… let's say that, purely by chance, we stumble across a celebrity, I don't know, waiting at a train station or something. Whereas a normal person might go up to them and make small talk or maybe ask for an autograph or a photo, *we* will bundle them.'

Out of nowhere, Gaz suddenly starts to show some real enthusiasm for the idea.

'Lads, this plan sounds like a good'un. I'm in.'

'Me too,' follows Yeti.

'How much have you lot had to drink?' questions Volk. 'Look, I can see how it might work, and that it could be fun…'

'Fun?!' I interrupt. 'It would be immense!'

'I can see how it could be fun,' repeats Volk, 'but there's one pretty major flaw. Bundling people was all very well when we were five foot tall. But bundling a fully grown man – or woman for that matter – is a whole different kettle of fish.'

'Why? We're bigger too, so it shouldn't make any difference.'

'Prove it.'

'OK, I will. Who shall we bundle?'

I survey the pub and find myself faced with an abundance of riches; everyone is a possible target. It's an important decision, though. I'll be proving a point and failure is not an option. Therefore, it can't be anyone too big. And it's essential to try and assess how the person might react to being bundled. Many people would take it in jest, but there are those that wouldn't and the last thing I want is for the exercise to degenerate into a brawl.

'It should be someone we know, even if it's only vaguely,' I say, taking the above into account.

'How about Dawn?' suggests Gaz. 'I bet you wouldn't mind being pressed up against her, hey Big D?'

He's not wrong. As a matter of fact, it's not a bad idea at all, especially if I could somehow manage to palm it off as an accident by pretending to trip or something. I imagine it would be quite enjoyable to splay myself across her voluptuous body, stomachs touching, my left arm resting against her heaving breasts. The very thought of it is enough to give me a semi.

'No,' I reply. 'She'd probably think I was trying to molest her.'

'Which is essentially what you would be doing,' accuses Volk.

'Give me *some* credit,' I protest. 'But seriously, I don't want to end up getting arrested for attempted rape, so I think we should choose a bloke. How about Bummole?'

They all nod slowly in approval.

'Any advance on Bummole? No? Good. Bummole it is then. It will serve the fucker right for almost boring Volk to death earlier on. But first, to christen the rebirth of bundling and the *birth* of celebrity bundling, I think it's only right that we drink a toast from the ear.'

We all turn to Gaz, who holds up his hands and backs away slightly.

'No way, guys. Not a chance. It took me fucking *hours* to rinse out the After Shock last time.'

'Then we'll drink something a bit less sticky. Like vodka.'

'No.'

'Come on, mate, it's a worthy cause. In fact, you should feel privileged. I almost wish I had a fake ear myself so *I* could do the honours.'

'Now you're just taking the piss.'

'I'm not, honestly. Come on, it's not as if we ask you all the time.'

'You ask me every bloody week! The answer's no.'

'Come on, Gaz, you know you love it,' bullies Volk, vigorously ruffling his friend's mop-like hair.

'No! Get the fuck off me, you weirdo!'

Volk retreats and we all lean back in our chairs and stare at Gaz with a combination of disapproval and disappointment, shaking our heads and raising our eyebrows at one another while making clicking noises with our tongues. We want to make it clear we think he's being a big baby about the whole thing and has gone way down in our estimation. It doesn't take long for him to cave in.

'Oh, for fuck's sake. Go on then. But this is the *last* time. Never again. You understand that? Never.'

'Until the next time!' I laugh, and scurry away to the bar.

I soon return with four shots of vodka and am pleased to see that Gaz's prosthetic ear is lying on the table as promised. They don't do proper shot glasses in this place, so I'm left carrying four half-pint glasses that hold so little liquid it looks as if someone came along and spat in some empties. This simple fact makes the ear thing all the more appealing.

'Who's going first, then?' I ask.

'You, I suppose,' proposes Gaz, 'seeing as this bundling nonsense was your bright idea.'

'But it's your ear,' I remind him. 'You should go first.'

'No, really, I insist. You go. And don't bite it like last time, 'cause it ain't funny.'

'Well, in the absence of pork scratchings… No, I promise I won't bite it.'

I take the ear and rub it briskly against my jumper to remove any remnants of Gaz's hair that might be stuck to it.

'Be gentle!' he protests, and I mouth the word "Sorry" to him across the table.

I transfer the ear to my left hand and hold it in front of me like an oyster shell. Resting the rim of the glass against the curl of the outer lobe, I slowly pour the vodka into the well at its centre. Like every other time we do this, the ear looks like it'll come up short in the capacity stakes and I'm going to end up spilling vodka all over the table. But the carefully crafted dips and valleys are deceptively deep and the whole twenty-five millilitres fits with room to spare. I hold the brimming, pseudo-cartilaginous shell triumphantly in front of me and propose a toast.

'*Ear's* to celebrity bundling,' I bellow in the deepest, manliest tone I can muster, knocking the vodka back in one swift gulp.

I wince almost immediately, the burning in my throat drowning out the applause from around the table. Vodka tastes like crap at the best of times, let alone the warm, cheap shite I just purchased. When I feel confident enough about opening my mouth without the fear of choking or retching, I offer the ear to the rest of the gang.

'Who's next?'

They take it in turns to toast the beginning of our new hobby: Gaz first, then Volk, and finally Yeti. Understandably, Gaz refuses to put the ear back on after the last of the shots, informing us that he'll have to go home and disinfect it first. I tell him I'd have thought the vodka would do that anyway, but he won't be persuaded, so he tucks it into his back pocket instead.

'You'd better hope I don't pull tonight,' he says.

'You won't,' I reassure him. 'Anyway, I guess it's time. Volk, call Bummole over, will you?'

'What the fuck am I supposed to talk to him about?'

'I don't know. He used to play tennis as well, didn't he? Get him started on that and let *him* do the talking.'

Volk stands up and beckons to Bummole while I whisper some brief instructions to Yeti. Bummole wastes no time in strolling over to us, and he's looking pretty damn pleased with himself at having received the invitation. Such innocence. It's like a lamb to the slaughter…

So as not to seem too suspicious, we let Bummole talk at Volk for a bit and continue to drink our pints as if everything is normal. After a couple of minutes, I call Yeti on his mobile and then hang up as soon as he answers. Yeti speaks to the imaginary person on the other end of the line, then gets up from his seat and walks to the left of where Bummole and Volk are standing. His spare hand is clasped over his ear, like he's struggling to hear above the noise of the pub. I get up about thirty seconds later and make like I'm heading to the toilet. I stop to talk to Bummole on my way past.

'How's it going, Bummole?' I ask with fake enthusiasm.

'Not too bad, mate. How about yourself?'

I can tell by his face that although he recognises me, he can't remember my name. This is a blessing in disguise, as it is yet another thing to distract him from what's about to happen.

'Pretty good, thanks,' I reply. 'Hey, I like your shirt. Where did you get it from?'

Bummole glances down to check which shirt he's wearing and as he does so, Yeti crouches down on the floor immediately behind him and curls up in a ball.

'Oh, this is an old one. It's from Topman I th– Aaaah!'

He cries out in fright as I shove him hard with both hands and he topples over Yeti, the human tripwire. His momentum sends him skidding a few feet across the floor, legs and arms flailing in the air like an upturned tortoise being used as a curling stone. Before he has a chance to gain composure, I'm on top of him, lying over him at right angles so that together we form a human St George's Cross.

'BUUUNDLE!' I holler through my excited laughter, as the weight of Yeti crashes in on top of me.

He's quickly followed by Gaz and then Volkan, Bummole yelping with surprise as each impact knocks the wind out of his nicotine-filled lungs. I expect it to end here, but a couple of randoms who happen to be walking past on their way to the bar jump on as well. A couple more thuds tell me the total has reached eight and Bummole now forms the foundation of a messy tower constructed from more than half a ton of solid bloke. I strain my neck upwards to see a huge man in a black jacket striding over in our direction. Someone could get seriously injured if this man mountain decides he wants to form the summit and I begin to panic. But then it twigs that his intentions are entirely different.

'Bouncer! The bouncer's coming!' I yell as best I can, the mass of bodies above me hindering my ability to achieve maximum volume.

The message seems to get through, though, and I feel the load lighten as people scarper in all directions to escape the reprimand that's about to be dished out. I didn't even know they had security in this place, but suddenly they're everywhere – at least four of them, all ready to inflict heavy-handed retribution on our prone frames.

I feel myself being hauled up by the collar and marched towards the exit. I try to dig my heels in, but soon realise that resistance is futile when faced with such brute force. I may as well have been wearing roller skates for all the difference it's making. I'm shoved out onto the pavement where Volk, Gaz and Yeti are already standing, all looking suitably ruffled up and agitated.

'You're barred, the fucking lot of you,' says one of the cavemen. 'You can't behave like that in here. It's not on.'

We shrug our shoulders and pretend like we don't care, like we've got better places to go and spend our money. The bouncer shuts the door and we're left out in the cold feeling sorry for ourselves.

'*Shit!*' exclaims Volk. 'That's just *fucking* great! We've been barred from our favourite pub. *Fucking* nice one!'

Everyone focuses in on me, expecting an apology, I imagine. But they're not going to get one. It's not entirely my fault. After all, it takes two to bundle, and then some. We stand there in silence for a bit, kicking our heels and walking in circles along the cracks in the paving slabs.

I'm not sure who started laughing first, but before I know it we're all doubled over in hysterics.

'"Nice shirt"? Where the hell did you get that from, Big D?'

Volk is laughing so hard he has to sit down on some steps, while my stomach hurts so much I'm beginning to think it might be possible to physically split your sides laughing.

'Did you see Bummole's face? I've never seen anything as funny in my whole life!'

This was no exaggeration on Yeti's part.

'Hey, I can't wait to do that for real, on a celebrity,' enthuses Volk. 'They're gonna write books about us, man!'

'Too fuckin' right,' I agree.

This was a fantastic finish to the evening, the abrupt ending making it all the more memorable. Everybody is still grinning to themselves about what has just happened. Everyone except Gaz, that is, who's looking worried.

'Hey, what's up Gaz? You're a bit quiet there.'

'I think I've lost my ear.'

The admission is too much for me and I collapse in a heap on the floor, Volk and Yeti fall over each other with hilarity.

'I'm *serious* guys, this ain't funny.'

'Sorry, sorry,' I splutter, trying to be helpful. 'Where did you last have it?'

'It was in my back pocket,' recalls Gaz, patting his arse. 'It must've fallen out during the bundle.'

I try to keep a straight face, but the thought of a prosthetic ear being kicked around the dirty floor of the pub is far too amusing. And judging by their reactions, the other two think likewise.

'Cocks,' spits Gaz as he approaches the door of the pub.

He doesn't get very far, because the way is blocked by the bouncer who had banished us a few minutes earlier. We all stop laughing for a second to listen to what Gaz is going to say.

'Excuse me, sir. I need to get back in the pub, please.'

'Oh you do, do you? Give me one good reason why.'

'I left something in there.'

'What?'

'My ear.'

My sides collapse once more. Surely a lie would have been preferable in this situation.

'Very funny, mate.'

'I'm serious.'

'Really. That's very original, but please stop wasting my time. You're letting all the cold air into the pub.'

'Look!' asserts Gaz, pulling back his hair to reveal the empty space where his ear should be.

The bouncer looks unimpressed.

'Listen, mate. I don't care if you've left your knob in there, you are *not* coming back in this pub. Not after what you did. If you've genuinely left your ear inside, and I'm not saying that you haven't, then you'll have to come back and get it tomorrow. But as far as tonight is concerned, I'm afraid your night is over.'

Gaz doesn't bother arguing; he has already played his last card. He mopes his way back to the group as I stagger up off the floor.

'How am I supposed to explain to my mum that I lost my ear?' he whinges. 'Do you have any idea how much that thing cost?'

'She won't even notice,' I comfort him. 'Just don't tie your hair in a ponytail.'

This wasn't supposed to be a joke, but the other two start laughing again and I'm left feeling slightly guilty. Gaz seems genuinely upset about the whole affair.

'Look,' I assure him. 'I'll come with you tomorrow to collect it. I'm sure somebody will have handed it in. There's no point worrying about it now.'

'Easy for you to say. You've still got a full pair!'

Gaz chuckles at his own statement and thankfully the tension lifts.

All of a sudden, there's a loud blast from a car horn and we look towards the road in time to see the Bertmeister pull up in his silver Audi TT. He winds down the window and sticks his head out. Based on the glimpse we get of his neck, he's wearing one of his awful white-collared shirts. Bertie is living proof that money cannot buy taste.

'Whassup, Bertie?' I call over to him.

He ignores my question completely and instead seeks an explanation of the scene before him.

'I was coming to join you guys. Why the fuck are you all standing on the pavement? It's fucking freezing.'

'Give us a lift home and we'll tell you.'

'Fair enough. Hop in.'

'Shotgun,' barks Volk. He jumps into the front seat, leaving the rest of us to pile in the back.

The warmth and lavish comfort of the Bertmobile is a relief and it feels good to close the doors against the night air. Volk decides it's up to him to assume the role of storyteller for the journey.

'Bertie,' he begins. 'You will not *believe* the idea Big D came up with.'

A Bundle consists of the coming together of the following parties:

a) The Victim
b) The Instigator
c) The Accomplice(s)
d) Others

The Victim is the only involuntary participant in a Bundle, and he or she forms the base of the structure. Theirs is a passive role that is decided upon, in advance, by the Instigator.

The Instigator, by definition, is the person who brings about the Bundle. The Instigator has a number of responsibilities. Firstly, it is the duty of the Instigator to identify the Victim. Once this is achieved, it is up to the Instigator to ensure that the Victim finds him or herself lying face up on the floor (this step may require the help of the Accomplice(s)). Once the Victim is in position, the Instigator must lie across him or her – face down and at right-angles to the Victim's body – and then deliver the signal. The signal is a clearly audible shout of the word "BUNDLE".

The signal acts as an instruction to the Accomplice(s) to join the pile. The Accomplice(s) must lie face down on top of the existing heap. The only restriction is that Accomplices must assume a different angle from the person below them to ensure an even distribution of weight and to avoid the development of an unstable 'wall'.

The group labelled "Others" comprises any unscheduled participants who choose to join the Bundle. While this role is a voluntary one, it is important to note that the identity of the Others is not known to either the Instigator, the Accomplice(s) or the Victim until after the Bundle has taken place.

What differentiates a Celebrity Bundle from a Standard Bundle is that the Victim must be a Celebrity. The term "Celebrity" is open to interpretation, but an acceptable guideline to follow is that, to be deemed a Celebrity, the Victim must be known, for whatever reason, to a large proportion of the population.

Below are the five rules ("The Rules") of Celebrity Bundling:

1. The Rules are to be obeyed at <u>all</u> times and <u>without exception</u>
2. <u>Nobody</u> is above being Bundled
3. To be classified as a Bundle, <u>at least four people must be involved</u> (including the Victim)*
4. <u>The Victim must be spoken to</u> before a Bundle can occur**
5. If a Celebrity is sighted and an Accomplice is present, an attempted Bundle <u>must</u> take place***

* This Rule dictates that a Bundle is reliant on the participation of Others in the case where there is only one Accomplice present.

** The verbal interaction described by this Rule is designed to minimise the chance that the actions of the Instigator will be mistaken for an attempted mugging or assault.

*** The only situation for which this Rule does not apply is one in which a large number of celebrities is present, for example, at a movie premiere.

Please note that the author accepts no responsibility for any injury, loss of limb, mental trauma, damage to clothing/jewellery, imprisonment or any other legal issues that may arise as a result of following The Guide.

Friends, Romans, Countrymen

As promised, I accompany Gaz back to the scene of the crime the next day in a bid to retrieve his missing body part. This was not the first time I had offered my services for such a cause, having been involved in many an ear-related treasure hunt in the past.

You see, he had a few problems with it back at school. Part of the trouble was that he always had to remove it before PE in case someone choked on it in the scrum or something and naturally it often went missing from the changing rooms. It always turned up in the end, usually pinned to the sixth form notice board or wedged between two slices of bread in somebody's packed lunch, but the intervening period would be one of high stress for Gaz while the rest of us did our utmost to be helpful without actually being any help at all. I tell you, I had to take my hat off to some of the ingenious uses that were found for that piece of rubber. Gaz never seemed to see the funny side, but you know what kids are like and besides, it's not every day you have another student's ear at your disposal.

We arrive at the pub at about three o'clock on Saturday afternoon, which Gaz and I deduced would be the least busy point of the day. It was late enough not to overlap with the serving of food and early enough that the majority of people wouldn't have started drinking. In fact, the only customers there were likely to be the hardened alcoholics and, to be honest, who gives a fuck about *them*?

Me and Gaz stroll in through the doors with an air of artificial confidence, half expecting to be accosted at any moment and told to sling our hooks someplace else. But our trip to the bar is uninterrupted and it appears our criminal status has been renounced during the course of the night.

'What are you drinking?' asks Gaz.

'Eh? I didn't know we were staying.'

'We might as well have one while we're here.'

'Wouldn't you rather just ask for it and then…'

'What are you *drinking*?'

I glance up to the bar and see the reason for the sudden change of plan. The only person serving is Miss Blonde Big Boobs herself, the object of Gaz's desire.

'Oh. Pint of Boddingtons please, mate,' I tell him.

Gaz relays my order to Big Tits along with his own selection and she sets about pouring the pints, filling mine halfway first then allowing it to settle while she pumps out Gaz's Stella.

'That's five pounds exactly, please,' she smiles.

Gaz hands over a fiver folded between two fingers and takes the glasses and we sit at one of the many vacant tables near the bar, Gaz taking the inner seat so he can perve on Ms Melons.

'Shit!' he mutters. 'Of all the fucking people to be serving behind the bar it had to be *her*, didn't it.'

'Sod's law, mate,' I chuckle. 'There's not a lot you can do about it.'

'Let's just get these down and come back tomorrow.'

'Be serious, will ya? What if she's in here tomorrow? Come back again on Monday? Besides, if you plan to go out with her she's gonna find out sooner or later.'

'I'd rather it was later.'

'If I were you I'd just get it over and done with.'

'Yeah right. You obviously have *no* idea how humiliating this is.'

He's right, you know. It's all too easy to picture yourself dealing effortlessly with other people's problems.

'I suppose. Tell you what. We'll give it until we've finished these drinks for somebody else to arrive, and if they don't you'll just have to ask her.'

'Deal. Somebody's bound to turn up,' says Gaz optimistically.

They don't. Even though Gaz drinks as if this is his final pint before being sent to the chair, his last rights as it were, Barbie is still the only member of staff in the establishment. She spends her time pottering about trying to find things to do so she doesn't have to exchange pleasantries with the leather-faced elbow benders that line the bar like cows at a trough. Gaz is too preoccupied to hold a conversation, so we kill time leafing through discarded tabloids for football transfer rumours and pictures of scantily clad women. But even this gets boring after a while and I start to get impatient.

'Drink up, Gaz. We can't stay in here all day. I've got things to do.'

'Ok, ok. Wait a minute, I've got an idea.' His face lights up. 'Why don't you do it, Big D?'

'No.'

'I'll pay you.'

'No!'

'Why not? I mean, it's kind of your fault, after all. You were the one who made me…'

'You can't guilt trip me, Gaz. Nobody *made* you do anything. Besides, I think you may be in luck.'

I nod in the direction of the toilets and Gaz looks over his shoulder to see one of the barmen coming through from the back entrance. He greets the *Baywatch* clone and takes his place alongside her behind the bar, subconsciously puffing out his chest in a pathetic attempt to exert his physical presence.

'I'll just wait until she goes to collect the empties,' Gaz informs me.

'Fair enough, but I'm sure he'll tell her after you've gone, anyway.'

'Thanks a lot, Big D! That makes me feel so much better!'

'Just telling it like it is.'

Sure enough, now that there's somebody else to look after the bar, Madam Mammary goes off on a glass-collecting mission, her chest thrust out in front of her like a battering ram. Gaz wastes no time in getting to the bar.

'How can I help you, mate?'

An Australian. How fucking predictable.

'This is going to sound a bit strange,' starts Gaz.

The barman takes a step back. He's probably worried he's about to be asked out on a date by a *man*, a request his macho Aussie mindset would find difficult to deal with.

'I don't suppose anybody handed in an ear last night?' mumbles Gaz.

'Pardon?' bellows the Aussie.

I sometimes wonder whether it's possible for Australian men to open their mouths without shouting.

'When you were cleaning up last night, I don't suppose you came across an ear?' Gaz asks more audibly.

'An ear? You serious, mate?'

Gaz nods. The Aussie looks a bit puzzled.

'Dunno, mate. I wasn't working last night. I'll have to ask Kate.'

'No, it's ok, you don't…'

'Kate! Hey! *Kate!*'

A pair of funbags poke around the corner, the remainder of their owner appearing shortly afterwards.

'Kate, did anybody hand in an ear last night?'

'Pardon?'

The busty barmaid returns with a stack of empty glasses, which she places on the counter behind the bar. Gaz looks like he wants the ground to open up and swallow him, his face a deep shade of scarlet as he frantically massages his temples with his right hand.

'This geezer wants to know whether an ear was left here last night,' says the barman, pointing at Gaz.

'What does it look like?' asks Kate.

'Er… like an ear?' replies Gaz, his tone echoing the Australian's accent.

'I don't remember anyone handing in an *ear*. Although… Wait there a second, I'll check for you.'

She rummages around on a shelf below the till and emerges with a grubby piece of moulded rubber, which she holds at arm's length between her finger and thumb in the same way she might have done if she had picked up a dead mouse by its tail.

'Is this it?' she questions.

'Yeah, that looks like it,' answers Gaz, his expression revealing a deep disappointment about both the condition of the ear and Kate's reaction.

'*Ear* you go,' she giggles, passing it to Gaz. 'Sorry, that wasn't funny. You must get jokes like that all the time, huh?'

'More than you could possibly imagine.'

'Sorry. It's just that… I've never… You know…'

'It's ok, I'm used to it,' smiles Gaz. 'Don't worry about it.'

'I found it on the floor last night, but it never occurred to me what it was.'

'Well, I guess it's not the kind of thing you expect to find on the floor of a pub,' Gaz chortles.

'I guess not!'

Kate, Gaz and the Aussie all stand there laughing heartily, and the scene begins to look a bit too much like the end of a *He-Man* episode for my liking.

'This is all too weird for me,' admits the Aussie. 'I'm going to wipe down the tables.'

'But I've already done them.'

'Then I'll do them again.'

Maybe the man is psychic, or maybe it's plain impossible not to notice the way Gaz is staring wantonly at Kate. Either way, it's an impressive display of tact from an unlikely source, and one that Gaz should probably thank him for one day. The two of them are left alone, and I pray to God that Gaz realises the opportunity he's been presented with. There is a horrible moment when it looks as though he's going to bottle it and walk away, but instead he loiters uneasily at the bar, his fingertips nervously fondling the newly retrieved prosthetic ear. It is agonising to watch, and part of me wants to rush to the jukebox and put on some laidback numbers penned by the late Barry White in order to give the lad a push in the right direction.

I find myself whispering, 'Go on, Gaz,' trying to will him into action.

Unsurprisingly, my telepathic coaching has little effect, and I consign myself to the fact that Gaz simply doesn't have the guts to do it. But then, maybe sensing the awkwardness, Kate suddenly throws him a lifeline.

'So… are you going to, er, put it back on?'

'Not yet,' replies Gaz, focusing intently on the ear in his hand. 'I need to wash it properly first.'

'Oh.'

I shake my head. The man is useless, an imbecile. Finally alone with the woman of his dreams and he transforms into a social retard! I stand up to go and bail him out, but again Kate comes to his rescue. She must have a big heart that girl. Mind you, it would demand an ample one just to keep the blood pumping around those massive tits.

'How did you lose the ear, if you don't mind me asking?'

'It's a long story.'

'Tell me.'

So he does. He tells her about the whole bundling idea, about the vodka (at which point she shoots me a disapproving look), about Bummole and about being thrown out. The story is an entertaining one, no doubt about it, and he doesn't even have to embellish it with the exaggerations people often use when they're recounting a personal experience.

'Wow,' she swoons. 'Sounds mad. You guys are *crazy*. Don't worry too much about the bouncer, he can be such a wanker at times. Don't tell him I said that, though!'

'Don't worry, there isn't much chance of that. If I never speak to that man again it will be too soon. So we're not barred then?'

'I don't think so. Usually when people are barred their names get added to this list.' She pulls out a dirty piece of paper from under the counter. 'What's your name?'

Clever.

'Gaz. How about you?'

'Kate.'

'Pleased to meet you, Kate.'

He puts the ear down on the bar and reaches across to shake her hand.

'Pleased to meet you too, Gaz,' she replies, gladly accepting the greeting. 'Well, there's nobody of that name on the list, so I guess you're free to come in here as *often* as you like.'

She's flirting with him! I don't believe this. All my bullying about him asking her out was with the sole intention of him getting it out of his system so he could find a more realistic target. It would have been amusing watching him being turned down as well, but that was merely an added bonus. Never once did it cross my mind that she might actually be interested! Don't get me wrong, Gaz is a nice guy, but he's certainly not the sort of bloke that gets birds like *that.*

'That's good to *ear*,' jokes Gaz.

It's an awful pun, but she seems to find it hilarious. How can a prosthetic ear possibly be used as a pulling accessory? It makes no sense.

'You'll see me in *ear* more than ever,' he continues.

Kate erupts into fits of laughter, clutching her stomach and doubling over so her breasts almost spill out of her top. I can't take much more of this. It's often said that sarcasm is the lowest form of wit, but after bearing witness to this display I would strongly argue the case for puns. I get up and walk over to where he's standing and tap him on the shoulder.

'I'll see you outside, mate.'

'No probs, mate. I'm going to stay in *ear* a bit longer.'

I try my best not to openly cringe, but it's impossible. The jokes are too bad. I leave the pub with their pathetic guffaws ringing in my ears.

I am left standing alone on the pavement like an ineffective rent boy for a good five minutes before Gaz remembers that I still exist and comes out to meet me.

'Guess who just got themselves a date with the *fittest* bird in Thame?'

I don't bother answering in case my jealousy is detectable. However, this doesn't stop him from carrying on.

'How cool is that? Me and Kate going out together on Wednesday night.'

Again I don't answer; my mind is too busy thinking up elaborate ways to sabotage his evening. And he still hasn't finished.

'Thanks, Big D,' he says, putting his arm across my shoulders. 'I never could've done it without you.'

'Any time, mate. I'm pleased for you, really pleased.'

'Thanks mate. It means a lot.'

Fucking jammy wanker.

Take *That* and Party

'What the fuck are we doing here?' moans Volk.

I can tell by their faces that the others are thinking along similar lines.

'I could've spent the day in bed with Michelle, but no,' he continues. 'Instead you've dragged us all to Heathrow airport. The *airport*, for fuck's sake!'

'Patience,' I say, trying to convince myself as much as anything.

'Patience my arse. I can't believe we're actually here.'

To be honest, neither can I, although I'm not about to admit to it. This should have been one of those ideas that was born in the pub and died in the pub, never to see the cold and sober light of day. But for some reason, we're standing around in the arrivals lounge at Heathrow airport waiting for nobody in particular. I can think of some pretty lame and unproductive ways of wasting away a Sunday afternoon, but this one wins by some distance.

I had decided to stay in on Saturday night to mull over how it was that Gaz, the one-eared wonder, had managed to score a date with a busty blonde beauty while I was approaching my ninth consecutive month as an unwilling bachelor. I pondered whether I had come even remotely close to achieving a break from single life during this time, but the sad truth is that, aside from being checked out on a couple of occasions and being given an incorrect (or deliberately false) phone number on another, I couldn't have remained further from a relationship unless I had become a monk and silently emigrated to a secluded mountain retreat.

After realising the desperateness of my plight, I sat down and had a good think about how this miserable situation had arisen. My ex-girlfriend had dumped me because she wanted to go travelling for a year and didn't want me to be waiting around for her all that time. How fucking considerate. That part of it, at least, was beyond my control. I suppose I could have gone with her, but I wasn't particularly overwhelmed by her chosen route; a real voyage of self-discovery. It revealed to me how different we were, and I'm pleased to say I'm not exactly counting the days until she returns. I expect she'll come back a cardiganed hippy with bongo drums, dreadlocks and sandals in tow. And hippy chicks are generally considered rough by everyone apart from their crusty male counterparts, so there's no great loss there. Apart from the sex, that is, which is never quite the same when it's with yourself. Not that I'd be particularly thrilled to sleep with a grubby beatnik, mind you. But anyway, we digress, and the last thing I want to do is sound bitter.

Having decided that a reunion with my ex in three months' time was out of the question, I set about forming a mental list of all the local girls I find attractive. This was easier than it may sound, as the community is fairly static and you see the same old faces day in, day out. Once the list was complete I worked my way through it, eliminating any women that were either known to have boyfriends, were lesbians, or were too young. This left me with about five names, two of whom were complete slappers. Despite being damn fine, they probably wouldn't be up to scratch as relationship material. So that left three.

'There's plenty of other fish in the sea, son,' my dad told me when I was moping around the house soon after the split.

Define 'plenty'. Is *three* plenty? Is it? The odds were so stacked against me it was hardly worth casting my net.

The depressing nature of the analysis forced me into a change of subject and I turned to another topic that was at the forefront of my mind, that of celebrity bundling. Expulsion from the pub aside, the bundling of Bummole had been an undeniable success, and I was keen to keep the momentum going by nailing a celebrity of some description as quickly as possible. The big question was where to find one.

And that's how we came to be here, leaning against the barrier in a line of five, watching returning holidaymakers drift past in their hundreds and not recognising a single one of them. A brainstorming session with the Yeti had seen the airport emerge as the most likely place we could think of to spot a celebrity. They're only human after all, and while they might not frequent the same restaurants or bars as the likes of us common people, they are nevertheless limited in their choice of places to fly from or to. Bertie kindly agreed to drive us here, which was a godsend as it's a stifling day and his car has air conditioning. Gaz spent most of the journey relaying the story to the others of how he had charmed Kate into going on a date with him, all of us pretending to be impressed but secretly hoping that it would go badly so that he might shut up about it. Volk sulked for the best part of the forty-five minute journey as he didn't really want to come and is only here because he couldn't think of a reasonable excuse not to be. Yeti was his usual subdued self, opening his mouth only when subjected to a direct question or to point out subtle flaws or factual inaccuracies in our arguments. He's a clever bastard is Yeti, a closet genius.

We've been here for coming up to two hours and the backs of my legs are beginning to ache. Standing in one place for any length of time is deceptively tiring, and I'm grateful to have the barrier to lean on. Without it, I feel like my lower back might stiffen up permanently, leaving me unable to tie my own shoelaces for the rest of my life. Every now and then, one of us is allowed to take a walk, maybe to buy a drink or go to the toilet. But each must go alone, for we need all the numbers we can get. Just in case.

There have been a couple of false alarms; times when my heart has started racing only to be slowed by an anti-climax. Excited screams are usually the trigger, the sound of which is enough to cause my muscles to tighten involuntarily as I scan the trolley pushers and suitcase draggers for the source of the sudden hysteria. Every single time I find myself disappointed – it's yet another mundane member of the general public being greeted by a pathetically overemotional friend or relative. As I watch the tears of happiness dribble down the cheeks of the peculiar women who are apparently overwhelmed to see their loved ones for the first time in a couple of weeks, it makes me wonder who in the world would be so pleased to see *me* if I had been away for a while. My mum, perhaps, if she were still alive. But that's about it.

The one thing that strikes me about the procession of people is how offensively *normal* the majority of them are. They've just come back from holiday and should be looking close to their best, yet most of the faces are instantly forgettable. I've often read how certain stars can instantly light up a room or boast such a level of charisma that they are instantly picked out from a cast of thousands for a lead role, but not a smidgen of this wow factor is evident in the people I see today. I guess this is why some people are famous and others are not. Another thing that amuses me is the lack of golden skin on show. Maybe it has something to do with the synthetic lighting, but there don't appear to be many tans in the vicinity. I can see some people have made the effort – necks and foreheads covered with painful-looking sunburn lay testament to that – but for the most part it's impossible to tell that these people are returning from warmer climates. I come to the conclusion that it's a hereditary flaw in the British complexion. Most of us are simply destined to be pale.

'This is a waste of time,' grumbles Volk. 'Let's go back.'

'Yeah, let's call it a day,' agrees Gaz. 'I don't think we're going to get lucky. I used all my luck yesterday getting a date with Kate.'

A date with Kate, a date with Kate. If I hear that name mentioned one more time I might have to kill him.

'Come on, lads. We're here now. We might as well give it another half an hour,' I say to them.

'Half an hour?' whinges Volk. 'We've been here for two hours already, for fuck's sake.'

'Watch the language, mate,' I tell him, aware of the disapproving looks we're attracting from our immediate neighbours.

His profanities have already forced a woman to lead her children to another part of the barrier so they're out of earshot and protected from his obscenity-laden outbursts.

'What do you fu–? I mean, what do you expect when you make us stand here for hours like idiots so you can bum a celebrity? Come on, Bertie, let's go. These jokers can get the bus back if they're so desperate to stay.'

'Ten more minutes, Bert,' I request.

'Don't let him talk you into…' protests Volk.

'Ten minutes, that's all I ask.'

'Ok,' agrees the Bertmeister.

'Oh, for fuck's sa– You wan–' groans Volk in disbelief, as if being unable to swear prevents him from forming proper sentences.

'Come on, mate,' says Bertie. 'What difference is another ten minutes going to make?'

'Fine!' Volk concedes.

Good old Bertie, always realistic. Mind you, for someone who works as many hours as he does, he's hardly likely to complain about a few more minutes of standing around doing nothing. With not a lot of it to play with, Bertie knows the value of free time, and I think part of him enjoys wasting what little of it he has, because that's his way of disconnecting himself from the world of work.

The minutes pass incredibly quickly. Four of them slip by without a single person emerging from the black hole of the luggage inspecting area, an inconvenient time for the first break in human traffic of the day to take place. It looks as though we aren't even going to get to see another batch of people, and I consign myself to the string of smug 'I told you so' remarks Volk is no doubt lining up as we speak. There's little in life I hate more than having to admit defeat in an argument just because events happen to conspire against me. I'm fairly certain there must be *at least* a couple of celebrities passing through this joint every day, and it's hardly my fault we happen to have picked a barren couple of hours. But this is pure speculation, and without any statistics to back me up I don't really have a leg to stand on. It is of considerable relief to me that part of the blame can be apportioned to Yeti, a man who is rarely wrong.

After six minutes, they start to trickle through; a few pacesetters out in front who were lucky enough for their bags to be spat out onto the conveyor belt first. I glance at my watch. A shade over three-and-a-half minutes left. The early leavers are followed by a denser, more constant stream of tired but happy families and couples. Three minutes. A man in sunglasses! A deliberate attempt to avoid recognition! But no, he's a nobody; he probably just had too much to drink on the plane. Two minutes. We're running out of time. A smile begins to creep across Volkan's lips. Smug bastard. Come on, come on. More people, but they're all anonymous. It looks like it's going to be a wasted trip.

But then he appears, stepping out of the darkness looking as familiar as a long-lost childhood friend. It's been a while since I've seen him on the telly, but he hasn't changed much. He's a bit older and maybe slightly heavier, but there's no doubt about it, it's definitely him. For a man who has seen so many crowds and so much success, he looks strangely apprehensive about the walk that lies before him. It's almost as if he's expecting to be mobbed at any second, but surely he should know those days are gone.

'Is that…?' Yeti has seen him too.

'Yeah, it's him,' I whisper, as though he might hear us if we talk any louder.

'And?' questions Volk.

'What do you mean, *and*? It's what we've been waiting for!' I hiss excitedly.

'Why the fuck are you whispering? He's not a celebrity. Not any more, anyway. He doesn't count.'

'Of course he counts!' I raise my voice in order to defend my corner. 'He might not be in the limelight at the moment, but that doesn't make him any less famous!'

'He doesn't even *do* anything these days,' argues Volk.

'Actually, I think you'll find he writes songs for other people now,' Yeti corrects him.

'Yeah, because he isn't famous.'

'Who gives a monkey's fuck how he spends his time?' I explode. 'It doesn't make him any less famous! None of us have met him, but we all still know who he is! Gaz, *you* know who he is, right?'

'Yeah, he's the fat one from Take That,' he replies immediately.

'Exactly. So he's a *celebrity*. And he's getting away. I'm going in, and you lot had better back me up or I'm gonna look like a twat. Bertie, start filming.'

Dirty Bertie is reduced to the role of chauffer and cameraman since, unlike the rest of us, he has a career and isn't prepared to sacrifice his professional integrity for what he deems to be another one of my harebrained schemes. The plus side lies in the fact that the Bertmeister is one of those people who believes that if a job's worth doing, it's worth doing properly, so I know we're in capable hands. He whips his mobile out of his back pocket and presses a few buttons to activate the camera function. I always knew there must be some use for this new mobile video technology, but I didn't think it would be this. I look into what I believe to be the camera lens and deliver my lines.

'Hi, my name's Big D. It's Sunday the 13th of July, 2003, and we're about to bundle Gary Barlow.'

A sudden surge of adrenaline makes my vault over the barrier seem like child's play, and I half jog, half shuffle over to where Gary is walking. I can sense that he has seen me coming, as he begins to visibly tighten up, the dragging of his suitcase becoming more laboured as he tries his best to ignore my presence. I don't want to frighten him into a hasty retreat, so I slow down a bit to put him at ease. I then stroll right up alongside him, mirroring the pace and rhythm of his footsteps with my own. It's the first time I've been this close to anyone famous and I find my heart thumping fast and hard, rather like the beat of one of Gary's previous pop classics in fact. Although I've never been a fan, I still find myself in awe of the man, and his sheer presence renders me completely dumbfounded for a few seconds. I keep opening my mouth to speak, but find that the words I had rehearsed so many times have gone missing and I'm left silent and gawping like some kind of gigantic fish. He glances over with a look that suggests I must have escaped from my nurse, and the brief eye contact snaps me out of my celebrity-induced trance.

'Er, hi. *Gary*, isn't it?'

It was the best I could manage under the circumstances.

'Yes,' he replies without averting his gaze from the path ahead.

'Hi, my name's Big D, pleased to meet you,' I declare, offering my hand.

'Pleased to meet you too,' he replies, and takes it.

In one swift movement, I take his right hand in a firm handshake, place my left hand on his right shoulder, step past him so that my left leg is behind his left leg and then push hard. It works perfectly – all those hours practising on Yeti this morning have clearly paid off. He swivels over and lands flat on his back, suitcase toppling to the floor soon after. Gary lies on the floor looking dazed and I make a quick visual check for any injuries. I did my best to make sure he didn't fall too heavily, but in case he's landed awkwardly there's still time to get away before security get wind of what has happened. But he doesn't appear to be in pain, so I get down on the floor and spread myself across him.

It's a surreal feeling, lying there in Heathrow Airport on top of Gary Barlow, and a feeling that I'm unlikely to experience again. But this is not a time for reflection. Everything is in position and there's only one thing left to do.

'BUUUNDLE!!!' I scream, as loudly and clearly as I possibly can.

'What the hell are you do–?'

It seems to take an age for the others to arrive. I wish they'd hurry up, because Gary's a big lad and I'm scared he might try to wriggle out from beneath me. But he appears to be in a state of shock and offers no resistance whatsoever. He just lies there, round and spread out like a hapless baby.

Gaz, Yeti and Volk arrive in quick succession: bang, bang, bang, and I become the meat in a testosterone-filled sandwich. Without the influence of alcohol, the crushing weight is more noticeable this time, Gaz's belt buckle digging uncomfortably into the small of my back. I try to shift my position slightly, but I'm completely wedged in, and I imagine the bruise darkening with each passing second.

'Hey, look! A bundle!' squeaks a high-pitched voice.

'Cool!'

A further two bodies join the pile, their lesser weight and excited giggles signalling their tender age. But they're gone as quickly as they arrive, quickly dragged away by their over-alert parents.

'Don't be so stupid!' they shout at them, although I'm sure a large part of the telling off is aimed at us, the people that should really know better.

We need to go if we're to escape without charge and I attempt to hoist myself up, but unsurprisingly my attempted press-up doesn't even make it off the ground.

'Go, go, go!' I yell, and the others start to squirm above me.

Untangling ourselves proves challenging and the ensuing panic that we're about to get arrested doesn't help. Hands grope for the same bit of floor space to use as leverage, while legs kick aimlessly in the air as we flounder about on the polished surface. Eventually we succeed in rolling off in all directions, the heavy heal of Yeti's age-old Doc Martens catching me agonisingly in the shins.

'Ah, you fucker!' I wince, the insult aimed more at my throbbing shin than at Yeti.

But Yeti is long gone, anyway. Having being at the bottom it takes me longer than most to get up and the others are already sprinting off in the direction of the car park by the time I hobble to my feet. I turn and run, taking a few painfully clumsy steps to go after them. Yet I find myself stopping in my tracks, overcome by a sudden urge to check that Gary is ok. I spin around on my good leg to where he's lying, only to find that he's now sitting up, looking in dismay at the crumpled, dirty state of his clothes and doing his best to brush himself into a presentable state. He no longer looks like the famous pop star he was two minutes ago. He looks like an ordinary human being like you or I: small, humble and covered in dirt. He looks up at me. He has stopped brushing and his face is expressionless. He stares vacantly, unable to comprehend what has just happened. I raise my right hand and point jokingly at his face.

'Take *that* and party,' I tell him.

His eyelids narrow, and for a split second I think he's going to deck me. This is not good. Although I'm a lot taller than Gary, he's better built and I wouldn't fancy my chances in a fight, especially with my injured leg. But then he smiles. And the smile turns into a chuckle and then he starts shaking his head. I stand there perplexed as I watch the chuckle turn into a bellow of laughter, and before I know it Gary is lying flat on his back again with his hands on his head, roaring with uncontrolled hilarity.

'I can't believe you bastards bundled me!' he hoots, and I too find myself starting to laugh.

Much as I'd love to stand here and have a good giggle with the driving force behind Britain's most famous boy band, I turn on my heels and scuttle as fast as I can back to the car, never looking back for fear of seeing the uniformed guards closing in with handcuffs and truncheons. When I arrive at the car park I'm greeted by the others, who are by now safely inside the Bertmobile. The engine is already running and the door is wide open for me so we can make a rapid getaway. I feel like we've robbed a bank or something.

'What took you so fucking long?' demands Volk as we pull away.

'Ask Yeti, he almost broke my leg!'

'Sorry, mate, it was an accident,' apologises Yeti.

'Yeah, I know. Don't worry about it.'

'So how did he take it?' Bertie shouts over his shoulder.

I put my hand on his seat and lean forward so I have a clear view of the road ahead.

'Oh, he loved it,' I grin. 'He absolutely fucking loved it.'

A Refuge for Those Who Have Nothing Better to Do

'Morning, Albert. Good to see yesterday's comments didn't put you off wearing that hat. It looks nice.'

Bertie was surprised to see Linda already sitting behind her desk. He thought that, at 6:32am, he would almost definitely be the first in. He certainly didn't expect to come second to a secretary in the early starter stakes.

'Morning, Linda,' he half-heartedly smiled back, removing the green beanie and straightening his hair.

'Well, *that* wasn't very enthusiastic,' said Linda with motherly concern. 'Rough night was it?'

Bertie covered his mouth to spare her the sight of his tonsils as he yawned.

'Not really, no. You are aware what time it is though, right?' He pointed at the clock on the wall. 'It's just gone half-past six and I've been up for over two hours. Don't expect much enthusiasm from me until at least eleven.'

'I don't know how you youngsters do it,' said Linda, shaking her head in disbelief. 'Don't you need sleep like the rest of us?'

'You get used to it. You don't have a lot of choice, really. Anyway, what are you doing in at this time?'

'I got "the call".' Linda clenched her right hand into a fist with her thumb and little finger protruding to form the shape of a phone. 'Hank needed some presentations to go out this morning, but he didn't finish writing them until 5am, so I was summoned in to get them printed.'

'Couldn't he have printed them himself?' asked Bertie.

'What do *you* think?' said Linda rhetorically.

'I guess I'd better leave you to it, then.'

Bertie sighed as he switched on his computer. Sometimes he didn't mind the early starts. When he was working on a big project and the hours got insane, he almost found a sick satisfaction when his timesheet reached triple figures for the week. Even the one-night, champagne-fuelled piss-up that followed the six weeks of sleep deprivation and malnutrition seemed like a just reward. But today he knew his time would be filled with menial work and a lot of it. This, plus the knowledge that he would probably still be here in fourteen hours' time, tended to put a dampener on things.

'Morning, Linda! Morning, Albert!'

Lorraine, the team's other secretary, waltzed in with a regal air about her that suggested she was entering the champagne tent at Ascot rather than an office.

'You're looking very clean today, Albert,' she commented as she sat down.

'What's that supposed to mean?' Bertie asked defensively. 'Do I normally look dirty?'

'I don't know,' Lorraine said, as if she were surprised that her comment warranted further justification. 'Maybe it's the white shirt.'

'But I've worn this shirt loads of times!'

'I've never seen it before. Perhaps it's because you're clean-shaven.'

'I'm always clean-shaven!'

'A combination of both, then. Whatever it is, you look different. Cleaner. When I see you in your dark shirts, I think, *'Ooh, I could live with that'*. But the white makes you look pale. Insipid.'

Bertie was dumbfounded.

'Leave him alone,' said Linda defensively. 'He looks alright. Don't listen to her, Albert, the shirt looks nice.'

'Dark colours suit you better, Albert.'

'If you say so,' replied Bertie as he squinted at the contents of his inbox. It never ceased to amaze him how many tasks could appear between the hours of two and six in the morning.

'You'll never find yourself a girlfriend wearing that shirt,' Lorraine continued, determined to have the final word on the matter.

'I'm not here to find a girlfriend,' Bertie muttered from behind his screen. 'I'm here to work.'

'I'm quite sure Albert has no problem attracting girls,' commented Linda. 'Isn't that right, Albert?'

'Maybe.'

Bertie exhaled audibly as he read Hank's email. A report that was originally scheduled for the following week was now scheduled to be on the client's desk for the following morning. This was exacerbated by the fact that he hadn't even started the report yet.

'What's the matter, Albert?' asked Linda.

'It's probably that shirt!' chirped Lorraine.

'Oh, for goodness' sake, Lorraine,' responded Linda. 'Will you stop going on about his shirt? There's nothing wrong with it.'

'There's nothing right with it.'

'You're not looking too great yourself this morning, you know,' Linda informed her.

'What? Why?'

'Your boobs have disappeared.'

Bertie allowed himself a faint snigger as he recognised the signs of what was about to commence. While Linda and Lorraine were undoubtedly good friends, they didn't hold back when it came to trading personal insults, and it was a testament to the strength of their friendship that their arguments never resulted in physical fighting. The closest it ever came to this was the fervent exchange of whatever food items were near at hand.

Lorraine stood up and looked down at her front. Bertie glanced over at her and had to admit that she wasn't looking quite as full-figured as she sometimes did, although he was not about to air this opinion in public in case he got dragged back into the firing line.

'I must've left them in my other blouse,' Lorraine replied.

There was a short silence as Linda bit her tongue, but the opportunity to attack was there and she wasn't about to let it pass.

'I'd like to say that your arse has disappeared as well, but it's still as big as ever.'

Lorraine placed her hands on her hips in mock exasperation and glared daggers at Linda.

'Well I never! You can talk, Mrs Rhinoceros Arse! How many chairs are *you* sitting on today?'

Linda erupted into hysterics as Lorraine continued her verbal assault.

'And look at your eyes! They're like piss-holes in the snow!'

'So would yours be if you'd been up since quarter past five.'

'Never!' Lorraine crowed defiantly. 'Anyway, enough of this silliness. Would either of you like a drink?'

'Coffee, please,' answered Linda, the mood suddenly returning to one more befitting of the environment.

'Yeah, coffee for me as well, please,' requested Bertie. 'And make it a strong one.'

No sooner had Lorraine left for the coffee machine than the cleaner entered. To this day Bertie didn't know his name. He had never been particularly good with names anyway; anything more unusual than David or Steve and Bertie would have more chance of remembering what he had eaten on a specific day seven years ago.

Linda winced as the cleaner bent down to pick up a bin and at the same time gave her a good four inches of ample builder's cleavage.

''ow do you lot get so much stuff on the ground?' he asked as he straightened up, gesturing with one of his thick fingers at the white confetti that bordered the printer and bin.

'I think those elves were in again last night,' replied Linda.

'Fuckin' elves.'

The rest of his profanities were drowned out by the sound of the hoover.

'Did you get my email?'

In typical fashion, Hank dispensed with what normal people would consider to be common courtesy and cut straight to the chase. His time was charged out in ten-minute blocks and he was not about to fill up one of these with something as needless as polite conversation with his staff.

'Yeah, I'm onto it,' replied Bertie. 'How come the deadline changed?'

'I touched base with the client yesterday and offered to move it forward, guessing that you would have some spare capacity to get it done. I would have emailed you sooner, but I had a presentation to finish. Let me know if you can't do it.'

There was almost a sneer in his last sentence, one that Bertie was used to. "Capacity" essentially translated to whether it was physically possible to do the work, to which the answer was nearly always "yes". In Hank's eyes, if you had time to go home and get four hours' sleep then you had spare capacity.

'I was planning to leave on time today as it's my friend's birthday, but I should be able to squeeze it in,' said Bertie.

Hank appeared slightly annoyed by this statement.

'If you're unable to do it, I'll get Nathan to do it when he comes in. He's *always* looking for extra work.'

'No, it's ok, there's no need for that. I said I'd do it.'

'Good. I knew I could rely on you, Albert. Linda, has that presentation gone out yet?'

Bertie cursed himself as Hank turned his attentions to Linda. He should have let Nathan do it; after all, it was only one report. But he knew Hank's selective memory would remember this one occasion he had turned work down rather than the umpteen times he had willingly cancelled social engagements for the sake of earning the company a few extra quid. Having said that, if it had been any name other than Nathan's that had been brought up, he might have been persuaded to change his mind, but giving the office golden boy a chance to gain extra brownie points was something Bertie wasn't prepared to do. While he did his best not to get sucked into the competitive nature of the work, Bertie found Nathan's shameless kissing of every remotely senior arse difficult to take. Nathan was actually quite a nice guy on a one-to-one basis and, were it not for the fact that he worked with him, Bertie could see the two of them being reasonably good friends. The problem was, he was the kind of guy who would discard you like a coffee-cream chocolate for the sake of his precious career, even to the point of refusing to be seen talking to people if they were out of favour with management.

'Let me know as soon as they've been sent out,' Hank bellowed over his shoulder as he marched away from Linda's desk.

'Good morning to you, too,' mumbled Linda when he was safely out of earshot. 'You'd think something as simple as a greeting wouldn't be beyond him.'

'He didn't get to where he is today by being a nice guy,' Bertie informed her.

'That may be, but there's no need to be like that. I've never seen anybody so full of arrogance.'

'It's part of the job description, I'm afraid.'

'What, being an obnoxious prick?'

'He's not *that* bad. I don't think he means it. It's just the way he is.'

'That's no excuse. You can't go around being an arsehole and then turn around and say, "Sorry, it's just the way I am".'

'You can when you're as important as he is.'

'It's not right. Tell me you won't be like that when you get to his level.'

'I'll try. I have to get there first, though. Which means getting this report done for starters.'

Linda took the hint and returned to her printing, while Bertie made a start on the report. Luckily it was nothing too complicated. Similar reports had been done for other clients, so it was a simple matter of digging one out and changing a few things. It shouldn't take him too long and if he worked through lunch there was every chance he would make it back in time to join the others at the pub.

It was almost twenty to eight by the time Nathan made an appearance; a veritable lie-in compared with the rest of the team. Just looking at him was enough to make the majority of people think "banker". He wasn't so much *born* to be an investment banker, he was *created* to be one; the result of years of top secret genetic research, carried out by a team of the world's leading scientists in the basement of the building. He had it all: the chiselled jaw, the old-before-his-time air, the broad shoulders, the pinstriped suit and the booming voice. He even had the braces and the waxed hair. Earlier prototypes had suffered from a limited lifespan, burning out after ten years or so, but this new model – this Nathan Version 2.0 – he would go on forever.

His first question was invariably, 'What are you working on?' rather than 'How are you?' and today was no exception. Bertie explained about the report and, as expected, Nathan offered to take it off his hands. Bertie thanked him for his selfless gesture, but explained that he wanted to see it through himself, quickly getting his head down while Nathan scurried off to see Hank in order to pass off an idea he had heard on the radio as one of his own.

Bertie normally lunched at his desk, but today he didn't even have time to do that. Instead he grabbed nothing more than a breakfast bar and a fruit smoothie on the return journey from his single, late-morning trip to the toilet. He purposefully rationed the amount of water he drank during the day as he got the feeling that time away from his desk was constantly monitored and a weak bladder could easily be interpreted as laziness. By this time of the day the morning's banter was long forgotten, the only conversation audible in the office was business-orientated and usually took place over the phone. The upside of this was that there were few distractions, so Bertie was able to make good headway with the report. At this rate he would be able to hand it over to Hank by mid-afternoon and, barring any major problems, there was no reason why he shouldn't be able to leave the office by seven.

This was wishful thinking. Somewhat predictably, Hank was too busy to look over the report straightaway, so it sat idle on his desk for a good two hours while he attended to more pressing matters. And once he eventually picked it up, it was too much to ask for him to be satisfied with the report in its present state, and Bertie was instructed to make some superficial changes that meant having to redo and hence realign all of the graphs and tables. This took him until seven o'clock, at which point Hank glanced over it once again. Luckily, he was happy with it this time. Bertie breathed a sigh of relief. If he left work now he would be back home by eight-thirty and in the pub by nine, something of a record for him, even on a "normal" night.

Again, this was wishful thinking.

'Get this printed and organise an overnight courier please, Albert,' ordered Hank.

Bertie couldn't believe it. This would take him at least another hour.

'Can't I get somebody else to do it? As I said before, I have a social engagement I need to make... If possible,' he added in response to Hank's raised eyebrows.

'Albert, in this business it's important to see things through from beginning to end. How would you feel if you left it to somebody else, only to receive a phone call from the client tomorrow telling you the report hasn't arrived?'

'I suppose. I'll get it sorted.'

'Good lad.'

Bertie picked up the report and moped back to his desk. He hated the way he became the wimpiest man in the world when it came to work. In any other situation he would have stood his ground and refused outright, but the moment he stepped into his boss's office he always felt ten years younger and about a foot shorter. He knew it was ridiculous. After all, they were both adults and of comparable intelligence, but the fact that Hank had the power to fire him meant he was prepared to take more crap from him than from any other person in the world, even his own parents. He would stand there and let himself be patronised or shouted at, even if he knew Hank was in the wrong or simply on another of his regular power trips.

For a split second, Bertie considered marching back in there and informing Hank that it shouldn't matter who printed and sent the report; if you couldn't rely on your fellow colleagues, what was the point in hiring them in the first place? But he knew it would be a waste of time. He would end up walking in there without any conviction, nervously making his point, getting shot down by Hank and leaving with his tail between his legs, having achieved nothing other than make himself look like a hot-headed fool. It was better to sit down and get on with it. Again.

Bertie left the office a little before half-past eight. He didn't announce his departure in case somebody found him something else to work on. He just fired off an email to Hank to say the courier had picked up the parcel. He didn't wait for a response either, shutting down his machine the moment the email left his outbox and rushing out of the office. He had about forty-five minutes to make the 21:10 from Marylebone station back to Haddenham & Thame Parkway, where the Bertmobile seemed to spend the majority of its life. This should be enough provided he got his skates on and there were no major delays. If he didn't make it, he would be left facing a half-hour wait at a station that wasn't designed for passing long periods of time.

The pavements of Bishopsgate were generally free of pedestrians, with those that hadn't fled the area either sitting in the pub or still at work. Bertie ran as fast as the awkwardness of his suit and work shoes would allow, the heavy soles sounding like hand claps as he lumbered down the street. It was a fairly short distance to Liverpool Street station, but his empty stomach and heavy briefcase made it feel like miles. His calorie consumption for the entire day had barely been enough to cater for a sunbathing session, let alone a fourteen-hour working day and a half-mile run. But he made it in good time, the only hold-up being the frustratingly long wait at the traffic lights opposite the station as the black cabs paraded past like a mutant ant trail.

Once through the underground ticket barriers he was on the home straight. It was only seven stops to Baker Street and then a brief walk from there to Marylebone. Bertie allowed himself to catch his breath on the escalator as it carried him down, smiling at the imaginative places people had found to put their flavourless chewing gum, which was stuck to the various posters that decorated the downward journey. But his heart sank as he stepped onto the platform and the electronic display informed him that the next train was not due to arrive for another six minutes. Bertie glanced at his watch. It was going to be close.

The journey itself was a stressful experience. The time on his watch seemed to be in fast-forward mode, minutes rather than seconds passing with each regular check. Yet, despite the anxiety, a journey without interruptions saw him arrive at the entrance of Marylebone station with a good four minutes to spare. He toyed with the idea of nipping into Marks & Spencer to grab a sandwich for dinner, but the risk of missing his train outweighed the risk of starvation, so he headed straight for the platform instead, jumping into the first available carriage. He closed his eyes as the train moved away. If he was lucky he would get half an hour's kip before he reached his destination.

When he came to, the train was sitting motionless at a station. Bertie jumped to his feet in panic. How long had he been asleep? Had he missed his stop? Rolling up his sleeve, he saw that his watch read 22:27.

'Shit!' he exclaimed. He was probably halfway to Birmingham by now. 'Shit, shit, shit!'

He peered out of the window to look for a station sign and was mystified to see the words "Gerrards Cross" sitting proudly above the platform. He was only about fifteen minutes into his journey. Bertie examined his watch once again, expecting to discover that he had read it incorrectly the first time. But he hadn't, it was almost half-past ten. His recently awakened mind was unable to deal with the complexities of the situation, so he set off down the carriage to seek the advice of a fellow passenger who maybe hadn't slept through whatever disaster had taken place. The first person he came across was an elderly man, a fellow suit wearer.

'Excuse me, sir,' Bertie said softly, trying his best not to startle him. 'I don't suppose you know the cause of the delay?'

'Signal failure,' answered the man. 'We've been sat here for almost an hour.'

'Oh, right. Have they given any indication of how long we might be here for?'

'Nope.'

'Thanks for your help.'

Bertie returned to his seat. There was no way he would make it to the pub now, not a chance. He would have to call Gaz and apologise for missing his birthday the second year running. He reached into his inside pocket to retrieve his phone.

'Shit!' he spat again as his searching fingers found nothing but material. In his haste he had forgotten to retrieve the phone from his desk, where it sat charging up in preparation for this very eventuality.

Bertie slumped back in his seat, running his hands through his hair and bringing them to rest at the back of his head, where his fingers locked together to support the weight. He let out a defeated laugh before leaning forward and banging his head repeatedly against the table. What a complete bastard of a day.

Yeti's Delicious Recipe for Chicken

You will need:

- Skinless chicken breasts
- Light soy sauce
- White wine vinegar
- Sesame oil
- Two cloves of garlic
- A thumb of ginger
- Salt, pepper and sugar

Pour a load of soy sauce into a hat-sized bowl and add enough vinegar so that the mixture is sufficiently tangy without tasting purely of vinegar. Roughly chop the garlic and ginger into smallish pieces and add them to the bowl along with a few splashes of sesame oil. Next, add a large pinch of sugar, then season with salt and pepper. Mix it all together and give it a taste. If it doesn't make you salivate and want to drink the whole lot like a cold soup, vary the quantities until it does.

Lay each chicken breast on its side and, placing one hand on top, slice along its length to create two flat fillets per breast. Score each fillet at regular intervals and on both sides, then place them in the bowl, stirring well so that each piece is properly coated with the mixture. Cover and refrigerate for a minimum of one hour and a maximum of twenty-four hours, stirring occasionally to allow an even distribution of flavour.

When it comes to cooking, remove the chicken pieces from the marinade and place them under a medium grill for about fifteen minutes, turning once at the halfway stage. For best results use a barbeque. Serve the chicken with whatever takes your fancy.

This recipe also works well with other chicken portions (thighs, wings, drumsticks or quarters) or with lamb neck fillets.

The Bigger They Are...

To me it seems like something of a miracle, but Gaz's enviable liaison with the buxom Kate has now entered its sixth week and is showing no signs of petering out any time soon. But while I still find myself experiencing a tinge of jealousy whenever he lays his hands on her (which he does fairly often, and who could blame him), I'm nevertheless coming round to the idea of the two of them becoming an item.

You see, I've learnt that there are a number of advantages to his continuation of what will surely turn out to be a temporary escapade. The most obvious one is that we frequently get to spend time in the company of a beautiful lady; something of a novelty in what has always been a male-dominated group. Nights down the pub have been infinitely better for her inclusion, the enforced censorship of conversation more than made up for by the presence of a heavenly cleavage to admire over the course of the evening. This is made all the more enjoyable by a combination of her unwillingness to cover up and her hyperactive nipples, which seem to spring to the fore if you so much as breathe in their general direction. Believe me, Kate's addition to a night out gives you a couple of things to think about when you go home, if nothing else.

A second advantage is that of popularity by association. I'm convinced other women must look at us in a new light now that we're regularly seen chatting away with and entertaining such a prime example of their own kind. Good-looking girls can afford to be picky about who they spend their time with, so to have one sitting at our table for an entire evening must send out a whole host of positive messages about our charisma.

The third real advantage is that fit women don't exist as standalone products; they come in multipacks. A gorgeous girl will no doubt roll with a selection of equally gorgeous friends (plus a token ugly friend for those times when they need to

boost their fragile self-esteem), and it doesn't take a genius to work out who the beneficiaries of this will be.

I mustn't forget to mention the other, most important advantage either, this being that Kate is a really nice girl and fun to talk to. I'm not completely shallow, after all. I don't really understand what she sees in Gaz, to tell you the truth. Maybe he's a good listener, despite only having half as many ears as the average bloke.

Tonight it's the third advantage that I'm most grateful for (although all the others still apply), as I find myself talking shit to a fine young lady who goes by the name of Sarah. Sarah is pleasant company by all accounts: she's sweet, attractive, funny, and the added bonus is that she seems genuinely interested in what I have to say. I must admit that it took considerable subtlety and forward planning to get myself into the position I'm in now; a complex series of chair swaps as people went to the toilet, jukebox or bar that saw me manoeuvre into the empty seat to her left. Not that I have much competition for her affections from the others at the table. Volk and Gaz are already taken and Bertie is working late. This leaves only Yeti and, as I mentioned before, we have our suspicions he might be seeking some further education at the school of hard cocks.

Having surpassed the necessary introductions and "How do you know so-and-so?" questions that plague early conversations when you meet a friend of a friend for the first time, Sarah and I are now at the stage where we're free to find out about each other. It is at this point that battles are won and lost. Anyone can be polite and ask a few pre-prepared, bog standard questions to make it beyond the first thirty seconds of an interaction, but the subsequent period requires wit, spontaneity and a considerable amount of skill. It should be easy. Two people who've never met before should have an almost endless amount of interesting conversational material at their disposal. After all, both parties have their entire lives to draw from, so it should be possible to find something decent to talk about. But first encounters are rarely that straightforward.

'So what do you do, Dom?' Sarah asks me.

Her reluctance to avert her gaze from mine as she waits for an answer makes me feel slightly uncomfortable, and I find myself looking at the floor as I begin to speak. It's times like this I wish I was a magician, a forensic detective or involved in television; anything but the reality.

'Er, I'm a waiter mainly,' I reply, wishing I could think of some way to glamorise the title.

'Whereabouts?'

'Don Luigi's.'

'*Don Luigi's?*' She's not impressed, and I make a mental note not to admit this so readily in the future.

'Yeah. Stupid name, ain't it. I think Luigi fancies himself as some sort of godfather figure.'

'So he's actually called *Luigi*?'

'Doubt it. I take it you've never been in there, then?'

'No. I always thought it looked a bit grubby from the outside. Is it?'

'Not really. In fact, it's pretty posh inside.'

'Yeah right!'

'Seriously.'

'With *you* working in there?' She laughs as she says it, so I take it as a joke rather than a slur on my character.

'I can be posh,' I assure her.

'Relative to what?'

'I don't know… Relative to the staff in here?' Glancing around I realise this is not a particularly impressive boast.

'Hmmm. Must be a *really* classy place, then,' mocks Sarah.

'What are you trying to say?'

'Nothing,' she flirts. 'Maybe I'll pop in some day. Next time the occasion calls for somewhere *special*.'

'I wouldn't bother if I were you. We don't usually serve your sort in there,' I tell her.

'What do you mean, *my* sort?'

'Common people.'

'*Common people?!* I'm not *common!*'

'If you say so. Maybe we could make an exception in your case, though, seeing as you know me. Don't stay too long, mind. Luigi might not like you lowering the tone of the place.'

'I'll just have a coffee then, shall I?'

'Yeah. I might even allow you a biscuit if you're nice to me.'

'Wanker,' she giggles, and playfully punches me in the arm.

I laugh, but resist the urge to retaliate. It's too early in the flirtation for such childish behaviour.

An arm brushes past the back of my head and it suddenly dawns on me that the pub is a lot busier than usual tonight. This summer the hot weather has hung around with a stubborn determination I can't remember ever witnessing before, and the local residents have turned to beer to quench their thirst. The place is heaving and we find our table surrounded by crowds of people who tower above us and nudge their elbows into our backs as they struggle to make way for the punters travelling to and from the bar.

'So what are you into, that is… what do you do when you're not working at the *posh* restaurant?' Sarah asks.

'Er… not a great deal,' I reply, which is pretty close to the truth. Too close, perhaps.

'So your sole purpose in life is to wait on rich people?'

'Well, when you put it like that...'

The worthlessness of my existence dawns on me all at once and I feel like a giant pigeon has shat on me from above. I have to ask myself *why* am I working? I'm not using the money as a means to support a more meaningful pursuit, such as a musical career, producing stained glass or writing a book. Neither am I saving it up for anything of note, like travelling or getting my own place. In actual fact, when I think about it, I basically earn it, spend a considerable proportion of it in the pub and shove the rest in the bank, where it sits idle and useless until I decide to blow it all on the occasional holiday or a luxury item that I later discover I don't really need. I begin to wonder how many other people live their lives in such a pointless fashion and quickly find myself faced with two other candidates for Mr Waste of Space 2003 in the shape of Gaz and the Yeti. Individually we suck, and as a group we seem to suck more than the sum of its constituent parts.

'Hey, cheer up,' says Sarah, gently placing her hand on my leg. 'I was only kidding.'

'I know you were. I was just pretending to make you feel guilty.' This is a lie – I didn't even realise my internal revelation was visible to the outside world.

'So… tell me, really. What *do* you do?'

Her persistence would normally be something to admire, but right now it's just fucking annoying. I can't really admit to her that I was serious when I said that I didn't do a great deal, as this would surely result in me being labelled a bit of a boring bastard.

'I, er… I bundle celebrities,' I answer, and immediately regret it.

'You what?'

'I bundle celebrities.' This time I try to say it with greater confidence.

'Really? I've never heard of that before. What does it involve?' she enquires innocently.

'Well…' I begin. 'You know what a bundle is, right?'

'I think so… You mean, like an orgy?'

'No!' I laugh, 'nothing like that! You've got a dirty mind, Sarah. Filthy. Well, there are some similarities to be fair, in that a bundle involves a pile of squirming bodies. But there's nothing sexual about it. Far from it, in fact. Everyone has their clothes on, for a start, although I suppose they might take them off if they were that way inclined.'

'You're not making it any clearer,' Sarah complains.

'Sorry. Ok… how can I explain this…? A bundle is where somebody is lying on the ground and somebody else lies on top of them and shouts "Bundle!" and then other people jump on until there's a mound of people on top of the person on the floor.'

'Oh! I know what you mean. Like a pile on. You see footballers doing it sometimes.'

'Yeah. Yeah, that's it. As you see, nothing like an orgy,' I smile.

'No,' she says embarrassedly. 'So how does the celebrity bit fit in, then?'

'The people we bundle are celebrities.'

'Who's *we*?'

'Us lot,' I reply, gesturing to the other lads sitting round the table. 'It's kind of like a club in a way.'

'A celebrity bundling club… how cute,' grins Sarah in an attempt to patronise me. 'So who have you bundled then, Dom?'

'Well, we haven't been doing it for that long, so… Gary Barlow was the first. Then Phillip Schofield. And a few weeks ago we got some bloke who used to be in *EastEnders*, but I can never remember his name. Oh, and Chris Evans as well.'

'All men I see. You trying to tell me something?'

'Ha ha,' I chuckle. 'Are you trying to suggest I'm a manhole inspector? No, it's merely coincidence.'

'They're not exactly A-list, are they?' Sarah points out.

'We have to start somewhere! Jesus…'

'I guess.'

'Good celebrities are hard to find, you know.'

'I'm sure they are. So how did you track them down, then? I don't think I've ever seen a celebrity in real life.' *In real life.* You'd think celebrities were make-believe the way she's talking.

Dawn and her crew have entered the building and have managed to wrangle their way onto the table adjacent to ours. She's looking good tonight is Dawn, yet for once I find I'm not distracted by her womanly charms.

'Well, it's been more luck than judgement on the most part,' I tell Sarah. 'We never go out with a specific celebrity in mind, we pick a place where we think we might find someone famous walking about. I guess it's a bit like fishing in that respect. I mean, people don't go fishing to try to catch a particular fish. At least, I don't think they do. They just go to a lake and hope they're lucky enough to land a big 'un.

'We got Gary Barlow at Heathrow airport. Schofield and the *EastEnders* guy were bundled in the Soho area; on the same day, in fact. And Chris Evans was had near Notting Hill. It's a matter of going to a trendy or expensive area and hoping you get lucky.'

'Are you having me on?' Sarah is suddenly suspicious that I'm being far from truthful.

'No, I'm serious,' I reply in my sincerest tone.

'I reckon you're making the whole thing up to try and make me look stupid,' she accuses.

'Why would I do that?'

'I don't know. It sounds a bit farfetched to me.'

'Look, I can prove it. Bertie has them all stored on his video phone... except that he's not here right now.'

'Conveniently...'

'Seems that way, doesn't it. But seriously, ask any of the others if you don't believe me.'

'No, it's ok, I believe you. I mean, as you said, who would ever make up something like that? It's too weird.'

'Tell me about it.'

We both take a break for a moment. I do so to take a swig of my drink, while Sarah busies herself lighting up a cigarette.

'But *why*?' Sarah asks after blowing a cloud of smoke over the top of my head. 'I mean, why would you do something like that?'

'I don't know. Because we can? Why do people do anything? I mean, why do people climb mountains? Because they're there. That's what people say, anyway.'

'That's different.'

'How? It's all the same thing. Take any pastime, any sport. Tennis, for instance. Think about what you're *actually* doing when you play tennis: you're trying to hit a bouncy ball past another human being within an area constricted only by lines painted on the floor. It doesn't make a lot of sense when you think about it.'

'If you say so. But why bundling? Why celebrities?'

'Why not?'

'I don't know. Because it's an insane, stupid thing to do?'

'Don't knock it 'til you've tried it.'

'Pardon?'

One of the bar staff must be a big KLF fan, because the amp has been jacked up and the electronic magnificence of *3 a.m. Eternal* makes it almost impossible for us to hear a word either of us is saying. I drag my chair closer to Sarah so that our legs are now touching and she doesn't make any effort to move away.

'I said… Don't knock it 'til you've tried it. You might enjoy it.'

'No, I'll pass if that's ok with you. No offence. I'm happy to leave it to the experts.'

'Probably a wise decision.'

Sarah takes another long drag, exhaling the smoke straight upwards this time, so that it swirls beneath the spotlight above our heads.

'So do you bundle every celebrity you see?'

'We try to, yeah. It doesn't always work, though. The last person we tried to get was a failed attempt.'

'Who was that?'

'Lennox Lewis.'

'I'm not surprised you failed!'

'I know! The problem is, one of the rules of the club…' I pause. I need to find something else to call it other than "club", because it sounds a bit gay. 'One of the rules of celebrity bundling is that if you see a celebrity you have to try to bundle them. Another rule is that the person who sees them first has to instigate the bundle. We all saw Lennox coming out of a nightclub in the early hours, but we all pretended not to see him as none of us wanted to be the one that had to tackle him. Understandably.

'Eventually it was me that caved in. I pointed him out and then went over to chat to him. I shook his hand and told him how much I enjoyed watching him pummel Tyson and stuff like that, while Yeti crouched down behind him so we could trip him up. The problem was, he noticed Yeti doing it and he went a bit ape shit. I think he might've thought we were trying to mug him or something. I mean, who the fuck would try to mug Lennox Lewis? He's huge!'

I hold my hand about a foot above my head, which is probably a slight exaggeration. But Sarah gets the picture, so I continue.

'We tried our best to bundle him, but he fought us off easily. It must've looked pretty funny, because he had Yeti pinned down with one foot while Volk was wrapped around his other leg like a child and me and Gaz were sort of hanging off his neck. It was a bit like playing rugby at school, when about five little kids would try to bring down the one boy who had already gone through puberty by the age of twelve, dragging him down through sheer weight of numbers.

'In the end we had to leg it before he beat the shit out of us. So if anyone ever says to you, "The bigger they are, the harder they fall", they're lying. We can laugh about it now, but it was pretty scary at the time.'

'Sounds it! None of you got seriously injured, then?' she asks with genuine concern.

'Thankfully, no. Aside from a few cuts and bruises we escaped unscathed. I think Lennox decided we weren't enough of a threat for him to use his boxing skills. Which is probably a good thing. Otherwise my boyish good looks might've been at risk.'

I strike a sultry pose and give her the eye.

'You wish,' she laughs, although I can tell she's impressed by the story. It's time to make my move.

'Sarah, I was wondering… This may sound a bit forward, but would you like to go for a drink sometime, just you and me?'

Her cheeks redden and she looks down at her feet. I can instantly tell by her body language that the answer is going to be negative. Why did I even bother opening my big mouth? We were sitting here having a nice little chat and I had to take it one step too far. I had to go ahead and open the box, only to find that the cat is well and truly dead.

'I'd love to – really I would – but I can't. I've got a boyfriend.'

Jesus wept! A fucking *boyfriend*! I feel like yelling at her that this is *precisely* the sort of information I needed fifteen minutes ago when instead she was testing my patience by telling me about her university course! That way I'd have known not to get my hopes up when she kept touching my leg, fluttering her eyelids and acting like a general prick tease. Typical fucking women. So goddamn friendly and flirtatious when all along they aren't even available. It makes me sick.

'Ah well,' I say awkwardly. 'I should've known you'd have a boyfriend. The good ones are always taken.'

'Aaah, thank you. It was really sweet of you to ask, though.'

This last statement is blatantly supposed to make me feel better, but it only makes me feel worse. *Sweet?* That's a term you use to describe an animal or a baby, for fuck's sake. I'm not *sweet*!

Sitting back in my chair I take a long swig of my pint. Looking at the glass, I see that it's moved from being half full to half empty in a matter of seconds, despite the level of liquid moving less than an inch. I need to make an escape so I can take time out. A trip to the bar is in order, I think. But Yeti beats me to it, already out of his chair and wriggling past me.

'Want another drink, Big D?'

I wonder whether he heard Sarah's rejection and this is his way of saying, "Don't worry mate, it happens to the best of us".

'Same again, please. Cheers, Yeti.'

'Boddington's, yeah?'

'Yeah, please.'

He leaves the table and I'm now isolated with the siren, an empty chair on her right and another on my left cutting us off from the rest of the world. I should have offered to help Yeti carry the drinks. Then at least I'd have had the opportunity to check out some other women who maybe didn't have boyfriends. Perhaps it's the drink or maybe it's the rejection, but all of a sudden the girls in here seem to be looking pretty fine tonight. Judging by the number of silky legs on show, I'm guessing miniskirts have come back into fashion and there seems to be an unspoken, unofficial competition going on for who can get away with wearing the least material. I for one am certainly not complaining. The pub attracts a fairly young crowd, so the flesh on show is slick: flat stomachs, firm arses and barely a waistline in sight. It almost makes me wish I was back in the sixth form.

'What did he just call you?' Sarah asks after a lengthy pause.

'Who?'

'Yeti,' she says uncomfortably, like she thinks she sounds stupid saying his name. She does. Most women do in truth. Nicknames always sound better coming from the mouth of a man.

'Big D.'

'*Big D*? Why do they call you that?'

I unfold my arms, glance down at my groin and then raise my eyebrows at her as if to say, "It's yours if you want it".

'Oh.'

I detect a glint in her eye, and I begin to fear for the future employment of her boyfriend. This game is far from over.

Message From Across the Globe

Hey there Rach

not sure where you'll be when you get to read this email, but hopefully you'll have found an internet café somewhere in the deepest jungles, deserts or swamps that you happen to be passing through right now.

How are u?

How long have you been away for now? 7 months (or is it 8)? seems like a lifetime anyway. Apologies that I haven't been in contact much for all this time. I'd like to say that its because I've been too busy doing really exciting stuff, but the truth is I'm still just drifting along doing the same old sh*t as always! Need you here to give me a boot up the asre!!!

you must have seen some pretty amazing stuff on your travels - will be hard to come back to thame after all that. It's only a month to go now right? Can't imgine your counting the days.

me and the others have got this new hobby. its called celebrity bundling. basically, its like autograph hunting, but instead of getting an autograpj you bundle them instead. we've bundled loads of famous people already. anyway, I'll tell you all about it when you get back.

on the subject of you coming back.......... was thinking. i think you and i should give it another go. i think we rushed into the whole break-up thing and having had time to think about it I can see now that it was the wrong decision. i've met other girls but none of them compare to you. It isn't the same and the truth is that I miss you like crazy. hope you feel the same way, otherwise I'm going to look pretty stupid!

anyway, glad to get that off my chest. look forward to seeing you when you get back if I don't hear from you in the meantime.

Look after yourself

Dom x

p.s. sorry if this email doesn't make a lot of sense - its friday night and im a bit drunk!!!

How to Win Friends and Bundle People

After the would-be success of using Celebrity Bundler as an occupation to wow the ladies ("would-be" in the sense that my morals prevented me from pursuing Sarah beyond our brief encounter on Friday night even though she was *definitely* there for the taking), I figured that the idea was worth sharing with a wider audience as a means of gaining some image-boosting notoriety. I called on the wide-ranging skills of the Yeti and together we came up with a plan to push the concept of celebrity bundling to the world stage. When I say "together", I mean that I told Yeti my ideas and he converted them into a meaningful/useful/realistic form and put them into action.

It is a compelling way to spend a Sunday, taking it in turns to swig from a couple of bottles of Krug that we skanked from Bertie's house a few years back and had never quite found an occasion worthy enough to warrant their use, while at the same time thinking up ways to conquer the world in as short a time as is humanly possible. I've never been a fan of champagne myself, and the case for this particular bottle isn't aided by the fact that neither of us could be bothered to wait for it to chill properly. We're left with a drink that tastes mysteriously like it's been laced with parmesan cheese as it slips down our throats, and I quickly reach the stage when I have to hold it in my mouth for a few seconds before swallowing. From my point of view, I may as well be gulping back carbonated piss. But for some reason I'm under the impression that drinking such an expensive liquid will aid my thought processes, so I soldier on regardless, the two of us admirably working our way through the preliminary stages of drunkenness and onto greater things by the time the *Hollyoaks* omnibus finishes at around midday. Such are the joys of being completely twatted at this early stage in the day that alcoholism is briefly discussed as a hobby we could grow to love. Until Yeti points out that it isn't a pastime we can afford to indulge in on our present salaries, especially since neither of us is prepared to climb down to the bottom of the well with cider or special brew. It's all or nothing and the latter prevails, our livers breathing an intoxicated sigh of relief.

While the champers initially helps to massage our dehydrated brains out of their ritual of Sunday morning inactivity, it also distorts our sense of reality, mine in particular. Time and time again ideas come blasting into my head like divine revelations and I excitedly gabble them at Yeti before realising halfway through that they make absolutely no sense whatsoever; my rallying speeches petering out without him even having to point me in the direction of rationality. However, we are able to extract a small amount of useful material from my otherwise nonsensical ramblings, and with a mixture of imagination, shrewdness and perseverance we come up with a plan of attack so brilliant that it could only have come from the mind of a drunk. Without wanting to bore you to death with the details, the plan goes something like this:

- We will digitally transfer the video clips of the four successful celebrity bundles to date (currently stored on Bertie's mobile phone) onto Yeti's computer and release them via email, in chronological order and at one-week intervals, from an anonymous email account.

- We will set up a website and ensure that if anyone does a search for "Bundle", "Bundling", "Celebrity Bundle" or "Celebrity Bundling", it will come out as the top choice on any of the major internet search engines. On the website itself there would be details of all the bundles that have taken place (where, when, who, how, etc), links to the aforementioned video clips, a forum where people can share their own bundling experiences and a set of in-depth profiles of me, Yeti, Gaz, Volk and Bertie.

- Once the website has received a large enough number of hits to suggest that we're attracting a reasonable amount of public interest, we will release *The Beginner's Guide to Celebrity Bundling* via email.

Yeti and I rub our hands together with great pleasure at having produced such a prodigious plan. The real beauty of it lies in its subtlety, the way that a tiny amount of information is trickled to a few unsuspecting individuals, who would then forward it to others and set about an avalanche effect that would see our work spread across the electronic globe in a matter of days. God bless the world wide web. We allow ourselves smug, self-satisfied smiles at what we've achieved over the last few hours and dream of the fame that awaits. Yeti proposes a toast, only to discover that we're out of the good stuff. No matter, though, as we're already drunk on glory. It's doubtful anyone else in the country has had as productive a Sunday morning as we have. In the same space of time that others sweated out hangovers or sang cheery songs with their fellow members of the God Squad, the Yeti and I have concocted a scheme of unparalleled vision. Sometimes I'm amazed by my own genius. Astounded even. Me and Yeti muse over how we must be up there with the greatest minds in the country right now, if not the world.

The sound of a key in the front door snaps us out of our woozy self-adulation.

'Shit! My mum's home!' panics Yeti. 'Quick, hide the bottles!'

'Where?' My mind isn't functioning as quickly as it might.

'I don't know… here, behind the magazine rack.'

I pass my bottle to Yeti and he hurriedly stuffs it down by the side of the sofa, then quickly turns on the television and starts surfing the channels for something we might realistically be watching. MTV would be my choice, and it happens to be the one he selects as his mum enters the room.

'Hi, guys,' she chirps cheerfully, her face glowing from having come in from outside. 'What are you two up to?'

'Nothing much, just watching MTV,' replies Yeti, a little too defensively for my liking.

'It's a wonderful day outside, you two shouldn't be cooped up in here all day.'

'We were about to head out,' says Yeti.

'Good, good. And how are you, Dom?'

'I'm very well thank you. How about yourself?' I reply, concentrating hard on pronouncing the words.

'Yes, I'm good thanks.'

Don't talk to me, please. I don't feel up to holding an adult conversation right now. I'd struggle to stand at the moment, let alone chat. Yeti's mum eyes us suspiciously. It's bad enough that we're both already looking so shifty, but the room probably stinks of alcohol as well.

'Have you two been drinking?' It's more of an accusation than a straightforward question.

'Er… yes. A little bit,' slurs Yeti.

'Let me see,' demands Yeti's mum and she holds out her hand.

Yeti reaches down the side of the sofa and presents her with an empty champagne bottle.

'And the other one.'

Yeti reluctantly gives up the second bottle. His mum inspects the label and raises her eyebrows in approval.

'This is expensive stuff. What's the occasion?'

'Er, Dom's received an offer to publish his book,' says Yeti, nudging me in the ribs.

'I didn't know you were writing a book, Dominic.'

'Er, well…'

'He's been keeping it a secret in case it never got published,' Yeti interrupts.

'Well, congratulations! I look forward to reading it. Do I get a signed copy, then?'

'Yeah, you and everyone else,' I manage to joke.

'Brilliant. Wow, Dominic Carter the writer. Who would have thought it?'

'Yeah, who would've?' I reply, looking at Yeti.

'What was the point in that?' I hiss when she's gone through to the kitchen and is safely out of earshot.

'Sorry, mate. Mum thinks I've been drinking too much lately and this…' he points at the champagne bottles, 'would've been too much for her to take. She'd probably have carted me off to rehab.'

'Really?'

'Yeah, she's a bit of a worrier my mum.'

'But now she thinks I've written a fucking book!'

'So?'

'Well what's she gonna think when it never materialises? She'll think I'm some sort of compulsive liar.'

'She thinks that anyway.'

'What? I've never lied to your mum! Well, apart from that time when she caught me rooting through your sister's underwear drawer, but that was pretty much a matter of life or death.'

'Remind me again *why* you were doing that.'

'Gaz used to *well* fancy your sister, so I was gonna give him a pair of her pants for his birthday. Don't ask me how I came up with the idea. I think her door was open when I was walking past to the toilet and it just popped into my head. Anyway, I told your mum Volk had hidden my keys in there and I was trying to retrieve them.'

'Oh yeah, I remember now. Volk was banned from my house for about three months and he never knew why. You're a sick bastard, you are.'

'Your mum believed me, though, so it doesn't explain why she thinks I'm a serial bullshitter.'

'Think about it, Big D. Whenever she asks you what you're up to, the sort of stuff you come out with can be pretty weird.'

'Like what?'

'Well, one time she asked you if you had any plans for the weekend and you told her you were going to sit and drink beer on the roof of the Co-op supermarket.'

'Which was true. It's a great place to drink beer.'

'And another time you said you were planning to photocopy a picture of Bertie's face, make some masks and then hand them out in the town centre to boost his profile in the local community.'

'Also true.'

'Yeah, but imagine what it must've sounded like to my mum!'

'I guess. Well, I'm glad my reputation as a liar has kept you out of rehab. Shame in a way, though. It would've been a good place to find celebrities. I mean, some of them are pretty much permanent residents there. They use it like a fucking holiday home.'

'That's a good point. Maybe I should start drinking for real.'

'Maybe you should. Anyway, let's go outside, I could do with some fresh air. We'll give the Bertmeister a call to get those video clips off him and you can start putting this master plan into action.'

'What do you mean, *I* can start putting this plan into action? What are *you* going to do?'

'Nothing. I don't know much about computers, I'd only slow you down. It's better if I leave you to it.'

'You can at least write *The Beginner's Guide to Celebrity Bundling*, seeing as you invented the whole thing.'

'No need, I've already done it. One step ahead, Yeti, one step ahead,' I say, tapping my right temple.

'If you say so.'

'Show some enthusiasm, will you? This is the start of something big! Huge!'

'Big D, I'm tired and I'm pissed. I think I'd struggle to drum up any enthusiasm if the dark-haired one from t.A.T.u. entered the room wearing nothing but the smallest of thongs.'

I'm about to ask him, '*Are you gay?*' but think better of it.

Like Father, Like Son

I return home one night to find the house in an unusually darkened state, the only light coming from the street lamps, which glow feebly through the uncovered windows. Dad is normally pretty obsessive about making sure the curtains are drawn, paranoid as he is about burglars sizing up our wares for a possible future visit. So I guess he must be out somewhere and shut them myself, blocking out the intrusive silence of the outside world. And now I'm in pitch black. I don't mind it like this – your own home is pretty much the only place in the world where the surroundings are familiar enough for you to be able to walk around in the dark without fear of bumping into things, even when the house is as cluttered as ours.

As is nearly always the case when I've had a few pints, I'm feeling a bit peckish, so I go into the kitchen to make myself a snack, flicking on the light as I enter.

'Jesus fucking shit!' I yell as I leap away from the figure that suddenly appears at the table. 'You scared the life out of me, Dad! What are you doing sitting in the dark?'

His reply is lost in a deep sniff and I instantly feel a lump growing in my own throat. You know how it is when you suddenly realise you've fucked up big time, when the dread fills you from the feet upwards until your head is full of it and your hair tingles and you can barely even see? That's how I feel right now.

'Oh man. I'm sorry, Dad. I'm really sorry.'

I walk up and put an arm around his shoulders. I try to pull him towards me, but he resists. He sits there motionless, rigid. It's obvious he'd rather grieve alone, in his own space. In one hand he holds an empty glass that, judging by the smell, was once full of whisky, and in the other he clutches a picture of a beautiful lady: my mother, his wife.

'One night,' he starts. I know what he's going to say and I don't want to hear it. 'One night of the year. That's all. I don't ask for much. One night a year.'

'I'm sorry.'

'I know you'd rather be out with your mates, that you don't want to be sitting here in the house with your dad,' he carries on. 'But tonight! You could've been here tonight!'

The emotion is too much for him and he breaks down, the photo frame slipping from his grasp as he brings his hands to his face. The noise it makes as it clatters onto the table is deafening.

'It's only been two years,' he sobs. 'How could you forget?'

He's right. How *could* I forget?

'I don't know,' I reply.

'You don't know,' he mumbles. 'So where have you been? Work?'

'No. I quit.'

'You quit? Why?'

'*Why*? I don't want to be working as a waiter for the rest of my life, that's why.'

'And what else are you going to do?'

I take a couple of steps back as I can sense his grief is rapidly turning to anger. He has a temper on him does Dad, and the whisky doesn't help.

'I haven't thought about that yet.'

'You haven't thought about it yet,' he sneers. 'Well that's the problem with you, isn't it? You never bloody think! And what do you expect to do in the meantime, eh?'

'I *said*, I haven't thought about that yet.'

'Typical!' he spits. 'And how are we supposed to pay the rent if you're not working? I suppose you expect me to support you while you *think about it*, do you?'

'I've got savings.'

'Yeah? And how long are they going to last when you spend the whole time out drinking at the pub with your dead-end mates?'

'Leave them out of this,' I warn him.

'And where are they now? Still at the pub are they? The anniversary of your mother's death and you're out drinking with that bunch of *losers*. I hope you feel guilty!'

I grab the glass from his hand and hurl it against the wall, where it obliterates in all directions, the fragments of glass catching the light as they scatter like an exploding firework.

'Of course I feel fucking guilty!' I yell at him and run upstairs to my room, slamming the door behind me.

I bury my face in my pillow and weep silently until I can feel the linen becoming saturated against my skin. You're never too old to cry, and I'm not ashamed to admit that I do it quite often. Always alone though. I don't want to share my grief with that *wanker* downstairs.

It's about ten minutes before I'm all cried out, at which point I roll over and just lie there staring at the ceiling, or rather beyond the ceiling, trying to imagine whether Mum is up there somewhere looking down on us. She'd hate to see us arguing like this, you know, but she'd appreciate that we've never really been close, me and Dad. And we're drifting further apart with each day that passes, episodes like this only acting to speed up the process. She'd probably say it's because we're so alike; a pair of stubborn bastards, basically.

There's a knock at the door, a pause, and then Dad enters. He doesn't step far into the room, unwilling to enter my space. He just hovers there in the doorway.

'I'm sorry, Dom,' he apologises, the tone of his voice exposing how painful it is for him to say it. 'It's the drink.'

'Don't drink then.'

'Yeah, that would be an idea, wouldn't it?' He makes a half-hearted attempt at a chuckle, but his acting is unconvincing. 'No hard feelings, eh?'

It's too easy to say that now, too easy to take back what's already been said. Said and meant.

'It was a mistake,' I tell him.

'Yeah, I know it was. I miss her, that's all.'

And you think I don't?

'And you're right to quit your job, too,' he goes on. 'You can do better than that. You've got brains… like your mother.'

I don't answer.

'But if you want to talk about it, your plans…'

'Yeah. Yeah, I will,' I tell him, to make him feel better.

'Good,' he nods pensively. 'Oh, and Dom.'

'What?'

'Don't end up like me.'

'I'll try my best,' I smile.

You bet your fucking life I'll try.

Dad leaves the room, quietly closing the door behind him, and I look once again to the ceiling for company.

The walk to St Mary's Church from my house isn't exactly a long one, but journeys have a habit of taking a hell of a lot longer when you know for a fact there's nothing particularly uplifting waiting for you when you get there. Plus I have to stop off and get some flowers from the local flower stall on the way. Fuck knows what I'm buying. I just point and grunt at what I perceive to be the nicest ones within my price range and the woman who owns the store does the rest. And they ain't cheap either – flowers in general, I mean – especially for somebody who gave up their job the day before.

I take a fairly roundabout route for the remainder of the journey in an attempt to avoid other people; not because I'm embarrassed to be seen carrying a bunch of flowers, but because I'm trying to avoid the exact kind of situation that I can see is going to materialise the moment I spot Heather, a classmate of yesteryear, walking down the road towards me. As soon as she spots the flowers (and to be fair, she couldn't fucking miss them), her expression immediately changes from one of indifference to an insanely cheerful grin. I try to contort my own expression into one that says, "Please don't say what I know you're about to say", but either I do a crap job of it or she doesn't seem to notice.

'Oh, Dom, you shouldn't have. Are those for me?'

No, they're for my dead mother, would've been my instinctive reply, but I bite my lip before the words slip out. After all, she's not to know where I'm headed.

'Maybe next time,' I smile politely.

'How disappointing!' Heather chirps. 'Who's the lucky lady?'

'That's none of your goddamn business, and I'd appreciate it if you stayed out of my personal affairs,' I smirk at her.

Although I say it in a way that can only be taken as a joke, my lame attempt at humour only partially disguises what is a very serious point.

'Well, whoever they're for… I hope she appreciates them,' smiles Heather.

'Thanks. See you around.'

'Yeah, see you, Dom.'

We go our separate ways, and I'm left wondering why some people feel the need to comment when they see you carrying or wearing something remotely out of the ordinary. Don't get me wrong – I know she was only being nice – but surely a simple "good morning" would have been sufficient. Ignorance is bliss, though, in her case especially.

It occurs to me as I pass through the graveyard gates that this is only the second time I've been here in the last two years. Not that many people choose to hang out in graveyards, mind you, yet by any standards my visits are beyond infrequent. One solitary visit on the same morning each year. Or roughly the same morning each year I should say, as on this occasion I'm a day late.

I stray from the concrete path and venture in amongst the graves themselves, finding myself staring at a tomb that's covered with those weird green stones you only ever see in graveyards. As a kid I thought they were the most precious stones in the world and would probably have stolen a handful were it not for the fact that I thought the dead person might come back in the night to reclaim them. To this day I couldn't tell you what they are.

Beneath the shadow of a tree and surrounded by headstones bearing the names of people I've never heard of, Mum's final resting place is hardly what you would call an ideal spot. Mind you, you could say she was lucky to get a place in the churchyard at all, especially when you consider the way the world is going. Everything revolves around greed these days, and it's true when they say money talks, even in a place like the church. The fact is, space is running out and graveyards are becoming overcrowded. They're already talking about making the graves six bodies deep, turning each plot into a kind of involuntary, morbid bundle. It's something of a miracle that some ruthless bastard hasn't swept in to make a quick buck or two out of the whole burial thing. I mean, it sounds to me like a pretty safe business to be in. After all, people are always going to die.

So how long will it be before we see www.easy-funeral.com? Book the whole thing over the internet using dropdown menus and then pick it all up on the day, selection limited to a choice of budget, standard or luxury casket; fifteen percent off if you book in advance; optional extra insurance cover in case you damage the coffin; £50 extra if you want anything other than the standard epitaph. That sort of thing. They've commercialised everything else, so why not death?

Being back here reminds me of the funeral service, and this probably has a lot to do with why I never come to visit. All the well-wishers lining up to hug me and to say how sorry they were, which made me feel about a thousand times worse. And I've never been to a wedding or christening either, so everything I associate with the church is negative: a mixture of sadness and boredom. I used to absolutely *hate* going to church. Having to sit there in a refrigerated, musty room listening to some charismatically challenged corpse drone on and on for hours on end, and not even being able to doze off because of the frequent, earth-shatteringly loud mutterings of "amen" and people coughing so goddamn hard it shakes the whole pew. And being expected to be able to sing songs nobody has ever heard of without the whole thing sounding fucking awful. And the few songs that you do recognise being completely ruined by the fact that when singing in a church you're only allowed to go at quarter of the speed because the old biddy on the organ can't go any faster due to her arthritic fingers. Every hymn lasts about twenty-five fucking minutes; supposedly happy songs with misleading titles like "All Things Bright and Beautiful" becoming such an arduous effort that the mere act of singing them makes you lose the will to live. Maybe things have changed since then, but to be honest I'm quite happy never to find out.

Upon locating it, I squat down by Mum's grave and carefully place the flowers against the headstone. They sit there alone; either Dad didn't get any yesterday or some fucking scally has already nicked them. I don't know which scenario is more likely. Crouching by the grave is always difficult for me, partly because I never really know what to say and partly because I've got bad knees. I reach down and stroke the ground with the palm of my hand. It's pretty dry, so I slump down and sit cross-legged like a boy scout, without the fear of having to walk back through town looking like I've wet myself. And then I sit there in silence. It's not as if I can say a prayer or anything, and talking to a slab of stone seems like a strange thing to do. So I just sit. I try not to even think too hard as the surroundings don't really inspire happy thoughts, but I can't help it, and my mind drifts back to what life was like a couple of years ago when life seemed easy and everything made sense. But that all changed after the accident.

It was bad enough losing Mum without the added blow of losing Rachel a couple of months later. You know, it can leave you pretty twisted suddenly finding yourself without the two most important women in your life. To be honest, I don't blame Rachel. We were already on the rocks and it would've taken some kind of saint to put up with me after Mum died. And as it turned out, Rachel wasn't quite up to the task. She came pretty damn close, but Mum was the only saint I knew, the only one who would have put up with my moods; the same moods she was inadvertently the cause of. Life has been, how can I say it, *problematic*, since then. When you lose things you previously took for granted you're forced to stop and take a look at what's left. And what *is* left?

A shadow looms over me, and without the warmth of the sun I momentarily shiver. I don't shift from my school assembly position, craning my neck back to see who it is and lowering my head once I realise it's only Dad.

'Thought I'd find you here,' he says, kneeling down next to me.

I don't answer him. To tell you the truth, I didn't even know people said stuff like, "Thought I'd find you here" in real life, only in the movies or on TV. Either way, Dad's confirmation of his own correct assumption marks both the start and the end of the world's shortest conversation. The two of us sit there staring through the ground at what lies beneath, motionless until Dad decides he's had enough and gets up to walk back to the car, me waiting for another half minute or so and then jogging to catch him up.

'Any of the nine people in the studio today could win up to £10,000. They don't know each other; however, if they want that prize money they will have to work as a team. *But,* eight of them will leave with nothing, as round by round we lose the player voted... The Weakest Link. Let's meet the team.'

After the combined disappointment of a) the abortive bundle attempt on Lennox Lewis, b) our total inability to track down any further celebrity victims, and c) the withering failure of my painstakingly planned publicity campaign, suddenly we found ourselves with the opportunity of a lifetime. This really was the big one; a chance to take it all to the next level.

You see, long before the whole celebrity bundling idea reared its ugly head, me, Gaz, Volk and Yeti had all applied to enter *The Weakest Link*. It presented itself as a means of earning a bit of extra money rather than any of us being closet fans of Anne Robinson, or even particularly wanting to appear on TV (though I suspect Volk has always secretly fancied seeing himself on the small screen). It was only Bertie who didn't bother entering as he claims to earn enough money without having to degrade himself by "being made to answer stupid questions on national television and at the same time be insulted by that ginger witch". Mind you, so extreme is the culture of competitiveness in his field of employment he probably would've been sacked if he didn't win; a chance he was understandably reluctant to take.

After months of waiting with no response, it was Yeti that received the phone call and after convincing himself that the offer was genuine and not the rest of us winding him up, he gladly accepted and graciously invited us along as his audience support. I'm not sure why they chose Yeti rather than any of the rest of us. I suppose it's possible that Volkan's application was identified as a hoax and thrown out immediately, purely on account of his name, and that mine was too dull for further consideration. This would have left a toss-up between Gaz and

Yeti. Maybe they thought that the latter's nickname would provide Anne with an abundance of material with which to insult him. Or maybe they thought that to belittle a one-eared man in front of an audience of millions was beyond the boundaries of good taste. Either way, it was a stroke of luck that Yeti was the chosen one as he's the most intelligent by some distance. The only time we ever stand a chance in the local pub quiz is when the hairy one is involved. He's also the only one among us who can consistently answer more than three questions correctly during an episode of *University Challenge*.

We take our place in the audience, our contestant connection granting us front row seats, placing us ahead of all the random people who are here for the sake of it rather than to support anyone in particular. I find myself wishing I'd drunk some water before I came in. All I can taste at the moment is the remnants of the foul beverage I purchased not more than fifteen minutes ago, it having deceived me by masquerading under the misleading title of "cappuccino". It isn't so much the repulsive taste that bothers me, more the knowledge that my breath must smell like I've got a dead cat lodged in my windpipe. But it's a bit late to do anything about it now.

After being briefed about what will happen during filming, the lights dim and we settle into our chairs to enjoy the show.

It's always advisable to identify your favourites (and those you loathe) for any contest that's about to commence. This adds an element of excitement to even the most tedious of game shows, since it is immeasurably satisfying to see that your prior labelling of somebody as "a bit of a knob jockey" is recognised, agreed with and acted upon by the other contestants. So this is what I do. After all, they say it only takes fifteen seconds to form an opinion about a person, and the fact that the contestant introductions are far shorter than this serves as an extra challenge to my many prejudices.

'I'm Nigel, I'm from Manchester and I'm a student.'

There's always one. Rather than getting a job to pay his way through university, this joker has decided to enter a game show in which the chances are he'll leave with nothing. Lazy, good-for-nothing students.

'I'm Brian, I'm forty, I'm from Newcastle and I'm a house husband.'

Brian doesn't look anything like a house husband. He looks like a house raider, sleeves rolled up to reveal massive, tattooed forearms. Volk, sitting to my right, nudges me with his leg to indicate he thinks Brian will go all the way, something I wouldn't necessarily disagree with. Brian means business; he's not a man to be messed with.

'I'm Margaret, I'm fifty-seven, I'm from Gloucester and I'm an events organiser.'

I don't really have anything to say about Margaret, as she conjures up feelings of pure indifference. If she were a type of food she would be a boiled potato. Nevertheless, Gaz seems to sense something behind the offensively bland exterior and labels her as champion material.

'I'm Amy, I'm twenty-four, I'm from Luton and I'm a taekwondo instructor.'

Now she's pretty tasty. Frizzy blonde hair and an impressively ample chest. And evidently she must be good enough at the old martial arts stuff not to have received too many blows to the face. Naturally, I want her to win, and I gesture to the others to make my feelings known.

'Kate's boobs were bigger than that,' sulks Gaz in my ear.

'I expect they still are, although they're of no benefit to you anymore,' I whisper back at him.

I know this is harsh, but it's been three weeks since their breakup and I'm all out of sympathy. He should count himself lucky he got to see her naked, a memory I imagine he'd be unlikely to forget in a hurry, and one that the vast majority of men would pay a princely sum to have in their wank bank.

'I'm Dag and I live in Ipswich, but I'm originally from the United States of America. I'm fifty-seven and a civil engineer.'

Dag struggles with his words. Maybe it's only nerves, but I can't help thinking this doesn't bode well for the times ahead. Plus he's a Yank, which will no doubt count against him at some point during the course of the game.

'I'm Dennis, I'm twenty-four years old, I live in Thame and I'm a waiter.'

The producers wouldn't allow him to use the name Yeti, so it's one of the rare occasions when he is referred to by the name his parents gave him. He *always* introduces himself as Yeti, so believe me when I tell you that hearing the words "I'm Dennis" coming from his lips is quite a novel event.

'I'm Gordon, I'm thirty, I'm from Edinburgh and I'm a lawyer.'

He looks a bit like a hamster, does Gordon; small, hairy and harmless with slightly puffed-out cheeks. This animal-like charm and soft Scottish accent could well endear him to the other contestants, making him a strong outside bet for the pot of gold. Bertie recognises this too and marks him down as *his* tip for the riches.

And that concludes tonight's betting. Despite being an intellectual colossus, none of us bet on Yeti. After all, he isn't in it to win it. At least, he'd fucking well better not be.

'I'm Zara, from Hertfordshire. I'm twenty-six and I'm sub-editor of a magazine.'

Zara's not bad either, not bad at all in actual fact. Tall, dark and elegant, the lady clearly has style, although she looks older than her stated twenty-six years. Maybe she's lying. After all, it wouldn't be the first time a woman has lied about her age. Either way, I'd still do her given the choice.

'I'm Doug, I'm from Leicestershire, I'm fifty-one, and… mine an, I'm entertainer.'

With his unkempt hair bordering on an afro and his ill-fitting brown polo shirt drawing attention to his saggy man boobs, Doug looks like he's stepped out of a special needs class, invited here by the BBC in order to comply with anti-discrimination laws. And judging by his bumbling, Doug is probably as dense as he looks. He makes such a hash of his lines that for a moment I think they're going to have to reshoot the entire opening. But they don't, and his verbal constipation is left in for the entertainment of the viewing public.

The retard's bungled words bring the formal introductions to an enjoyable conclusion and the camera swings back around to Anne, her black clothes contrasting starkly with her pallid complexion and rusty hair, like someone has cracked an egg on top of a police riot baton. In the spotlight once again, she speaks her lines like the true professional she is.

'And now the rules. Each round, your aim is to answer enough questions correctly to reach your £1,000 target within the time limit. The fastest way is to create a chain of nine correct answers. Get your question wrong and you break the chain and lose all the money in the chain. But if you say "Bank" before the question is asked, the money is safe; however, you start a new chain from scratch. Remember, at the end of the round only money that has been banked can be taken forward.

'In round one there will be three minutes on the clock. We will start with the person whose name comes first alphabetically. That's you, Amy. Let's play, *The Weakest Link*.'

Music sounds and the lights perform acrobatics before settling on the contestants, who form an inward-looking semi-circle with the ginger dominatrix acting as the focal point.

'The first question is for £20. Start the clock! Amy, who is the mother of Prince Edward, the Earl of Wessex?'

'Pass,' says Amy, without a moment's hesitation.

Well done, Amy, off to a real flyer there. You really done me proud. I start to think that maybe I should have gone with Zara instead.

'The Queen,' Anne informs her, and then turns to the next contestant. 'Dag, in security, what's the instrument that is inserted into the lock and turned in order to operate the mechanism?'

Dag leans forward as she speaks, concentrating intently on every word. Great furrows appear in his forehead as though a tiny farmer has taken a plough to his skin.

'The key?' he answers speculatively.

'Correct. Dennis, before eating a banana, people usually remove the what? The seeds or the skin?'

Jesus wept! I know it's only the first round, but that's a pointlessly straightforward question, even without the additional help of narrowing it down to one of two answers. I try my best to envisage who might get such a question wrong, but I can't think of anyone over the age of three. Surely only an absent mind or a complete slip of the tongue would result in an incorrect answer.

'Skin.'

'Correct. Gordon, on a greetings card, which word usually appears before the word birthday or between the words many and…'

'Happy,' Gordon butts in before Anne has a chance to finish the question, clearly undeterred by the cumbersome presence of all the food he's storing in his cheeks. The flying Scotsman is obviously keen to stamp his authority on the game early on.

'Correct. Zara, in family life, which colloquial word for mother is a word meaning silent?'

Zara looks completely blank before reluctantly uttering the word 'Pass.'

'Mum!' chirps Anne in a "you really should have known that" tone.

Zara allows herself a wry smile, knowing Anne will be using this to belittle her come the end of the round.

Anne seamlessly works her way around the rest of the group. Doug gets his question wrong, which comes as no surprise to anybody (including himself, judging by his reaction). Nigel answers his question with a smugness that says, "I'm in higher education, you know. Don't insult my intelligence". Brian and Margaret both answer correctly and it's back to Amy again, and I'm pleased to say that she goes some way to redeeming herself by accurately identifying "horse" as the odd one out among a group of words otherwise consisting of types of vegetable. And so the game continues, the questions jumping between the ridiculously easy to the plain ridiculous.

'Time's up. You banked £650,' states Anne without even the slightest hint of congratulation. 'But whose head is in the clouds? Which fool is fooling nobody? It's time to vote off, the weakest link.'

It amuses me the way she says 'theweakestlink' like it's a single word, especially as she pronounces everything else so goddamn slowly and precisely.

The contestants set about scrawling names on large pieces of cardboard. Take your fucking pick. The level of general knowledge on the show is pitiful and you could choose one of about six obvious targets. Personally, I'd plump for Doug, who is clearly a stupid man. Yet to my disbelief it is Amy who receives the highest number of votes. The fools have voted off the fitty! Getting the first question of the whole quiz wrong must have stuck in their narrow minds. This means we're left with Zara as the solitary source of eye candy, and while she is irrefutably an attractive woman she comes up comparatively short in the chest department. Put simply, she has nothing on Amy's mighty gozongas and I feel my interest in the show beginning to wane.

With a one hundred percent record, Yeti receives no votes and is one of only two people to recognise Doug as the weakest link. You can always count on the Yeti to put in a good showing. Cool as an Indian cucumber salad, he spends most of the time with his hands clasped behind his back looking as calm and confident as if he were taking an aural maths test for five-year-olds.

Anne uses the break in play as an opportunity to pour scorn on the various contestants, attacking them with a calculated composure that can only come from having access to all the quiz answers and a string of pre-determined putdowns. As expected, Zara is her primary target.

'So, Zara, you're a sub-editor. That's a big job. What does it involve?'

'Um, we rewrite very poorly written copy from so-called celebrity writers, so er…'

'Oh, do you?'

'Yeah,' replies Zara in her slightly nasal, I'm-better-than-you tone.

'So you must have to have a large vocabulary?'

'Certainly do, yeah.'

'Right. Never heard of *keeping mum*?'

'I have, yeah, but er, mum's too short a word.'

'For what?'

'Well… my long vocabulary.'

Not a bad answer. Zara appears to be holding her own against the orange terror and she looks pretty pleased with herself as a result. Anne pauses before making her next attack.

'What magazine do you write for?'

'Er, *She* magazine. It's for thirty-something women. I don't know if you'll have heard of it.'

This is a first-class insult, but the audience seems almost afraid to laugh. Zara bites her lip, knowing she may have overstepped the mark. If you dangle food in front of a lioness then you run the risk of getting bitten. But Anne looks down submissively. Has she met her match?

'Why Amy?'

Maybe she has, but I doubt it. You get the feeling she has plenty left in her verbal arsenal and is merely biding her time, and I find myself fearing for the future wellbeing of Zara's self esteem.

Anne goes on to pick on Margaret and Gordon, slating them on everything from their employment, educational background, perceived intelligence (or lack of) and even their physical appearance. Resistance is futile, and the best way of putting an end to her spoken bullets seems to be grinning and bearing it. Personally, I'm not sure how I'd respond to being publicly berated by the flame-haired dictator, and in a way I'm glad it's Yeti standing there in the firing line. Dag cops it next.

'Dag. That's an interesting name. Isn't that used as a derogatory term in Australia?'

'That may be the case, but we're not *in* Australia, Anne.'

'Are you sure about that, Dag? After all, you Americans aren't known for your geographical knowledge.'

Ooh, it's close to the bone that one, and the studio is filled with the sound of a hundred people sucking air through their teeth. Dag should have known better than to answer back to Anne. He lowers his gaze and bites his tongue; it's important for him to hold on to his dignity. National pride is at stake here.

'That's bordering on racism, Anne,' he warns her.

'Not at all!' she dismisses him. 'It's merely an accurate observation.'

And that's the end of the matter.

Last of all, Anne turns her attentions to the lovely Amy, and I find myself hoping she goes easy on the girl. In a way she does, pointing out that Doug was statistically the round's weakest link and that she was unlucky to be voted out. This is a cyanide-laced compliment, though, equivalent to saying, "You weren't *actually* the thickest – you just came across that way".

'Maybe it's the blonde hair?' speculates Amy.

Or the big tits, darling, but it all amounts to the same thing in the end.

'Amy, you are the weakest link. Goodbye!'

And Amy is gone, bouncing out of our lives forever. She must be gutted. Whatever your expectation upon entering a game show such as this, one thing is for certain: you don't want to be the first to take the walk of shame. Whether you deserve it or not is irrelevant.

And so the second round kicks off. We're down one contestant and ten seconds, but otherwise it's more of the same. This time the group gets off to an equally bad start, with the previous round's strongest link Margaret finding herself unable to add 18 and 23. Dag is up next and, in spite of Anne uttering his name with a heavy dose of derision, he manages to keep his composure for long enough to answer correctly. Yeti, Gordon and Zara get their questions right and once again it is down to monkey boy to keep the momentum going.

'Doug, in the English language, when an apostrophe is used to indicate ownership, it is usually followed by which letter of the alphabet?'

Doug takes a deep breath. He clearly doesn't know.

'A.' It's a guess and a fucking awful one at that.

'S,' mocks Anne, and I sense a hint of disbelief in her voice.

Doug shakes his head and well he might. It was a truly shocking answer. On the next passing he guesses "chippy" in response to a fifty-fifty question concerning a word that describes a rough sea, and I'm afraid to say that his fate is sealed. Now it's just a matter of seeing how much money the others can drum up despite having a complete fuckwit in their midst.

'Nigel, a granny smith is a type of what?'

'Apple,' answers Nigel, nose held aloft and with a private-school accent that turns my stomach.

The sheer arrogance! Quite how anyone can be so smug about answering such a piss-easy question is beyond me. I'm sure he wants and expects to win the money so he can buy an even bigger, shinier silver spoon to stick up his arse. And I'm pretty positive he thinks that when he victoriously sets foot back on campus they'll be carving the suckling pig for the returning prodigal son. He would undoubtedly experience a level of popularity for a time as other tight-arsed students tried to benefit from his newly bulging bank balance, but this wouldn't last. Money only buys friends in the short term. But nevertheless, I still hope the smug twat doesn't win. Plus there's always a chance Anne will drag him down from his high horse kicking and screaming. That's what she's being paid to do, after all.

'Time's up, and that was a disaster. You only banked £170. So, who is the bonfire in your igloo?' It's a clever metaphor and I wonder whether Anne made it up herself. 'It's time to vote off, the weakest link.'

Doug, Doug, Doug, Doug… It seems like the obvious answer to me, but still some of the other contestants get nominated. Not enough to prevent the brainless wonder from being voted out, though, and he lumbers off in the same direction as Amy, having realised his dream of appearing on television if nothing else. At least, I assume this was the reason he entered. Surely he couldn't be deluded enough to honestly think he could win? It would have taken exceptional luck on his part to find himself up against eight more dim-witted people than him.

'What's Yeti doing?' Volk whispers in my ear as Doug disappears from view.

'Give him time,' I reply in equally hushed tones, steering my breath away from his nostrils to avoid intoxicating him with the putrid stench. I tell you, I've had enough bad experiences involving reprimands from angry teachers straight after their coffee breaks to know that I don't want to inflict the same suffering on one of my mates.

I appreciate Volk's concerns about Yeti. He has yet to answer a single question incorrectly and his success has granted him virtual immunity when it comes to the voting. I guess it must be tough for him out there. He must know he has the beating of these clowns and the money is his for the taking if he wants it. And I'm sure he does want it, too. Who wouldn't? Ten thousand pounds is not an amount to be scoffed at. Not that the prize pot will ever make it that high, but still. I can probably find it within my heart to forgive him if he decides not to go through with the plan, but I'm not sure the others will.

'We'll start with the strongest link from the last round. That's you, Dennis. Start the clock. Dennis, which is closer to the Earth? The moon or the sun?'

'The sun.'

Good man! I knew I was a fool to doubt the Yeti. Leaning forward in anticipation, I catch a glimpse of Volkan's hands rubbing together in my peripheral vision. It's almost time.

'The moon,' Anne gleefully corrects him. 'Gordon…'

Yeti's fall from grace is a dramatic one. Watching someone fail sensationally can be every bit as breathtaking as watching somebody break a record, and Yeti doesn't disappoint. He sucks dick on a grand scale, fucking up questions across all disciplines: science, history, sport and music. And he doesn't just get the answers wrong, he gets them spectacularly wrong. He gets Anne to repeat the questions, *three times* on one occasion, and he even tries to bank money when there is nothing there to bank. If truth be told, it might have seemed a bit over the top were it not for Doug's dismal showing in the previous round. We all sit there in the darkness of the audience trying not to piss ourselves laughing, while Brian and Margaret exchange bemused looks at what they are witnessing: the hasty unravelling of a previously infallible mind.

By the end of the round the team has only banked £70, and this is almost entirely as a result of Yeti's full-blown display of incompetence.

'Whose lock has been picked?' asks Anne. 'Whose shelf has fallen down?'

I don't think there can be much doubt in anyone's mind.

'Dennis,' says student scum Nigel.

'Dennis,' agrees tattooed Brian.

'Dennis,' echoes the charismatically challenged Margaret.

'Dennis,' concurs the American dream.

'Nigel,' says Yeti, breaking the chain as he had done so successfully during the game. I'm glad that of all the people he could have voted for, he voted for that conceited twat.

'Dennis,' declares gopher Gordon.

'Dennis,' mimics sexy-but-not-quite-as-sexy-as-Amy Zara.

And that concludes it. Yeti is found guilty of being a complete muppet by the rest of the jury. And by the look on Anne's face you would think that Christmas, New Year and her birthday had all come at once.

'Dennis, your friends refer to you as *Yeti*, don't they?'

'That's correct, Anne, yes.'

'I see. And why is that, do you think?'

'Your guess is as good as mine, Anne.'

'I hope not, judging by the standard of your guesses in the last round.' There is a murmur of appreciative laughter from the audience. 'So you've never seen a Yeti, *Yeti*?'

'No, Anne. That would be impossible as the Yeti is a mythical creature.'

'You mean it doesn't exist?'

'Yes, Anne.'

'Rather like your general knowledge, then.' Again the audience shakes with laughter, but Yeti remains unruffled, seemingly at ease with his newly acquired status as a figure of fun. 'It was a spectacular demise, Dennis. What happened?'

'I don't know. Pressure got to me I guess.'

'But you have a degree in biochemistry from Cambridge; a first, no less! You're *supposed* to be intelligent.'

'General knowledge is only one small part of intelligence, Anne. You of all people should know that.'

'But in this show, general knowledge is the only part that counts, Dennis. You of all people should know *that*. You are the weakest link. Goodbye.'

She's good is Anne, hard as nails.

Hands still behind his back like a cuffed felon, Yeti leaves his plinth and heads towards the exit. His eyes are trained on Anne, but she's dismissively looking the other way. As far as she's concerned, he no longer exists. But Yeti's gaze doesn't falter, for he craves one final confrontation with the brass-headed harpy. As he makes it past Nigel and is about to leave the glare of the studio lights he pauses and turns to face her.

We begin to wriggle forward in our seats and I feel my heartbeat quicken. Anne still doesn't turn around. Her head is held low, composing herself, waiting for the lights to change to signal the beginning of the next round. Yeti remains in position, unwavering, defiant, his foot tapping impatiently in the darkness. A word in her ear from the producer, maybe a sixth sense, or perhaps she's fed up of waiting, but Anne finally lifts her head and swivels it like a bird of prey, pointing her beak in Yeti's direction.

'Still here?' she questions.

Yeti nods calmly.

My palms turn clammy as a stare-out ensues. We all edge forward a little more, bums hovering above the uncomfortable plastic seats as we await the battle cry. My eyes dart excitedly between Yeti and Anne, but it's clear from the start that this is one competition Yeti has no chance of winning. Anne is well-practised at this sort of thing, make no mistake. Her stare is harder, more intense, and I envisage her standing in front of the mirror for hours each day perfecting its sharpness; right down to the slight puckering of the lips and the subtle scrunching of the right eye. Gaz gasps as Yeti begins to turn to stone before our eyes.

'You are the weakest link,' she reminds him. '*Goodbye!*'

He is defeated. His will is shattered and his poise has left the building. Yeti walks away a smaller man, while Anne turns back triumphantly to continue with the show.

'He's fucking bottled it,' whispers Volk, and he slumps back in his chair in exasperation. 'And now we have to sit through the rest of this shit!'

He gestures with his arm at the stage in front of him, just in time to coincide with Yeti making his move. As I said before, you can always count on the Yeti to put in a good showing. You see, it was a double bluff all along; a cunning ploy to lure the red baroness into a false sense of security. Facing the other way and with her guard lowered, Anne is a sitting duck, and Yeti sprints up behind her and throws his arms around her waist. Like a lion leaping onto the back of a stricken wildebeest, he hauls her to the ground, the expression of pomposity torn from her face as she helplessly claws at the air. Despite his nickname, Yeti is not exactly the hulking animal you might imagine, but he is nevertheless more than a match for the likes of Anne Robinson and he wastes no time in pinning her down and climbing on top of her.

'BUUUNDLE!'

Dag is the first to join in the carnage, beating us all to it by a considerable distance. We're barely even out of our seats when Yankee Doodle comes steaming in with a big smile on his face.

'You can't speak to me like that! I'm an American!' he bellows as he crashes down on top of Yeti. I guess Anne's comments had been taken to heart.

And he's not the only contestant to join in, either. Zara is the next to offer her body to the cause, shuffling over on her high heels with rapid, tiny steps before slumping down on top of Captain America with an excited squeal. She's clearly spent a lot of time and effort on her appearance and outfit, but she seems more than willing to sacrifice both for the chance to flatten a defenceless Anne Robinson. Her arrival gives me renewed incentive to be next on the pile and I push my way past Gaz and Volk to beat them into fourth place. I soar through the air like a rugby player searching for the try-line and come crashing in with such momentum I almost knock over the existing stack, the people beneath me groaning in complaint.

'*I said, goodbye!*' shrieks Anne from the bottom of the pile and the audience erupts into hysterics, thinking this is all part of the show.

Volk and Gaz are not far behind me and there are now seven bodies amassed on the studio floor.

'What are you doing?!' wails Nigel in desperation, recognising that the show will almost certainly have to be abandoned and that his chances of personal and financial glory are slipping away before his eyes.

'You're next!' I yell at him and he flees the studio as if somebody has pulled out a gun.

'Goodbye!' Anne screeches at him as he races past, bringing an appreciative round of applause from the audience.

Once the on-set security team realise Ashton Kutcher is not going to suddenly appear from nowhere and reveal the mayhem to be some elaborate prank, they move swiftly and efficiently to end Anne's suffering. We're lifted off one by one and made to stand in the corner of the studio, where we're told to wait patiently like school children waiting to receive further punishment. At the same time, Anne is escorted to the dressing room in a state of shock, mumbling the word 'goodbye' repeatedly under her breath.

It always feels awkward being told off as a fully grown adult, and this time is no exception. On another day I might have used the opportunity to chat to Zara, but I fear my coffee breath will act as an insurmountable obstacle. Besides, I think I've spotted a wedding ring loitering on her left hand, so it may well be a lost cause anyway.

The group stands quietly, heads hung in shame, until Dag eventually breaks the silence.

'Hey, you guys rule, man,' he chuckles. 'That kicked ass!'

He holds a hand aloft and we deliver some half-hearted high fives.

'Yeah! Alright!' he says, pumping the air with his other fist. I really don't think he understands the seriousness of the situation.

Filming is terminated for the day and the audience is asked to leave, filing out row by row.

'See you outside, lads,' calls Bertie, waving his camera phone. We give him the thumbs up.

We're left waiting in the studio for about fifteen minutes before a BBC spokesperson comes out to meet us. I fear the worst. The police have probably been called already and are busy preparing a cell for us as we speak. However, my worries are premature. Apparently, Anne has decided not to press charges, although the spokesman informs us that she has strong grounds for having us arrested for assault. In fact, no legal action will be taken against us whatsoever. Result.

We don't get off completely scot-free, though, and as punishment for the cancellation of the show we are required to reimburse the travel expenses of all the other contestants. In addition, Yeti, Dag and Zara are banned from taking part in any future broadcasts of *The Weakest Link*. It's hardly the end of world.

'Consider yourselves *very* lucky that Ms Robinson has a sense of humour,' the man tells us.

We do our best to look repentant, but it's easier said than done under the circumstances. She had it coming to her.

They all do.

RE: Message From Across the Globe

Hi Dom

Am having an amazing time thanks and am doing really well. Sounds like things are still drifting along for you as always. Don't worry about it tho, there's nothing written anywhere that says you should be out there doing "meaningful" stuff. The most important thing is that you remain true to yourself.

It's been eight and a half months actually, so you were pretty close! But I'm having such a good time I've decided to keep going for a few more months. I figured I might as well try and see more while I'm out here. And I've decided not to come back to Thame when I get back. The thing is, I've met this guy, and we're going to rent a place together in Brighton. I think you'd like him - he works in television and shares your sense of humour.

Don't be silly about looking "stupid". You were only being honest and that's one of the most important things to be. I miss you too, but my time away has shown me that what we had just wasn't meant to be. I've moved on and you should too.

Sorry I can't end on a more positive note! All I can say is that you're a very special person and that you'll find somebody else one day.

Say hello to the guys for me.

Take care

Rach XxxX

p.s. Celebrity bundling sounds like fun!

'Come on, Volk! You've got to do better than that!'

Me and Yeti laugh as the ball skips off Volk's shin and goes straight out of play, the cause of the barracking from his manager. He stands there with his hands on his hips for a moment, staring down angrily at the offending piece of turf that caused the ball to bobble up and make him look like a bit of a cock in the process.

'Get your head up!' yells the manager, and Volk jogs back to the halfway line in anticipation of the next attack.

It's a pretty nice day by all accounts, and with nothing better to do with ourselves on a Saturday afternoon, me and the Yeti have come to offer our "support" to Volk and his team. We do this every now and then, but not *too* often as Volk never looks particularly pleased to see us walking towards the touchline. I can't begin to think why. Plus if you think I'm going to watch this kind of shambles on a cold winter's day then you can forget it.

Recent wet weather has made a mockery of my decision to wear white trainers, and I'm annoyed to see the mud creeping up the sides of my shoes and even threatening to soil the backs of my jeans as well. Yeti showed more sense when he opted for his Doc Martens – not that he ever wears anything else, mind you. So while he trudges around without a care in the world, I'm left tiptoeing between the muddy patches like some kind of pansy. I'd be lying if I said it hadn't occurred to me that maybe it should be the other way around.

'I got an email from Rachel last night,' I tell Yeti as Volk is shrugged off the ball by a defender twice his size.

'Yeah? What did she say?'

'She's met someone else.'

The words hurt when I say them out loud.

'Really? That doesn't matter though, because you're over her, right?'

'I thought I was. Now I don't know what to think.'

Yeti doesn't say anything. To be honest, I doubt he knows *what* to say. I wouldn't either if I were him.

'You know, it's weird,' I tell him. 'I haven't really thought about her for ages. But then, all of a sudden, I started having these dreams. And since then she's been on my mind all the time.'

'You guys *were* together for a long time,' Yeti tells me. 'You've got to expect her to enter your thoughts sometimes.'

'Maybe. But why now? Why after all… Volkan, you donkey!!! Who is this clown? He couldn't finish his dinner! Get him off!!' I yell as Volk cocks up a one-on-one chance with the goalkeeper.

Volk turns around and gives me a two-finger salute, so I wink at him sarcastically and give him the slow handclap.

'Sorry, Yeti… Yeah, anyway, I sent her this email asking her in a roundabout kind of way if she wanted to get back together when she got back. But then it turns out she isn't even coming back.'

Yeti nods thoughtfully.

'You never told me you sent her an email. When did you do that?'

'After that night in the pub when I was chatting to Sarah.'

'When she turned you down, you mean?'

'If you want to put it like that.'

'How else would you put it?'

I shrug my shoulders.

'That explains why you emailed Rachel, then,' he says.

'What does?' He has well and truly lost me.

'You got rejected and your pride was hurt. You wanted to feel there was somebody out there that cared about you. And who better than your ex-girlfriend?'

'You been reading your sister's magazines again, Yeti?'

'No. But I bet that's the reason.'

'Possibly.'

A knee to the small of the back causes Volk's gangly striking partner to drop to the floor in a manner that suggests he'll never walk again.

'You only think about the past when you're not happy with the present,' says Yeti, as the manager lumbers onto the pitch clutching a bottle of water and a large sponge; a versatile combination of equipment that I believe cures 99.9% of all Sunday league football injuries. 'If Sarah had said yes you wouldn't be pining after Rachel like you are now.'

'I'm not pining!'

'No, not much!'

'I'm *not.*'

'If you say so. But anyway, following the initial humiliation of being dumped…'

Humiliation. Nice choice of words, mate.

'…you didn't seem all that bothered. You were quite happy with single life in the beginning. You only started missing her when you discovered you couldn't pull.'

'Thanks a lot!'

'It's true and you know it.'

He's probably right. The idea of single life is always far better than the reality: no commitments; sex on tap with a string of different women; and being able to stay in bed with your hangover rather than being dragged like a zombie around Miss Selfridge or Gap. But it never really works out like that, well not for most people anyway. And the fact is, if I'd had sex with anyone other than Palmofthe Handerson in the last eight months, I very much doubt we'd be having this conversation.

'The problem is, I can't see myself getting anyone better than Rachel. What if she was The One?'

'Now you're being melodramatic. Personally, I don't buy into the theory that there's only one perfect partner out there for each person. Statistically it doesn't work. Besides, you said yourself there were more bad times than good with Rachel towards the end of the relationship.'

'The problem is I can only remember the good times.'

'The sex you mean? Three minutes, twice a week?'

We both laugh. Yeti has a way of making you see sense about these things.

All of a sudden, a miss-hit clearance sees the ball fly over in our direction, bouncing about two feet away from where we're standing and continuing all the way over to the children's play area that's currently home to nobody other than a couple of leisurewear teenagers sharing a fag. A member of the opposition gives me a dirty look as he runs past to retrieve the ball, presumably because I made no effort to stop it when I easily could have done so. I just stare right back at him. If he expects me to get my shoes dirtier than they already are to save him having to run fifty yards, he can fuck right off. Besides, he looks like he could do with the extra exercise. Fat fuck.

'What about you, then?' I ask after the throw-in has been taken. 'Any ideas about who would make a good Mrs Yeti?'

'Dunno,' he mumbles. Despite being a fountain of knowledge when it comes to everyone else's love life, Yeti is never comfortable talking about his own. 'I don't really have time for that at the moment.'

This is a bit of a copout answer, especially coming from a man who spends as much time bumming around as I do (not in the literal sense, I might add; as far as I know at least).

'You're wasted as a single man, Yeti. You've got a lot to offer.'

'Like what?'

'Well, for starters you're by far the most intelligent person I know.'

It's true, you know. Yeti is a right clever bastard. Although the funny thing is, he doesn't really use his intelligence; he doesn't *enjoy* it, so to speak. Not that the rest of us particularly revel in ours. But the thing is you will rarely hear him make a witty remark or throw a one-liner into the conversation. Everything he says has a point to it.

'That may be,' he replies, 'but where's it gonna get me? I don't see Jon Tickle beating them off with a stick.'

'To be honest, mate, and without wanting to sound gay, you're a lot better looking than Mr Tickle.'

'Thanks,' says Yeti, giving me a puzzled look. 'Oh yeah… there's one thing I definitely have going for me.'

'What's that then?'

'I have a quality recipe for chicken,' he grins.

'You certainly do,' I nod in agreement. 'That really is a delicious recipe for chicken. Anyway, why are we stood here watching this shit?'

'It was your idea to come,' he reminds me.

'Me and my fucking ideas. It's obvious Volk's team's gonna lose. I mean, it's men against boys out there. *Literally*, men against boys… Look!'

I point at the guy marking Volk to demonstrate my point.

'Check out this guy here,' I continue. 'What chance has Volk got against him? He's a *man*, for fuck's sake.'

Yeti nods in agreement. It doesn't matter that Volk is sporting three-day stubble growth and is of quite muscular build, you would still only ever refer to him as a "lad", "geezer" or "bloke". The guy he's up against, on the other hand, is indisputably a "man".

'At what stage do you become a man, then?' ponders Yeti. 'It's certainly not an age thing.'

'No, you're right, it's not an age thing. Forearms have something to do with it. Men always have bigger forearms, whether they work out or not.'

We both inspect our own forearms and conclude that neither of us can claim to have reached manhood yet.

'Attitude has something to do with it, too,' I add. 'For example, a man would never wear trainers. When a man goes into a shoe shop, he doesn't even look at the trainers… he heads straight for the sensible shoes.'

'Yeah, I think I see where you're coming from. A man will only enter a sports shop to buy sports equipment… for actually *playing* sport. If a man buys some jogging bottoms, it's because he plans to go jogging.'

'Exactly. A man won't care so much about how he looks because he's that much more confident and mature. A man will have no problem saying to himself: "Yes, it is fairly cold today, so I *will* wear this vest." And what's more, he won't give a shit if people can see it under his shirt. A man doesn't care about stuff like that. Come to think of it, being settled has a lot to do with being a man. Having a career, that kind of thing.'

'So would you consider Bertie to be a man, then?' poses Yeti.

'That's a tricky one… a young man maybe. But not a man. Bertie likes watching wrestling. And he listens to East 17. A man would never openly talk about something like wrestling. He probably wouldn't even entertain the topic. A man talks about current affairs or his latest projects in the garden.'

'So who of this lot would you consider to be men, then?' says Yeti, gesturing towards the football field.

We do a quick tally up of each side. There's no real science about how we decide which players qualify for the title of "man", but it's generally pretty obvious purely by looking: a certain leathered look about the skin or something in the way they walk. As it turns out, Volk's immature team has a mere two men (both defenders), whereas the opposition can boast a manly eight. Like I said, it's men against boys.

'And?'

Yeti has summoned us all to his house to "tell us something important". It crosses my mind that maybe he's finally going to come out of the closet or something, and how we will react to this momentous (if not entirely unexpected) news is the main topic of conversation in Bertie's car on the way there. We all say it will make no difference to our friendship, but I sense that Volk finds the whole thing a bit awkward. The problem stems from his football changing room mentality and I think he's worried about the repercussions of being friends with a gay bloke; of being tarred with the same brush, so to speak. It makes matters worse when we begin to speculate on which of us he fancies and before we know it we've started to read homosexual connotations into previously innocuous things Yeti has said or done in the past. Perfectly innocent statements or actions suddenly take on a whole new meaning in light of the information we think we're about to receive. It's ridiculous really, as I'm sure it would be possible to construct a strong case for any one of us being a regular visitor to the Vegemite Valley.

But as it turns out, Yeti's news is of far greater consequence than a long overdue confirmation of his sexuality.

We arrive at his house with a strong sense of communal trepidation, ambling towards his front door at a speed that suggests none of us particularly want to get there. We repeatedly swap between who is leading the way, finding all sorts of excuses to stop and let someone else overtake, like tying our shoelaces, pretending to spot something of interest in the undergrowth or pausing to double-check we've remembered to take our mobile phones from the car. These underhand tactics see the lead change countless times, and as we near the door it looks like it's to be Gaz that's going to have to ring the bell. That is, until he accidentally drops his keys on the floor and then farcically struggles to pick them up. Without any further delay tactics up my sleeve, it is me that ultimately puts finger to buzzer. I give it a long, hard press.

Yeti arrives at the door so swiftly it's clear he must have been eagerly awaiting our arrival for some period of time and he looks extremely excited to see us. Come to think of it, I can't recall him ever being this animated in his entire life, as he's normally the epitome of placidity. This is a good sign. I can't imagine he'd be this enthusiastic about admitting to us after all these years that he's gay. Or maybe he would. You can never tell with the Yeti. Anyway, he invites us in and ushers us towards the lounge, where we sit uneasily on his two sofas.

Normally, I would welcome the opportunity to come round to Yeti's because his house is pretty plush, albeit in a fairly tasteless kind of way. Just walking about on the carpet is a pleasure in itself because it's so goddamn deep. I tell you, small children could play hide-and-seek in its fibres it's that dense. And he has these floral-patterned spongy sofas that swallow you as soon as you sit down, so your arse gets sucked back into oblivion while your feet are hoisted off the floor. Believe me, they're the best sofas in the world and I'm going to get myself some as soon as I can afford to. Maybe in a different colour, though. But today there's way too much anxiety in the air for me to appreciate the luxurious upholstery.

'Is your mum in?' asks Volk.

'No,' replies Yeti.

'Good.'

'How about your sister?' asks Gaz.

'*No*,' replies Yeti.

'Shame.'

These are the only words that are spoken while Yeti goes about setting up the video player. I find myself wondering what the fuck is going on. Maybe the news is too difficult for him to say out loud so he's pre-recorded it for us to view at our leisure. I glance around the room and see that the others are as uncomfortable with the whole affair as I am: Volk's right hand is rubbing agitatedly at his stubbled chin; Bertie is rolling a two pound coin over and over on the backs of his fingers; and Gaz is fiddling obsessively with his prosthetic ear. I suddenly feel like I'm sitting in the waiting room of a clinic for the mentally disturbed.

'Watch this,' instructs Yeti, and we all lean forward in wrought anticipation.

'Why the fuck have you recorded the news?' Volk wants to know as the opening credits twirl and spin before our eyes.

'Just watch,' commands Yeti with a huge grin on his face, prompting Volk to cease his questioning.

"This lunchtime on 5 News…"

A sharp-suited man reads out the main headline of the day from an autocue while we sit and speculate as to what Yeti considers so significant about this latest development in Iraq. Does he really think we're *so* ill-informed about global events that he needs to spoon-feed them to us using pre-recorded episodes of the Channel 5 news? Yet the item ends and we're none the wiser as to why the hell he's dragged us over here to watch this crap. If there's a cryptic message in there somewhere, he's obviously overestimated our intelligence if he thinks we're going to get it.

"Other stories to make today's headlines…"

Yadda, yadda, yadda. More uninteresting guff about rail strikes, record-breaking temperatures and such like. I've heard it all before and my mind begins to search out more stimulating pastures. I pick up a gossip magazine from the coffee table and begin to flick through its pages. My eyes are blind to the words, seeing only the glossy images of the beautiful people, while the newsreader's droning is relegated to background noise.

"…And finally, celebrities are on their guard following a series of bizarre attacks involving a phenomenon known as 'bundling'."

'Hey! Stop! Wait-wait-wait-wait-wait, play that back,' I call out, hurling the magazine to the floor.

Yeti rewinds the tape for a few seconds and then presses play, and this time I watch as intently as if my life depended on it.

"...And finally, celebrities are on their guard following a series of bizarre attacks involving a phenomenon known as 'bundling'. Paul Johnson has all the details. Over to you, Paul."

The scene cuts away from the studio to a man standing around in a dirty-looking street. The caption informs us he is in "Soho, London". In a manner suggesting years of practice, the reporter speaks his lines impeccably as he walks along the pavement towards the camera, not once glancing downwards to detect obstacles in his path.

"This Soho street, full of cafés, restaurants and bars, is ever popular with the rich, famous and those involved in the media business. However, today they tread its pavements with a feeling of trepidation, as *this* is the spot where *This Morning* presenter Phillip Schofield was victim to what has been termed a 'celebrity bundle'. I have here with me Chief Inspector Richard Morris of the Metropolitan Police. This is not the first time such an incident has taken place, is it Richard?"

"No, Paul, that's correct. We've reason to believe this is just one of a number of similar incidents that have taken place over the past few months."

"And how did this phenomenon come to your attention? Did Phillip Schofield report it to the police directly?"

"Firstly, Paul, I'm reluctant to label what has happened as a *phenomenon* at this stage, as the assaults – which is how we're treating them at present – remain isolated events. But in answer to your question, no, Mr Schofield did *not* report the incident to the police. Mr Schofield came forward after we contacted him in relation to another attack that took place on television quiz show *The Weakest Link*."

"And do you have any idea who is behind the attacks?"

"We believe them to be the work of some form of 'celebrity bundling club', the members of which are filming the attacks and then releasing them on the internet. At this stage we've requested that media outlets do not broadcast any of the material or give out any details of this *club*, as the last thing we want is a spate of copycat incidents."

"Do you consider these people to be dangerous?"

"As far as we're currently aware, nobody has been injured during any of the attacks. Causing harm to celebrities does not appear to be the club's motivation. However, while I wouldn't describe them as dangerous individuals, there is certainly an element of danger involved in what they do."

"And finally, to sum up, should celebrities be worried about walking the streets while these attacks continue to take place?"

"No, Paul, I don't believe there is any reason for undue panic, although I *would* recommend that celebrities exercise a greater level of caution than they might have done in the past."

"Thank you, Richard. Well, celebrities, you have been warned. Back to you, Steve…"

Yeti switches the television off and we sit there dumbfounded by what we've witnessed, like when the credits start rolling at the cinema after a really powerful film and the audience remains silent and rooted to the spot. Despite the fact that I possessed enormous faith in the publicity plan when it was conceived in this very room all those weeks ago, the fruitless intervening period had seen me begin to doubt its merits. I thought success would be instant, that I'd be approached by people in the street on a regular basis, all of them eager to ask me if I was the guy that had bundled Gary Barlow and all the other celebrities. But nothing had happened. The website Yeti had spent so much time creating barely mustered up more than a few hundred hits, and a large number of these were the result of my frequent checking in the early stages. And yet here we are now, sitting in Yeti's lounge on a Wednesday evening watching a video of the news; news about us! My mind is reluctant to accept what has happened and it is likely to take me a bit of time to get my head around it. In this respect, it's probably a good thing nobody's talking.

'Jesus fucking Christ!' Volk shatters the peace right as I'm beginning to get used to it. 'We made the national news. The fucking *news*! We're famous! Well… kind of.'

'That's incredible,' Gaz agrees with comparable disbelief.

'I can't believe one of your schemes actually worked, Big D,' says Bertie.

'Ye of little faith,' I reply. 'In the words of Hannibal Smith, I love it when a plan comes together. Fetch my cigar and my black leather gloves will you, B.A.?'

This marks a moral victory of considerable stature for me and the Yeti, as the others were less than enthusiastic about our publicity plan when we first told them about it.

'Our emails must've made it into the hands of the police, then,' I say, stating the obvious.

'You don't think we're in danger of getting arrested, do you?' worries Gaz.

'I doubt it. If they were planning to arrest us, surely they would've done so already. I mean, it wouldn't take a genius to link the emails to the website and seeing as all our details are on there… I wonder how the website's doing, by the way.'

'Approaching five hundred thousand hits,' Yeti answers immediately. 'That's almost one percent of the entire population. Ignoring multiple hits from the same person, that is.'

'Fucking hell! That means approximately one person out of every hundred knows who we are,' says Volk after doing the maths.

'If you want to look at it like that, then yeah, I suppose,' agrees Yeti.

'Well I never…' Volk leans back with his arms folded to contemplate his overnight fame. It seems to me that he's happier with the news than most.

Everyone has a friend who is desperate to be famous. And today's society gives these people the glimmer of hope they never had before and don't particularly deserve. For we live in the age of reality television and fly-on-the-wall documentaries, where nobodies are hoisted up to the dizzy heights of D-list celebrity status for no better reason than they have an unorthodox hairstyle or maybe happen to be a bit camp (the two not necessarily being mutually exclusive). I can't think of anything more tedious than watching staff go about their everyday jobs at an airport or something, where the climax of a week's worth of footage compressed into half an hour is something as mundane as an irate customer whose flight has been delayed by a few hours, or a rogue bird that repeatedly evades capture. If I really wanted to watch people trying to catch a pigeon I'd much prefer it was Dastardly and Muttley rather than some overweight woman called Sandra.

Yet this doesn't even scratch the surface; it doesn't even break the skin of the rotting celebrity corpse. *By far* the worst thing to come out of this movement is the notion of accessible fame. All of a sudden everyone's a would-be pop star, turning up in their thousands to a televised audition with twinkles in their eyes and heads brimming with delusions of grandeur. Fucking losers.

Now don't get me wrong, I don't disagree with the concept as a whole. I can see there's some merit to be squeezed from events such as these, that they present an opportunity to a handful of talented youngsters who otherwise might have gone unnoticed. But for every potential king and queen of pop there are a thousand village idiots and it is this group of degenerates that I have issues with. To me, these people are nothing short of pathetic. Anyone who turns up to a pop talent contest who is ugly, cannot sing and then cries when they get rejected should be taken out the back of the studio and bludgeoned repeatedly in the face. Yet such is the extent of some of these morons' misguided belief in their ability to be the next Robbie Williams that a warning of "Those who do not reach a minimum standard will be executed" would unlikely result in a significant drop in numbers. It makes me sick.

I'm all for people following their dreams, provided their dreams are realistic; in other words that they're ambitions rather than fantasies. I'm sure most of the contestants would agree with me that it would be ludicrous for a one-legged man to harbour dreams of playing upfront for Manchester United, but they cannot recognise how they are similarly limited by their own physical shortcomings. What they can't seem to grasp is that, by simple definition of the word, it isn't possible for everyone to be famous. Some of us have to accept that the best we can hope for is to lead a healthy, comfortable life and that we should leave the fame game to the professionals. After all, we can't all be movie stars or TV presenters, in the same way that we can't all be married to Brad Pitt or Britney Spears. More's the pity.

'You never told us why you were recording the news,' I remind Yeti. 'And why 5 News? Look at that guy, he doesn't even have a chair. He has to sit on his desk!'

Yeti laughs as he gives us his excuse. 'I was going out and wanted to record *Home and Away* but couldn't be bothered to set the timer, so I just pressed record and left it running.'

'Why couldn't you watch the later edition at six o'clock?' asks Gaz.

'I would've done, but it doesn't work like that. The episode they show at lunchtime is the one from the previous evening.'

'Oh.'

I'm surprised Gaz didn't know this seeing as he watches so much goddamn TV.

'I'm just thankful the video was the reason you called us over,' chuckles Volk. 'We thought you were going to tell us you were gay.'

I shake my head in disbelief at Volkan's lack of tact, while poor old Yeti looks distraught at the accusation.

'What? I'm not… Do you guys think…? I'm not *gay*. For fuck's sake, man. Jesus! What made you think…? I ain't *gay*.'

'Good. That's alright then,' continues Volk, as if he hasn't said enough already. 'You see lads, I told you he wasn't a haemorrhoid hitman.'

If I was sitting near enough I'd kick him, but from my position across the other side of the room it would require go-go-gadget legs.

'A haemorrhoid hit... I don't believe this. Have you guys been *discussing* whether I'm gay?'

'Don't worry, mate,' Bertie comforts him. 'We wouldn't think any less of you if you were, would we boys?'

'But I'm not! For fuck's sake, what's your problem?'

'You know you can tell us if you are,' I wind him up. 'We've been friends for a long time and I think I can deal with it.'

'I'm not fucking *gay*!' screams Yeti, probably loud enough for the neighbours to hear.

'Ok, ok, I understand,' I assure him.

'Good!'

'Yeah, I understand. You're in denial. Don't worry, mate. One day you'll be able to admit to it.'

Yeti attacks me with a cushion as we fall about the place clutching our sides.

'Ok! Calm down, the joke's over,' I splutter as the dusty blows rain down over my head and back.

Yeti ceases his attack and I sit up to straighten my ruffled clothes.

'We should go out to celebrate the success of celebrity bundling,' I suggest as a means of changing the subject.

'Yeah, good plan. We also need to celebrate Yeti's return from the dark side,' jokes Volk.

'Ha fucking ha.'

'Where shall we go?' Gaz asks.

'How about Luigi's?' I suggest.

Despite all our months of working there we've never used it as a place to eat. Now seems as good a time as any.

'Are we still welcome there since the triple resignation?' queries Yeti.

'I don't see why not. We parted on good terms. If you can call, "You were crap anyway. I was going to fire you at the end of the month but you've saved me the bother" as parting on good terms, that is. But our money's as good as anyone else's, even if our work ethic isn't.'

'I suppose you're right,' Yeti agrees with me.

He seems to have calmed down a bit now, although he appears to have subconsciously adopted a more masculine, iron-wristed stance.

'I'm gonna have to bail I'm afraid,' Bertie apologises. 'I've got to get to work early tomorrow morning to finalise a report, which means leaving before five.'

Six months ago we would have tried to persuade him otherwise, but we're so used to his fleeting visits now that we've learnt not to bother.

'I can drop you guys there on the way home, if you want?' he adds half-heartedly.

'Cheers, mate,' I thank him. 'Come on, lads. Let's get going. Bagsy not sitting next to Yeti.'

'Fuck off,' he sighs.

'So if you *were* gay,' says Volk as we walk out of the front door, 'and I'm not saying you are. But if you were, which one of us would you fancy the most?'

'I'm not even going to dignify that with an answer.'

Bertie drops us at Don Luigi's at about half past eight. It's spitting with rain for the first time in about a month, so for once the streets are devoid of people. Usually the al fresco drinkers are out in force at this time of year, not to mention the countless souls who wander between estate agent windows to peer at the inflated prices within. We make a last ditch attempt to persuade the Bertmeister to join us, but it's to no avail as his loyalty rests with the people who pay his wages. It's not surprising really as there are people queuing up to take his job from him, whereas the same can't be said for his place in our social circle; he knows we'll always be here.

When we enter the restaurant Luigi doesn't look particularly pleased to see us, standing there with his immense gut hanging over his belt like he's swallowed a couple of bowling balls and turning his nose up at me, Gaz, Yeti and finally Volkan (who he's never met before, but instantly dislikes due to his association with the rest of the group).

'Come to beg for your old jobs back, 'ave you?' he sneers. 'Well don' bother 'cause you'll be wasting your time.'

He's a right cunt is Luigi.

'Pleased to see you too, compadre,' I respond. 'We're here to eat.'

'To eat, eh?' he eyes us suspiciously. 'Do you 'ave a reservation?'

'No. Doesn't look like we need one, though,' I say, standing on tiptoes to peer over his shoulder into the almost empty restaurant.

Luigi smiles at me sarcastically. 'Let me check the book.'

He waddles off to the counter, pulls out the reservations book and pretends to study its contents, running his finger down an imaginary line of bookings and repeatedly checking his watch. He then pulls out his mobile phone and turns his back on us so we can't see what he's doing. Once he's put it back in his pocket he strolls back over to where we're standing looking smugger than J-Lo's nipple tweaker.

'I'm sorry, but we…' He's interrupted by the sound of the phone on the counter. 'Excuse me one second…'

He skulks away once more and picks up the receiver.

'Don Luigi's, 'ow can I 'elp you? Ok… Oh dear… Yes… No problem… Ok… Thank you, goodbye.'

He comes back over again.

'You are in luck,' he announces on his return. 'We just 'ad a cancellation. 'ow many of you are there?'

'Just the four of us.'

'Ok. Table for four. Come this way.'

He begins to lead us into the dining area, but then suddenly appears to think better of it.

'Wait,' he instructs. 'Do you 'ave cash? I will only accept cash.'

'What? Why? It says you accept cards on the door,' argues Volk.

'The machine is broken. I'm waiting for the engineer to come an' fix it.'

'Yeah right,' replies Volk.

'Take it or leave it, my friend,' says Luigi, raising his voice.

'We'll fu…'

'It's ok,' I reply quickly before Volk can get any further. 'We're happy to pay cash.'

I give Volk a nod to tell him everything is under control.

'Let me see it,' demands Luigi.

'Pardon?'

'Let me see your money. I want to make sure you 'ave enough.'

I open my wallet to reveal about thirty quid, with Gaz and Yeti showing Luigi similar amounts. And now it's Volk's turn.

'This is bullshit,' he protests, but presents the contents of his wallet anyway.

'Good,' chirps Luigi. 'This way please…'

He ushers us over to a table in the corner so we're away from the majority of the other diners.

'Enjoy your meal.'

'Say it like you mean it,' Volk mutters under his breath.

'Pardon, my friend?'

'Nothing.'

Luigi walks away from the table while Volk uses the internationally recognised hand signal for "wanker" behind his back.

'What a fucking tit!' he exclaims. 'I can't believe you guys worked for him for so long.'

'Neither can I,' agrees Gaz. 'I'd almost forgotten how bad he was.'

'*I* can't believe he phoned himself to make us think the restaurant was busy!' I add.

'Is that what he did?' asks Gaz.

‘I’m pretty sure that’s what happened, yeah.’

‘What a cock,’ declares Volk.

Exactly. What a cock. What a complete dick. What a total and utter penis. He isn’t even Italian, for fuck’s sake! He just likes to call himself Luigi and speak with a stupid accent. I think he might have an Italian great-grandmother, but that’s about as strong as the connection gets. I mean, Gaz has some Mongolian somewhere in his family tree, but I don’t see him walking around calling himself Genghis and raping women.

‘The food had better be pretty special to make up for having to put up with all that shit,’ moans Volk. ‘What sort of a restaurant makes you show them your money before they give you a table?’

‘I don’t think old Don Luigi trusts us,’ says Gaz.

‘Oh really? I’d never have guessed,’ replies Volk cynically.

While they continue to slate the pseudo-Italian, I take the opportunity to survey the other diners. The place has never been one to attract regulars, so I’m unsurprised to see a room full of strangers, or half-full as the case may be. It’s reassuring to see that the new waiters look as young, inexperienced and inept as we were when we first started. It serves to confirm what I’ve always suspected: that Luigi is a cheapskate who will cut every corner he can for the sake of a few extra quid.

‘Are you ready to order?’ asks one of the waiters.

‘Can you give us a few more minutes, please?’ I request.

‘Certainly, sir.’

I bet he hates having to call people like us “sir”. I know I did when I used to work here. It takes a great deal of self-control to be respectful to people when you know they’re probably taking the piss out of you when your back is turned.

If truth be told, we haven’t even looked at the menus yet. This always happens when we go to restaurants (which isn’t very often, admittedly). We sit down and start talking shit and it isn’t until an impatient waiter comes along and asks the question that we remember why we’re here.

By the time he comes back five minutes later we've made our choices. All except Gaz, that is, because as usual he's being an indecisive bastard, torn between one of about five different dishes that are all subtle variations on the same theme anyway. But he's just about ready by the time the rest of us have relayed our orders, either that or he's simply forced into making a decision by being put on the spot. Whichever the reason, he continues to fret about his chosen items long after the waiter has gone away.

'I was posed an interesting question at work the other day,' begins Volk after all the toasting is out of the way (the toasts were given to celebrity bundling (again), the absent Bertie, and of course Yeti's heterosexuality).

'What was that then, mate?' I ask him.

Volk puts on his serious face and points at us using the index and middle fingers of his right hand. 'Which would you rather lose? Your legs or your eyes?'

Having put the question forward he leans back in his chair, raises his eyebrows and folds his arms while he waits for our answers.

'Well, that's easy,' answers Yeti. 'Legs every time.'

'Why?' Volk is far from satisfied with Yeti's concise answer.

'I'm pretty sure I'd get more pleasure out of seeing than standing, that's all.'

'Fair enough. What about you, Gaz?'

'Hmmm. Well, speaking as a man who knows what it's like to lose a body part, I'd probably go with eyes.'

'Are you crazy?' I ask him. 'Surely legs are less important?'

'But think about it,' says Gaz. 'As a blind man, you'd have access to places a man with no legs couldn't go. Like buildings with stairs but no lift, for instance.'

'Eh? And what would you do once you got there?' I question. 'Aside from shouting, "Hey, legless people! Look at me up here!" I mean, it's not as if you could even enjoy the view.'

'I didn't think of that,' admits Gaz.

'And…' I haven't finished yet, not by a long shot. 'I think you'll find that false limbs are likely to work better than false eyes. Plus, if you were fully clothed, nobody would be any the wiser if you had false legs. But if you had false eyes you'd have to wear sunglasses all the time. And people that wear sunglasses indoors always look like twats. Well, P. Diddy excluded. And worse still, when you took the sunglasses off you'd look like a psychopath because you'd be permanently staring in one direction. And you'd never blink!'

'I'd agree with Big D on this one,' says Volk.

'But just think, Volk,' Gaz argues. 'You wouldn't be able to play football any more.'

'And how many blind people do you see playing football?' replies Volk.

'I don't know. Don't they have that special version for blind people where the ball has a bell in it and they crawl about on the floor?'

'That's not football! Blind people rolling about in the dirt swinging their legs about… that's pretty screwed up. Who would want to watch that? I bet even their families nip off after the first five minutes and then turn up again at full time. They wouldn't be any the wiser anyway 'cause they're fucking blind!'

'But think of the advantages of being blind.' I don't know why Gaz doesn't admit defeat on this one.

'Advantages? I think you're gonna have to help me out on that one,' I reply, almost dreading what he's going to say.

'Well, any bird can look how you want her to look because you can't actually see her. That way, every bird you go out with could potentially be Britney Spears.'

'I doubt it's that straightforward,' I reason with him. 'I mean, closing your eyes doesn't suddenly make an ugly girl attractive. You'd still be able to *feel* the greasy hair, bad skin and rolls of fat, even if you couldn't see them. So unless you were involved in a relationship that involved no physical contact… but what would be the point in that? Plus you'd know deep down that they'd more than likely be ugly. After all, you don't see fit birds queuing up outside the local school for the blind do you? And think of all those pop stars that are only successful because of their looks. With your sight taken away you'd only be left with their terrible music and those same people would become like the antichrist. Sorry, Gaz. You can argue there's no right or wrong answer to this kind of question, but I can assure you that "eyes" is the wrong answer.'

'Or to put it another way,' adds Yeti. 'Who do you think would generally be happier? A blind man or a man in a wheelchair? I reckon a man in a wheelchair.'

'Ok,' concedes Gaz. 'You win.'

Thank fuck for that.

'Maybe legs versus eyes was a bit obvious,' muses Volk. 'Ok, I've got another one for you. Which would you rather lose? Your eyes or your knob?'

'You serious?' I sigh.

'Absolutely. I'd be intrigued to hear your thoughts on this matter.'

Eyes versus knob is a much closer contest, with all of us unsure as to which would be preferable (or rather, less soul-destroying) to lose. Predictably, sex is the main argument in favour of retaining the penis, although Yeti shrewdly points out that if you lost your eyes then you could masturbate as much as you wanted without the fear of going blind. And Gaz wants to know if losing the penis means sacrificing the whole package, his reason being that he can draw some comfort if he still has his balls to play with. But in the end, common sense shines through and we all agree we would rather keep our eyes, given that they're far more useful pretty much all the time, even if this means living a life of enforced celibacy.

This stimulating debate is drawn to a close by the arrival of our starters and there's a break in conversation as we attack the plates in front of us. This is the kind of stuff that probably should be savoured, but it's late in the day and we're all fucking starving, so it doesn't last long. It tastes pretty damn good, too. Despite being a complete tosser, Luigi's got it going on once he dons an apron and picks up a knife. I'd almost be tempted to say it's one of the best meals I've had in a while, but my enjoyment of it is slightly tarnished by the sneaking suspicion that the fat Italian has probably spat in it. Or worse.

'Hey, look who it is,' announces Volk and nods towards a young couple who are being led to a nearby table.

It's Sarah, the girl I was talking to about celebrity bundling that night in the pub. And it looks like she's brought her inconvenient boyfriend with her, too (assuming he's the same one, of course). He's a big fucker, probably a rugby lad, and I thank my lucky stars I didn't take my interest in her any further than my initial inquiry. As Sarah takes her seat she happens to glance over at our table and we briefly make eye contact. I smile politely but she doesn't acknowledge it. I guess that now Gaz and Kate have split up there's no need for her to pretend she likes us anymore.

'Isn't she that girl you tried to pull, Big D?' asks Volk.

'I didn't try and pull her,' I protest in an attempt to retain my pride. 'I merely asked her out for a drink. I reckon she was interested, anyway.'

'Sure. I can see that now. I mean, she looks like she can barely resist your animal magnetism.'

'Fuck you.'

Volk starts laughing and I wish I could say something to shut him up. But the fact is he has a girlfriend and I don't, so it would be an argument I had little chance of winning.

'Do you think Kate will go out with me again now that I'm famous?' asks Gaz.

'Gaz, you're not exactly famous. The only two people in here other than us who know who you are Sarah and Luigi,' I inform him. 'Maybe if you progress up the fame ladder a bit more and obtain the riches that go with it you might have a chance, but otherwise I think you should look elsewhere.'

'Yeah, Gaz, get over it man,' says Volk in his typically unsympathetic tone. 'It's been well over a month and you two weren't exactly together for long. Move on, will ya?'

'It's not that easy, you know,' sulks Gaz.

'Of course it is,' Volk reassures him. 'There's no shortage of large-breasted blonde girls around here, so just get on another one.'

'I didn't like her just because she had blonde hair and big boobs,' gripes Gaz.

'If you say so, mate.'

'I didn't!'

'I believe you. I'm sure she had a great arse as well,' teases Volk.

'You're such a fucking perve,' Gaz accuses him. 'I don't know how Michelle puts up with you.'

'Must be my legendary charm.'

'Of course. Why didn't I think of that? But seriously, you shouldn't talk about women like that.'

'Ooh!' mocks Volk. 'Look at mister *sensitive*. Gentleman, it appears we have a new-age man sitting with us at the table. You can cut the act, Gaz, there are no women around for you to impress.'

'I'm not trying to impress anyone. You just shouldn't talk like that. It's not right.'

'It's not right?! What are you on about?'

'I don't know. It's something I began to notice when I was with Kate…'

'I might've guessed!' scoffs Volk.

'No, let him finish,' I assert. 'I'd like to hear this. Go on, Gaz.'

Gaz looks less confident of his beliefs now that he's been put on the spot.

'It's just… talking about women like they're sex objects… I don't know, I find it a bit offensive these days, that's all.'

Volk's jaw begins to lower in disbelief as Gaz continues.

'And when you listen to it, listen to what you're saying, it's sad. That's what it is, sad.'

'In what way?' demands Volk.

'Saying, "Phwoar, I'd like to get my hands on those" and stuff like that. It's like speaking your most sordid fantasies out loud. Because that's what they are, fantasies. You're talking about an unobtainable woman in a way that suggests she'd jump into bed with you if only she was aware of your interest!'

'So?'

'Well, imagine if every time you walked past a group of women they leered at *you* and said, "Check out that guy's butt. I'd like to get my hands on that".'

'Sounds good to me,' grins Volk. 'What do you reckon, lads?'

We all nod in agreement. I for one can't really see the downside of groups of women wanting to grab my arse.

'But what if those women were ugly?' questions Gaz.

Immediately the thought becomes less appealing; a horde of mole-ridden trollops crawling towards me with their hands outstretched, groping, grinning, dribbling. I begin to see what he's getting at.

'You saying I'm ugly?' accuses Volk, his words thankfully interrupting my vision.

'No, I didn't say that. I'm just making a point.'

'But wait a minute,' I butt in. 'Surely it doesn't make any difference, because they can't hear what we're saying anyway. Ignorance is bliss and all that.'

'They don't have to. It's written all over your faces.'

I must admit that Gaz's last comment is slightly worrying. I was always under the impression my leering was subtle enough to be passed off as an accidental glance or a case of misplaced recognition, so to find out after all these years that I potentially have the word "sleaze" stamped across my forehead is of some concern.

'And you learnt all this from Kate?' asks Yeti.

'Not *from* Kate,' affirms Gaz. 'And none of this really applies to you, Yeti...'

We exchange smirks as it dawns on Gaz what he's said.

'No, no, no, I didn't mean it like that. I meant that Yeti is the only one that has any respect for women out of you lot.'

'I have the highest respect for women!' I protest.

'Maybe you do,' says Gaz. 'But you'd never know it from the way you talk. Or act. It's no wonder you're single.'

'In case you hadn't noticed, *you're* single as well!' I point out.

'Not for long, though. Kate revealed to me the errors of my ways.'

'Your shortcomings in the sack, you mean,' laughs Volk, and we all laugh with him.

Gaz shakes his head in defeat.

'You lot are a lost cause,' he sighs. 'Forget I said anything.'

The waiter comes to collect our empty plates and while he's at the table he tops up our wine glasses, elegantly rotating the bottle to catch the drips that run down its neck.

'Was everything ok, gentlemen?'

'Yeah, great thanks,' we reply.

As he turns to walk away I can see from the back of his shirt that the same old tricks we used to employ have been adopted by the new team; a line of floury finger marks dissecting the black material. Subtly defacing each other's uniforms was the kind of depths we had to sink to in order to keep ourselves entertained. That and trying to trip each other up while we were carrying piles of dirty dishes. Come to think of it, it's no surprise that Luigi was thinking about sacking us. I had always planned to sneak Gaz's ear into a customer's minestrone soup, but I never had the opportunity to do it. It was to be my pièce de résistance, but try as I might I couldn't get Gaz to remove it. I used to flick pizza dough or tomato sauce at it so that he'd have to clean it, but he would never take it off. I guess he knows me too well.

Our main courses arrive some time later, along with another bottle of wine that was deemed essential to get us through the evening. Me, Volk and Gaz have all opted for pizza, whereas the Yeti has gone for some creamy pasta dish.

'So, where's the next hunting ground to be?' Gaz asks me.

'What for?'

'Celebrities.'

'Oh! For a second there I thought you meant women. Celebrities… I was thinking we should maybe try somewhere in North London. Islington maybe. I've heard a fair few TV personalities hang out in that neck of the woods.'

'Yeah, I've heard that too,' Yeti agrees. 'When are you thinking of going?'

'Saturday? Provided the Bertmeister is free to give us a lift, that is. It's a bit of a trek to that part of London from here unless you have a car.'

'Shame Dirty Bertie couldn't be here tonight,' states Volk.

'It is a shame,' echoes Gaz. 'He probably would've paid.'

I almost forget that I'm sharing a table with Ebenezer Scrooge himself. But Gaz is right, he probably *would* have paid, since the Bertmeister is a generous man and can afford to be so. I think he realises he's being a bit of a monkey for working every spare hour God gives him (and preparing for work every hour that he isn't), and buying us drinks, meals or cinema tickets is his way of making up for neglecting us. Some people might argue this is all a bit superficial and a bit of a copout on his part, but they'd be wrong. It's Bertie's way, that's all. And he's doing alright for himself, too, especially for a man whose parents were short-sighted enough to christen him *Albert Hall.* I tell you, when people like you and I are all still slogging our guts out at the age of forty-five, he'll already be retired and lying on a beach somewhere with some fit Hispanic bird twenty years his junior. It's all a matter of priorities, and while many encourage you to "live for the now", Bertie believes in working for the now and living for the fifty-year retirement. It's not the path I would choose, but I've the utmost respect for Bertie and his long-term financial planning.

A familiarly repugnant scent drifts across the restaurant. Sarah and her brute have ordered the pecorino spaghetti.

'Ah, man!' exclaims Gaz. 'I thought I'd seen the last of that rancid cheese. That smell still gives me nightmares to this day.'

His discomfort is shared by me and the Yeti. Of all the things on the menu, the pecorino spaghetti is the one item all of us hated having to serve. The maximum input any other dish required of us, other than carrying it to the table, was to sprinkle some fresh parmesan or grind some pepper on top. But not the pecorino spaghetti. Oh no. The house special meant having to wheel out the sacred *formaggio*, a thing of such weight it has to sit atop a reinforced trolley. It really is fucking huge; a gigantic bowl made out of stinking cheese, wide enough to wear as a helmet and deep enough for babies to take a bath in. And judging by the smell of it, it's probably about a hundred years old as well; older than Luigi himself.

We watch as the pan of hot pasta is emptied into the hollow shell of the cheese, the waiter tossing it about like a stringy white salad and wincing as the foul-smelling steam rises into his face. Believe me when I tell you that the process is analogous to standing over a saucepan of simmering sick.

'I think I'm gonna throw up,' declares Yeti.

'It can't be *that* bad,' says Volk.

'Try doing it a hundred times or so,' grimaces Yeti. 'Then tell me again that it's not that bad.'

'I'd quite like to try it,' says Volk. 'Maybe I'll cancel my dessert and have that instead.'

'If you do I'll pick up that fucking cheese and break it over your head,' I warn him. 'And I'm not joking.'

'I'll stick to the profiteroles then.'

'Luigi loves that cheese like it were his own son,' Gaz informs Volk. 'It's his pride and joy. I lost count of the number of times he told me the story of how he brought it all the way back from some remote Italian village.'

'When he dies he'll probably have his coffin made out of that stuff,' I joke.

'It wouldn't surprise me,' agrees Gaz. 'Where are these bloody desserts?'

The family at a nearby table are paying by card and I find myself hoping Volk doesn't notice.

The puddings are every bit as nice as the rest of the meal was and I slump back in my chair feeling satisfied and bloated. We decline the offer of coffee and ask for the bill.

'I'm just going for a piss,' I inform the others. 'I'll leave you lot to work out how much we all owe.'

I get up and shimmy away from the table. I've been needing to go for some time but couldn't really be bothered, and the delay has left me fairly desperate. You know how it is. It's always preferable to go in the comfort of familiar surroundings, so you find yourself thinking, "I'll just wait until I get home". Under normal circumstances this is what I'd have done, but the urgency to urinate is always immeasurably greater when alcohol has been consumed.

I push my way through the spring-mounted door and head down the corridor towards the toilets. There are only two of them and thankfully both are empty. I burst into the nearest one and barely have time to unzip my fly and take aim before the flow comes gushing out with great velocity. The piss is both a marathon and a sprint, the result of almost a bottle of wine and half a jug of water, and I feel my bladder shrinking back to its normal size. The relief is indescribable.

I wash my hands but refrain from drying them on the soggy towel that hangs by the sink. It looks so goddamn dirty I wouldn't be surprised if it had been used to wipe an arse. Instead, I shake my hands in the direction of the wall, the droplets of water smattering the crudely painted surface. When they're dry enough not to leave a trail of drips by which somebody could trace my steps, I exit the toilet and am surprised to be greeted by a familiar face.

'Hi there, *Big* D,' a tipsy Sarah greets me.

'Oh, hi Sarah. You made me jump there.' She did, you know. The last thing I was expecting when leaving the lavatory was to bump straight into another person, especially a failed former conquest.

'What have you been up to?' she probes, smiling naughtily and running her finger down from my neck to my chest, where its progress is halted by the fastened top button on my shirt.

'Er, I've just been to the toilet…' I reply.

'Oh *really*…' Sarah purrs. 'Why's that then?'

She's standing so close I find myself pressed up against the wall, but not so close that I don't notice how her blouse is unbuttoned way too low to allow her any degree of modesty.

'Because I needed to take a leak?' What other reason could there have been?

'*Did* you now…'

Sarah takes another step forward, and is now as close as she can get without literally standing on my toes. Her chest is thrust against the bottom of my ribcage and her head is tilted back so that her hot breath keeps buffeting my face and I can feel the plumpness of her boobs and the silkiness of her bra rubbing up and down against my shirt as she breathes.

'Sarah, what are you…?'

My words are halted by the index finger of her right hand, which she places provocatively over my mouth, its tip pressing softly against my lips.

'Shhhhhh…'

Her left hand finds a far more intimate area of my anatomy to hold and her gentle fondling makes me gasp with a mixture of shock and excitement.

'I saw your website,' she whispers. 'You're famous, you know.'

She leans towards me and licks my neck, the fragrant sweetness of her hair proving the most alluring scent in the world as it brushes against my face. I want her bad, but while her hands drift over my body, mine stay idle by my side, afraid to touch; as though I'm receiving the most exclusive of lap dances and will be thrown out of the club if I make any physical contact. And then all of a sudden she pauses. She lifts her head and looks submissively into my eyes, then takes a couple of steps back so I can see her properly.

My mouth hangs open in disbelief as she starts undoing the remaining buttons on her top, and even though she virtually does it in slow motion, it doesn't take her very long because there are so few left to undo. Once the two sides of her blouse are hanging unrestricted, she coaxes them over her shoulders and extends her arms out behind her so the garment slides effortlessly to the floor. I swallow hard. This whole situation is beyond my wildest dreams and I can't help but stare at her semi-naked body, totally in awe of the uninhibited display of female flesh. It's been almost a year since I was this close to a woman in her underwear, and I could never have imagined that the first encounter since Rachel would be anything like this, anything like as *good* as this. Sarah's body is amazing: fit, toned and sculptured, but with a soft covering of flesh to accentuate her femininity. Her breasts are big, *really* big, and firm too, suggesting they'll retain their shape if she removes her bra. Or should that be, *when* she removes her bra. Something tells me it's only a matter of time. Her skin is faultless, too, tanned and smooth. I notice she has an outie, but I guess you can't have everything.

Sarah approaches me in all her glory, taking my hands in hers, and before I know it she has forced them against her breasts. They gladly remain there as she puts her own hands behind my head and pulls me towards her. She kisses me, and this time I can't resist, our tongues meeting a split second before her lips come closing in.

'I've never kissed a famous person before,' she gasps as she takes a break for air.

I don't answer because I don't want her to stop. We kiss again and this time I pull her hard towards me, my left arm locked around her midriff, holding her in place, while my right hand gropes her arse through the thin material of her skirt.

'I've never screwed a famous person before either,' she whispers.

'What?'

'Come with me…'

She grabs my collar and shoves me back in the direction of the cubicle, stopping briefly to pick up her discarded shirt before following me in.

'Wait,' I stammer, but she's already shutting the door behind her and trying to pin me up against the wall, her legs and arms forming a restricting cage around me.

'Get off me!' I yell and push her away.

I'm careful not to shove her too hard, but it takes her by surprise and she's sent crashing against the opposite wall. Luckily, it is her back rather than her head that takes the force and she isn't hurt, just humiliated, and she stands there looking angry and dazed.

'What the fuck is wrong with you?!' she bellows at me, her arms covering her breasts, suddenly conscious of her own nakedness.

'What's wrong with *me*? What's wrong with *you*, more like?!' I shout back at her. 'Your boyfriend is sitting there in the restaurant waiting for you, for fuck's sake!'

'So?'

'What do you mean, *so*?'

'He doesn't mean anything to me.'

'He meant enough to you that time in the pub!'

'That was then. This is now. I want *you*, Big D.'

'What? Why? Because you think I'm *famous*?'

She doesn't answer.

'That's fucked up,' I tell her.

'Why?' she questions. 'He'll never amount to anything. But you, you're going places, I can tell. And I want to be part of it.'

'You want to be part of it?' I repeat. 'Then check the fucking website. You'll find details on how to be part of it on there. But don't hold your breath for any personal treatment.'

Sarah starts to giggle, laughing with an arrogance that must come from going through life being able to have any man she wants.

'I know you want me, Big D.'

I try my best to laugh the comment off with a similar level of arrogance, but the truth is I *do* want her. I want her more than anything else in the world I can think of right now.

'*Did* want you, Sarah, *did.* That was before I realised you're nothing more than a shallow, self-centred slut.'

She goes to slap me, but I block it and push her in the direction of the toilet, where she loses her footing and slumps down on the seat with a surprised yelp. All of a sudden she doesn't look so sexy. Her bra is crooked and her sassy confidence has deserted her. She looks like the slapper she is, sitting there in her natural habitat, the public lavatory.

'And another thing,' I say as I open the door to leave. 'Your breath stinks of pecorino spaghetti. You might want to chew some gum or something.'

'Wanker!' spits Sarah, but I'm already on my way back to the dining area.

'What the fuck took you so long?' demands Volk on my return. 'Were you trying to break the record for the world's longest piss?'

'And why is your shirt all creased?' asks Gaz.

'You wouldn't believe what happened back there,' I begin. 'Sarah pretty much tried to molest me.'

The others all burst into hysterics at my admission.

'Yeah right!' mocks Volk. 'Is that what you were thinking about when you were out there spanking the monkey? That's pretty sick, Big D.'

'Very funny. Look, I'm not gonna try and convince you. But it *did* happen.'

'Sure it did.'

Sarah emerges from the toilets and we all turn to look at her as she walks back to her table. She's put her blouse back on and straightened out the rest of her clothing, but her outfit still looks messy and crumpled like mine. The others eye her thoughtfully and then look back at me once more. I can tell they're entertaining the idea that I might actually be telling the truth, but I'd rather not discuss it here in the restaurant, especially since her bulky boyfriend is present.

'Come on, lads, let's make a move. How much do I owe?'

'We thought we'd split it equally four ways. It's twenty-six quid each including tip,' Yeti tells me.

I pull out my wallet and throw in a tenner and a twenty, pocketing the three pound coins already sitting in the dish.

'Luigi can have the extra quid,' I announce. 'Let's go.'

As we vacate the table I can't help but notice Sarah's man pulling out a black velvet box and the sight of it, combined with Sarah's tearful acceptance of the ring held within, makes me feel physically sick. I cannot get out of the restaurant quickly enough and I forget all about my plan to steal and destroy the pecorino cheese. The coldness of the air outside brings me some refreshment, but I still feel like I could do with a drink.

'Pub anyone?'

'Thought you'd never ask,' replies Gaz. 'I've had more than enough sophistication for one evening.'

We head over to our usual haunt and as we draw nearer I begin to relax. It's only now that I can see the positive side of what took place at the restaurant. A woman I barely knew had seen what we were doing and was impressed enough to want to shag me, even though she already had a boyfriend; a boyfriend who was only a couple of doors away no less! I think you'll agree that this is quite a result. And something tells me this is only the tip of the iceberg, that there will be more recognition, more success, more women. And the best thing about it is not all of them will be scrubbers like Sarah.

Extract from The Intelligent Press

Ban the bundle!

- **Government urged to end craze after sixth child is hospitalised**

Tony Blair is under increasing pressure to tackle the problem of schoolyard bundling after a boy of 13 was committed to a South London hospital. The boy, who cannot be named for legal reasons, suffered fractured ribs and heavy bruising to his lower back.

John Swift, headmaster at the school where the incident took place, spoke of his concerns. "This was an unfortunate incident and one that regrettably comes at a critical stage in his [the boy's] education," said Swift. "Although no permanent injury has been caused on this occasion, it is only a matter of time before somebody is permanently disabled, or even killed, if this bundling craze is allowed to continue."

This latest injury will embarrass ministers, who had earlier dismissed bundling as "a harmless fad that children will soon tire of". Worried parents and teachers voiced their concerns following each of the previous incidents, but the government has been slow to react, seemingly reluctant to lend credibility to the growing phenomenon.

This is not the first time there has been a call to arms to counter a potentially dangerous schoolyard game. Schools experienced a similar problem in the early 1990s, when a child was left deafened after being subjected to a 'Tango Slap'. This particular prank was based on a television advert depicting a bald, fat, orange man attacking a member of the public by slapping him in the face simultaneously with both hands after the unsuspecting victim took a sip of a fizzy drink. The advert was later banned from television and the Tango Slap became punishable by suspension from school.

Many schools have already taken similar steps to remedy the current situation by banning bundling from taking place on school premises, but many feel this is not enough. "Bundling is something we are taking very seriously, and anybody found to be involved in a bundle will face firm disciplinary action," said Rosie James, headmistress of a comprehensive school in Buckinghamshire. "However, there is only so much we can do. This problem needs to be stamped out at its roots."

The main challenge facing the government is that the roots of this trend lie in the highly influential world of celebrity culture. Bundling itself has been around for decades, but it has only recently grown to such a level of popularity following a spate of highly publicised attacks in which a host of celebrities have been targeted. These incidents, rumoured to now be well into double figures, were originally carried out by a select group of people, but now it seems the entire nation has caught the celebrity bundling bug. While people would have previously settled for an autograph or picture, they now want to physically lie on top of the celebrity and invite others to do the same.

Some people have suggested that the celebrities themselves are not doing all they can to avoid being bundled and in some isolated cases are even encouraging it. Amanda Rimmer, chief features writer at *OK!* magazine spoke out about the subject in a recent interview. She explained: "Certain people in the media game have got it into their heads that you aren't really famous until somebody has tried to bundle you. I don't think they fully appreciate the dangers involved, not to mention the message they're sending out to youngsters. Bundling is unacceptable behaviour under any circumstances, and it doesn't help matters when the likes of Jordan and Jodie Marsh are publicly competing with each other to be the first to be bundled."

Yet the majority of blame has been apportioned to Dominic Carter, the self-proclaimed originator of celebrity bundling. The elusive Carter, 24, has developed something of a cult status among young people the world over, although not everyone is eager to shower him with praise. "Look at all the trouble he has caused," said a government spokesperson. "I hope he's proud of himself." One suspects he probably is.

'So… have you used a gym before, Mr Carter?'

'No.' I thought this would have been obvious, but I guess she has to ask the question anyway for insurance purposes or something. 'And please call me Dom.'

'Ok, Dom. Let's get you started, then. Please come this way…'

Seeing as I'm going to be appearing on TV I figure the least I can do is get in shape. Admittedly, I've left it a bit late, especially when you consider that it's now 10am and filming takes place this evening. But I'm hoping I can achieve something in the next couple of hours and it's got to be better than nothing, right? And anyway, it's about time I did some regular exercise, having been completely inactive in that regard since the age of sixteen.

The girl giving me the induction fulfils the stereotype of gym workers to such an extent that part of me thinks she must have been artificially created by a team of scientists purely for this role. And the mouth-watering combination of cover girl looks, toned body and the knowledge that she probably goes like the clappers makes it kind of hard not to fancy her. I'm sure her very presence results in an unnaturally high reading when she takes my resting pulse rate. Or maybe I'm even unhealthier than I first suspected. Either way, she looks far from impressed by my score of 89bpm, and her comment that 'This could be due to any number of reasons' is sympathy that, quite frankly, I could do without. She asks me what I intend to achieve by going to the gym and I tell her I want to be fitter and more toned, trying my best to phrase it in such a way that suggests I'm already nine-tenths of the way there. I don't know why I bother, really, because she's going to see me in my shorts and t-shirt sooner rather than later, and when she does it will become immediately apparent that I'm not even close to being the near-perfect physical specimen I claim to be.

She shows me around each piece of equipment in turn, taking her time to explain which particular muscle groups are involved and demonstrating how to use the machines by clambering on herself. Throughout the course of the induction she puffs and pants, bends herself into a whole host of wonderful positions and gyrates various parts of her anatomy in my general direction. By the end of it I don't particularly want to do a workout anymore, I feel more like having a wank.

'Right, that's it then,' she announces. 'Feel free to have a play with the equipment yourself and shout if you want me.'

'Thanks,' I reply, hoping that I'm not visibly blushing.

I check out her arse as she walks back to the desk and then look down at the training card she's filled out for me. I must admit that the task that lies ahead looks pretty daunting: five minutes of this, ten minutes of that, twelve repetitions of one thing, twenty repetitions of another. To me the fitness programme looks like it's been designed for the likes of AC Slater or Steven Seagal. But then again, the girl said it shouldn't take much more than an hour, and how much damage could I realistically do to myself in such a short space of time?

The answer is quite a lot. I'm on the verge of fainting by the time I've finished on the hand bike and that was only supposed to be a warm up. My muscles are already beginning to feel the effect of being cultivated on a diet of beer, doner kebabs and curry. My supposed forty-five-second rest period soon turns into more than five minutes as I wait for my head to stop spinning enough for me to risk standing up. I already feel like enough of a twat sitting here doing nothing but sweating profusely without having to endure the additional embarrassment of collapsing in a heap on the floor like some kind of retard. Once my legs are up to it, I go and do my stretches in the furthest corner of the gym, facing the wall so nobody can see how pale I'm guessing I must be right now. Being away from the claustrophobic seat of the hand bike makes me feel a little better and I approach my resistance training with a slightly more optimistic outlook than I had a few moments ago. Surely it must be a downhill ride from here.

But it isn't, and the energy flows from my body as quickly as the sweat. My carefully planned pre-gym breakfast hasn't transformed me into the athlete I thought it might, and even the puny weights the girl has started me on are more than a match for my feeble muscles. And I can't begin to describe to you how demoralising it is to be the least fit person in a room in which the majority of people are overweight housewives or men of retirement age. I hit rock bottom as I find myself having to reduce the weight on the shoulder press when using it directly after the bloke who used to work in the chip shop, and I decide it's time to call it a day and head for the exercise bike for the cool-down period.

As I sit there, outpaced by a woman old enough to be my grandmother, I vow that I'll cancel my membership first thing tomorrow morning, claiming I've broken my leg or something. I really don't think I'm cut out for this exercise bollocks, and I anticipate a fuckload of pain for very little gain. It simply isn't worth it. While these pensioners may be able to run further than me, I have little doubt as to who would win in a fight, and I tell myself that's what counts at the end of the day.

Besides, I'm sure these gym places can't be good for you. I mean, I've only been here the once, yet I've already been confronted by a visibly wet seat on more than three occasions. And the worse thing about it is that you know the *exact* source of this liquid; more often than not it's the sweaty crack of an old man's arse. I can't think of any other situation where people would find this acceptable.

I vacate the bike, kindly leaving behind a nice big sweat patch of my own for the next person to mop up with their shorts. Some people might consider that a privilege, you know, especially given my current status. I do a few more half-hearted stretches and then gladly head for the door.

'See ya,' calls the girl from behind the desk.

Her tone sounds almost mocking and part of me suspects it's supposed to, but since she's so good looking I decide to give her the benefit of the doubt.

'Yeah, see you around,' I smile back, and already I'm reassessing my decision to cancel my membership.

'Here it comes now,' declares Yeti.

I don't know how the fuck he can see the bus from here, but he has an uncanny knack for spotting things that are a long way off. I can see a bus myself, but I can't make out whether it's of the park-and-ride variety, the one that goes back to Thame or the one we actually want. But Yeti seems pretty certain it's the required Oxford Tube bus and as it draws nearer he is proved to be correct. A lucky guess, perhaps, but I doubt it. Legendary eyesight is another line on the long list of his many talents. Hawkeyes Yeti.

'Looks pretty full,' I comment as the big red machine pulls up alongside us.

'Yeah,' he agrees.

The coach is of the older variety, not the ultra-modern, double-decker style ones you usually see these days. I have to hop back to avoid being knocked over by the door as it hisses open and I wince as I step up into the coach's vast interior. My hamstrings are already beginning to feel the effects of the morning's workout.

'Day return to London, please,' I instruct the driver.

'Are you a student?'

'No.'

'That's nine pounds then, please.'

I dig my wallet out of my pocket and find it empty. I forgot to go to the fucking cashpoint! I knew there was something I had to remember to do before we set off and now I'm left with no money to speak of.

'Do you take cards?' I ask the driver, knowing full well they don't.

'I'm afraid not, mate. It's cash only.'

'Bollocks,' I mutter under my breath.

I catch sight of some repetitive movement out of the corner of my eye and I look up to see an old woman at the front of the coach sitting there shaking her head. I almost explode. What fucking business is it of hers if I've forgotten to get some money out? But I don't want to make a scene, so I blank her out and turn back to the driver.

'Would it be possible for me to leg it to a cashpoint when we get to London and pay you *then*?' It doesn't sound like a totally unreasonable request to me.

'I'm afraid not. You have to have a ticket in case an inspector comes on. If you're caught without a ticket it isn't only you that gets fined. I'll get fined as well.'

'Sure, I appreciate that, but can't you just print me a ticket and then I'll pay you when we get there?'

I glance to my right once more and *still* the miserable old hag is shaking her head in disapproval. I fix her a stare, but she's undeterred. She stares right back, eyebrows chiselled into a frown and lips pursed together like a cat's arse. Fucking coffin-dodger.

'I'm sorry, mate, I can't do that.'

'Here,' Yeti butts in. 'You can pay me back later.'

He hands me over a tenner and I pass it on to the driver.

'Cheers, Yeti,' I thank him. 'You saved my life.'

'No problem. It wouldn't be the first time.'

The driver gives me my ticket along with a pound coin and I stick them both in my pocket. I turn to look for a seat, but all I can see is that scaly old trout sitting up there on her high horse. A quick glance at the other passengers reveals that nobody else could give a monkey's about my little mistake, so why the fuck should *she* be so offended by it? I slowly begin to walk towards her, but her display of condemnation doesn't cease. Stopping alongside her chair, I'm about to open my mouth to ask what her fucking problem is when Yeti prods me in the back and hurriedly pushes me down the gangway. I turn back to protest, but we're already halfway towards the back and he's forcing me into one of the vacant seats, swiftly sitting down next to me so that I'm trapped.

'What's the rush?' I ask him. 'Didn't you see the way that woman was shaking her head at me? What the fuck is her problem?'

'Parkinson's disease.'

'*What?*'

I stand up and peer down the aisle and, sure enough, the old woman's head is still shaking from side to side.

'Oh shit,' I say guiltily as the realisation of what almost happened dawns upon me. 'Oh shit, oh shit, oh shit.'

'You see my point now?'

'Yeah. Jesus, that was too fucking close. Shit!'

Yeti grins that impeccable grin of his.

'That's twice I've saved you in one day, Big D. Next time I'm gonna have to charge you for it.'

After a bus journey of over an hour and a brief ride on the underground, we arrive at the BBC studios in plenty of time. It's the second occasion that me and the Yeti have been here this year (which is twice more than in any other year), except this time it's me who is taking centre stage.

'Thank you. On the show tonight, the film star so in demand his fellow actors call him the Lord of the Universe. He is Ewan McGregor. Then there's the actress, comedian and impressionist whose imitation of Victoria Beckham is better than Victoria Beckham's. She's Ronni Ancona. Music from one of the most successful young singer-songwriters of present time. She is Dido.

But first up, a man who has become famous… or should that be *infamous*, not only for what he has done, but for what he has inspired others to do. In his first live appearance on national television, the creator of the phenomenon that is 'celebrity bundling'… Ladies and gentleman, please put your hands together for Mr Dom Carter!'

I emerge triumphantly from the backstage area, grinning like a lunatic as I step into the garish glare of the studio lights. The band to my left is almost big enough to pass for a small orchestra, and they play me in with great enthusiasm, their efforts matched by the equally upbeat reaction of the crowd. While the applause certainly gives me a buzz, their flattering appreciation is partially wasted because I'm having to concentrate so goddamn hard on negotiating the studio steps in a seemingly relaxed fashion. You see, my exertions in the gym this morning have really come back to haunt me over the last couple of hours and right now I feel stiffer than a Viagra-fuelled penis. I try my best to adopt a casual strut, but I have this horrible inkling I'm walking in a manner that suggests I've shat myself. Thankfully, the steps come and go without me falling arse over tit and I approach the purple carpeted area where Michael Parkinson is waiting, beaming from ear to ear and looking genuinely happy to see me. I greet him like I suspect I would a long-lost grandfather, grasping his hands in a heartfelt, double-handed shake.

This is one occasion where a bundle is *definitely* out of the question; the old guy might not be able to take it. Mind you, I'm not sure I'd be able to take it either, not in my present state. And besides, it would have been so clichéd, so predictable.

He gestures to the seat behind me, one of those rotating office chairs, but this one has cushioned armrests and a purple trim to match the carpet. Such is the extent of the aching in my limbs that I sit down far more gingerly than Parky does, something the viewers might find surprising given our respective ages. There's nothing between us other than a small black coffee table that plays home to two glasses of water, one for me and one for Parky.

'Welcome to the show, Dom.'

'It's a pleasure to be here, Michael.'

'Just to get it out of the way before we start… I noticed you were walking awkwardly as you came in,' he smiles at me. 'Why is that? I mean, answer as you may, tell me to mind my own business…'

'Mind your own business!' I laugh, and the audience laughs with me. 'To be honest, I was hoping you wouldn't notice, wishful thinking I guess… No, seriously, I went to the gym this morning and let's just say I overdid it a bit.'

'First time in a while, was it?'

'First time ever, more like!'

The audience laughs again. It's easier than I thought this interview bollocks. I guess that because I'm sitting here in front of the cameras they're *expecting* me to be funny, so any wit is amplified purely through the power of expectation. Plus with an audience of this size, at least a *few* people are bound to find even the lamest of my remarks amusing and the rest of the sheep will laugh along with them for fear of appearing that they didn't get the joke. With this in mind I feel myself slip into a state of relative comfort.

'Dom, you've become famous for what you…'

'*Am* I famous?'

'Wouldn't you consider yourself to be famous?'

'Well, I suppose so. More famous than I *was* at least. But I'm not exactly famous in the real sense. Not a big star like yourself, Michael.'

I wait for the laughter to die down before I continue.

'People have heard of me, but this is my first real public appearance. All my other sightings have been as blurry pictures on emails. I guess I'm like a writer in that sense. I can walk the streets without being recognised, but when people hear my name they're suddenly impressed. Things might've changed when I wake up tomorrow morning, though!'

'Well they might,' grins Parky. 'And how would you feel about being famous; famous in the '*real* sense', as you put it? And with yours being an unexpected fame, if you like, and a particular kind of fame as well?'

'You know what… it's kind of hard to say. I'd like to think it would be a good thing, but I guess it depends how the public perceives me. I might be a national symbol of hatred for all I know. Ask me again in a year's time… if I'm still famous, that is.'

Parky chuckles away to himself and then takes a sip of water. I'd almost forgotten until then that they had supplied us with drinks, so I do the same.

'Tell me about this bundling thing,' he says. 'It sounds like an unlikely pastime to me… How did it come about?'

'Hmmm,' I muse. 'Where did it all begin…? It seems so long ago now, a lot has happened… But like all of history's greatest ideas, it was born in the pub, under the influence of alcohol. And we kind of just went from there.'

'We?'

'Yeah, me, Yeti… who incidentally, is in the audience tonight… Gaz, Volkan and Bertie. Have I left anyone out…? I hope not, they're supposed to be my best friends… No, that's the lot.'

'Sorry, run me through those names again… Gaz, Yeti…'

'Gaz, Yeti, Volkan and Bertie.'

'Sounds like science fiction gone crazy,' comments Parky and the audience bellows with laughter. 'A strange group of nicknames.'

'Only one is a proper nickname, though,' I inform him. 'They're a great bunch of lads.'

'I don't doubt it… So this bundling thing… and for the benefit of those who aren't sure exactly what it is… You throw somebody on the floor… then you, you lie… on top of them… and then you shout the word "bundle" and other people jump on top to form a pile of bodies. Is that an accurate description?'

I notice he always looks at the floor as he speaks, so much so that I peer down there myself to see whether there's an autocue hidden under the carpet or something. There isn't.

'Couldn't have explained it better myself, Michael. It's probably best to give a demonstration, but I wouldn't want to subject anybody here to it! But yeah, the mound of bodies is the real key… That's the bundle itself, so to speak. The shouting of "bundle!" isn't really necessary, but it adds to the fun. I'm trying to think of images that people might remember… There's a gigantic bundle at the end of *The Naked Gun*, during the baseball scene… Do you remember that?'

Parky nods his head thoughtfully, but I get the feeling he thinks I'm talking bollocks.

'And there was a great bundle in the World Cup of 1990, the one in Italy,' I continue. 'It involved the Cameroon team… They bundle the striker after he scores a goal… can't remember who they were playing… might even have been England.'

'I think it may have been,' confirms Parky. 'Bundling has become a bookable offence in football matches now, you know. They don't want to encourage kids to do it.'

'Yeah, and I think the FA got a bit worried after Michael Owen missed that World Cup qualifier after being injured during a bundle at Anfield.'

'But that had nothing to do with you.'

'Fuck no! Oops… Sorry, slip of the tongue there. Can they edit that bit out?'

'I expect so.'

Unnecessary swearing on a chat show, how embarrassing. And in front of Michael Parkinson as well. That's like swearing in front of your grandparents. I picture Yeti sniggering in the audience.

'Sorry, where were we?' I ask.

'Michael Owen.'

'Oh yes, Michael Owen. No, that had nothing to do with me… despite what some of the tabloids said at the time.'

'So who *have* you managed to bundle?

Parky holds his hands in his lap as he awaits my response. It occurs to me that at no point in the interview has he leant back in his chair; he's always perched forward on his feet instead. This is in stark contrast to my own position, reclined back with my arms up on the rests, almost exactly as I would if I was watching television in my armchair at home. He makes you feel at ease, does Parky.

'Let me see… In chronological order: Gary Barlow, Phillip Schofield… the *EastEnders* guy whose name I can never remember… er… Martin Kemp, yeah, that's the guy… Chris Evans, Anne Robinson – two gingers in a row, funny that… wasn't planned that way – er, who else… John Barnes, Denise van Outen, Joe Pasquale, Michelle Heaton from Liberty X… and one more… who was the most recent one…? Oh yeah, Jamie Oliver. That's it I think. Any more I can think of…? No, that's the lot. We tried to bundle Lennox Lewis, but he was just far too hard. And we wanted to bundle David Blaine when he came out of his box, but we couldn't get near enough. Probably a good thing really 'cause he might've disintegrated or something.'

The audience erupts once again. Jokes about the mental magic man always go down well with a British audience. I'm about to follow it up by saying that Paul Daniels should have outdone him by simultaneously embarking on a non-stop, forty-four-day public marathon sex session with the lovely Debbie McGee, but that would have been pushing the boundaries of taste.

'I didn't hear you mention Jordan in that list.'

'Jordan? Why would I?'

'The girls in the office tell me you bundled her. She was quite proud of the fact, apparently.'

'Not guilty I'm afraid. Must've been somebody else… Everybody's doing it these days. It's becoming *so passé, darling,*' I say, putting on my poshest voice and making a dismissive gesture with my hand.

'So which of those bundles did you find the most enjoyable? Which was the best?' enquires Parky once the audience has settled down.

'That's a tough one,' I reply, blowing air through my pursed lips. 'Joe Pasquale? No, seriously… I'm tempted to say Gary Barlow, because that was the first one, the one that got it all started… But I'd probably have to say Anne Robinson.'

'And why's that?'

'It was the whole build-up to it. Yeti was a contestant on *The Weakest Link*, so he had to endure a load of abuse from Anne before she eventually got her just desserts. It was a classic moment. Maybe they'll screen that episode one day when everything's died down a bit. It's funny, because there was this really stupid guy on there called D…'

'I'm going to have to stop you there before you get yourself sued for libel,' Parky interrupts, and there's yet another roar of amusement from the audience. 'So, Dom, you must have, if you like, an ideal target. If you could bundle anyone, anyone in the entire world, who would it be?'

'Aside from yourself, Michael?'

'Yes, aside from me,' he chuckles.

'Oh that's easy. The Queen. Imagine her lying on her back saying, "We are not amused." Priceless.'

This is a lie. The truthful answer would have been Britney Spears, but I wasn't about to admit that on national television. To do so would have put an end to any chances of it ever happening, because she would have been ready for it. Bundling relies on an element of surprise and she probably would have taken out a restraining order or something. Oh, to bundle Britney Spears…

'What if I had said dead or alive?' Parky pries further.

'I don't know… Jesus Christ perhaps?'

'You would have bundled the Son of God?'

'Yeah. I don't see why not. Nobody is above being bundled. That's rule number two of celebrity bundling.'

'There are rules to what you do?' he says with surprise.

'Oh yes. We're true professionals!'

'I won't ask you what they are,' states Parky. 'But joking aside… there is a serious element to all this, isn't there? There are risks involved. The child… the young boy who had his spine broken… What would you say to him if you met him? What *could* you say?'

'I don't know. I'd tell him that he was extremely unlucky... That's about it, really.'

'What I'm trying to say is... are you pleased with what you've created? I mean, there are many celebrities who are afraid to leave their houses for fear of being bundled. I've heard some have even left the country.'

'That's ridiculous. Firstly, I don't believe I've *created* anything. Bundling has always been around. What I did was remind people that it's still there, that's all. It's one of those sad facts of life that some people will always find a way to misuse even the most innocent of information. I don't accept responsibility for what has happened, because *personally* I haven't hurt anyone. You can't blame me if a young child has been permanently disabled, in the same way you can't blame Ronald McDonald for all the fat people in the world. I'm not going to come out here and make a statement to the nation that everybody should stop bundling, because I don't believe they should. Anyway, David Beckham has already done that.'

'I wasn't trying to pin blame...'

'I know you weren't, but a lot of people are. I didn't ask for any of this to happen... it was just me and a few mates having a laugh. I just got lucky. Or unlucky, depending which way you want to look at it.'

'Lucky,' suggests Parky.

'Yeah, I'd like to think lucky,' I smile.

'So what's next for you, then? What's next for Dom Carter?'

'To be honest with you, I have absolutely no idea. Answers on a postcard to... Really, I'm not sure. I think I might write a book or something, an autobiography. That seems to be the thing famous people do these days. But first I'll need some scandal to put in it.'

I bring my finger and thumb to my chin and cock my head to one side.

'What are you thinking about?' asks Parky.

'I'm trying to think whether anyone famous has ever done anything to me that I could pass off as sexual harassment.

That's always good for a bit of publicity… But I can't. Everybody I've met has been really nice. Although maybe Graham Norton was a bit too nice… I'm only kidding by the way; I've never even met the man.'

'So no big life plans, then?'

'Not really, I'm afraid. Right now I'm happy to drift along doing what I do and wait to see what happens. That's the good thing about life, you can do that. You can be a drifter; providing everything is going ok, that is. Otherwise it sucks. I guess you could say life is like a bundle… it's great unless you're one of the people at the bottom.'

I'd been waiting to get that one in for the whole interview.

'Life is like a bundle,' repeats Parky, smiling wistfully and nodding his head. 'I like that… Life is like a bundle… What a lovely way to finish. Ladies and gentleman, Dom Carter!'

'Five quid says he doesn't show up,' says Gaz, offering his hand for me to shake.

'You're on.' I grab his hand and shake it vigorously. 'You seeing this, Yeti?'

'Yeah, I see it.'

Our good friend Volk is the subject of tonight's bet, and if ever there was a test of his metal then this is definitely it. A certain girlfriend of his, or *ex*-girlfriend I should say, has taken it upon herself to give what can only be described as an up close and *extremely* personal interview in one of the country's leading tabloids. And let's just say that it doesn't exactly paint him in a good light. Gaz is convinced the revelations will be enough to turn Volk into a shamed recluse, with my side of the bet relying on the fact that he's probably the world's most stubborn man and will venture out.

So the waiting game starts and I can think of worse places to have to wait than where we are now, sitting at our usual table by the jukebox in our usual Friday night haunt. I tell you, it's something of a blessing that our newfound fame hasn't prevented us from enjoying an uninterrupted pint here like we used to, as I really don't know how we would manage without this place. It would mean breaking the habit of the last seven years and finding somewhere new to go. I admit, the local drinking crowd is a fickle one and, like everybody else, we've flirted with a handful of the town's other twelve public houses. But we always end up back here eventually; life wouldn't be the same if we didn't.

Being on TV is quite a big deal to most people these days, so you would expect a bit of hassle from the other punters, good-natured or otherwise. But to tell you the truth, nothing much has changed. We get the occasional shout of "Bundle!" as we walk to the bar, usually towards the end of the night when the alcohol has had time to push back the British qualities of politeness and self-restraint, and people seem more keen to chat to me as I stand next to them at the urinal taking a piss. I swear I've had the same goddamn conversation about fifty-seven times since the Parkinson interview, always beginning with, "You look familiar. Have you been on TV?" But aside from that, things are as they always were. It's kind of nice to get pointed at every now and then, or to receive a smile of recognition from a fit girl; however, things have yet to progress any further than that. I guess it takes a certain kind of person to approach a group of friends sitting at a table and interrupt their conversation for the sole reason of announcing that you recognise them, and this type of person doesn't seem to exist around these parts. Furthermore, the fact that we were familiar faces anyway probably has something to do with the lack of reaction. Everyone has seen us a hundred times before and the fact that we appear on daytime television or in a national newspaper from time to time doesn't make a great deal of difference. We're just the local lads that got lucky.

'That's five quid you owe me then, Gaz,' I smugly announce as Volk is sighted entering the pub.

My first reaction is to wonder whether he's even read the article, but his body language suggests he most definitely has. For a start, he's turned up the collar of his coat, something I've only seen him do once before when he was trying to cover up the mother of all love bites, a bruise so big it looked like he'd been sucked on by a camel rather than his then girlfriend, Becca. And gone is the usual man-about-town swagger he usually adopts; this has been replaced by a head-down, purposeful stride that carries him quickly to our table.

'Evening, gentlemen,' he grins sheepishly, sitting himself down in the spare chair that previously played home to Yeti's jacket.

'Bar!' we bellow at him in unison.

'For fuck's sake. Usual, yeah?'

We give him the thumbs up. Volk gets up and goes back to the bar, returning shortly afterwards with three pints and a bottle. None of us bother to get up to help him as we know he's the one person in the group that can easily do the four-drink carry.

'Alright, Volk?' we reply as he sits down again, trying to disguise our smirks.

'What's so funny?' asks Volk defensively.

'Nothing,' we reply.

'No seriously, what?'

'Nothing,' we repeat.

'You've all read it, then,' he mutters through gritted teeth.

'Read what?' I ask innocently.

'You know very well what.'

'What are you talking about?' I shrug.

'The article.'

'What article?'

'*The* article.'

He's quickly losing patience, but I'm not prepared to ease off quite yet. Winding up Volk is one of life's simple pleasures.

'I'm not sure what article you're talking about, mate. Gaz? Yeti?' They both show me their empty palms. 'You're gonna have to elaborate.'

'Michelle's article.'

'Michelle's article? No, I haven't read that one. What's she got to say for herself?'

'Quite a lot, unfortunately,' Volk says grumpily. 'She, er… criticised my performance.'

'But I thought you were quite good at football?' I respond, while Gaz and Yeti look away to hide their smiles.

'Not *football*,' Volk corrects me. 'My, er… *performance*.'

He clenches his fists and delivers a very restrained pelvic thrust.

'Oh!' I exclaim, pretending to see the light. 'She said you were crap in bed!'

'Hey, not so loud, will ya!' hisses Volk angrily.

'Sorry, mate,' I apologise, before adding, 'so which paper was that in, then?'

'*The Sun.*'

'Hmm… it has quite a large readership, *The Sun*,' I muse.

'Too fucking right.'

A group of girls enter the pub and journey straight to the back, passing by our table in a five-strong parade of perfume, pouts and perfect pins that turns every male head in the house. There's something there for everyone: the peroxide blonde leading the way; the tall brunette following close behind; the small but perfectly formed Mediterranean-looking girl coming in third; and even an attractive redhead who narrowly misses out on a podium finish. Come to think of it, they would make a passable girl band were it not for the rogue fifth member, a girl who hadn't been blessed with either looks or glamour and who walked with her shoulders hunched. I get the feeling she must have been friends with them from an early age, as I can't imagine the rest of them giving her the time of day if they were to meet her for the first time now.

Volk gives them his seal of approval as they saunter past. 'Yep, yep… definitely yep… yep… er, probably… What the fuck, yep.'

'First the worst,' I comment. 'Second the best.'

'Third the one with the treasure chest!' leers Volk, making groping gestures with his hands.

'Fourth the ginger eagle… I mean *golden* eagle,' I laugh.

'What about number five?' asks Volk.

'Dunno,' I reply. 'I never knew the rhyme went that far.'

'Fifth the cowboy in the west,' Yeti pipes up.

'Hmm, doesn't really work, does it?' says Volk, scratching the back of his head. 'Although she was the most masculine of the five, I suppose. That short one though… fucking hell! How do I go about getting myself one of those?'

'Well, plastic surgery would be a good place to start,' I tell him. 'Then a couple of years in the gym should help. And then it'd be time to start thinking about a personality transplant.'

Volk extends his middle finger and stares at me with a sarcastic, closed-lipped smile.

'You could start by getting yourself some social skills,' Gaz advises him.

'I've got all the social skills I need right here.' Volk raises his eyebrows as he points down at his diminishing beer. 'You can't beat a pint of Social-Skills.'

'You ain't wrong,' I agree with him. 'A couple of pints of Social-Skills is the only way to start off an evening down the pub. It paves the way for other drinks… like a pint of Elaborate-Dance-Moves, for instance.'

'Ah yes! I love a good pint of Elaborate-Dance-Moves!' laughs Volk. 'That and a pint of Find-Crap-Jokes-Really-Funny. Once you've got those down your neck you've got the makings of a good night.'

'But unfortunately, that's also where the problems start,' I warn them. 'You never really know what you're drinking after the third or fourth pint. I've lost count of the number of times I've ordered a pint of Enhanced-Attractiveness-In-The-Eyes-Of-The-Opposite-Sex, only to discover once I've finished it that the bastard behind the bar has served me a pint of Make-A-Twat-Of-Myself instead. And then it's all downhill from there. Before you know it you've had a bottle of I-Must-Wear-Yeti's-Hat, a pint of Buy-Some-Random-Strangers-A-Drink, and a couple of shots of Send-Numerous-Text-Messages-That-I'll-Be-Sure-To-Regret-In-The-Morning. Or in Gaz's case, a pint of Sudden-Urge-To-Take-A-Crap-In-The-Pub-Toilet-Even-Though-There-Is-No-Lock-Or-Toilet-Paper.'

'Jesus, yeah,' sighs Gaz. 'That barman always serves me a pint of that last one.'

'Do they serve Make-A-Twat-Of-Yourself in here, then?' Volk asks me.

'Yeah, they've got it on tap. It's good stuff, actually. I'll get you a pint of it later.'

'Cheers, ma… Aargh!'

'Volkan!'

Volk receives a heavy slap on the back that almost causes him to spill his drink.

I look up to see who it is, but it's not anybody I know. He looks familiar, mind you, probably one of his mates from football.

'Oh, it's you,' says Volk without enthusiasm. 'Lads, this is Chris. Chris…'

He waves his arm in our general direction. Chris cocks his head in acknowledgement and then turns back to Volk, grinning as though he's been told Beyoncé Knowles is waiting for him out the back, dressed in leather and legs akimbo.

'Well, well, well…' he begins.

Volk's eyes drop self-consciously to the floor in anticipation of the humiliating abuse he's about to receive.

'Well… well… well,' Chris says again, more slowly this time.

'Spit it out will ya, Christophe?' appeals Volk.

Chris turns to the rest of us.

'Has he told you guys about his problems between the sheets?'

I shrug my shoulders, and Gaz and Yeti do the same. It's all very well *us* taking the piss out of him, but I don't particularly want to see him getting belittled in front of an audience.

'Nice article in *The Sun* today, mate,' Chris chuckles as he sympathetically pats Volk's back. 'I always thought you lacked stamina on the football field, but I never thought it affected you in other areas as well.'

'You shouldn't believe everything you read, mate,' Volk sighs.

'Don't worry, mate, I'm sure you'll improve with time. Practice makes perfect and all that. Not that the women are going to be queuing up after that report!'

Chris bellows with laughter as he walks away and Volk is left shaking his head.

'Hopefully that'll be the worst of it,' is my lame attempt at moral support.

Unfortunately for Volk, that particular encounter is only the beginning. Word of his blink-and-you'll-miss-it bedroom performance soon gets around the pub and our conversations are interrupted on no fewer than seven different occasions by a whole range of random people. Old schoolmates we haven't spoken to in about six years make a point of coming over to give their ten pence worth, predictable jokes about "sex being a race in which Volk always comes first" and phrases like "one-minute wonder" are soon in danger of becoming clichés due to their overuse. Volk responds with sarcastic replies of "I'll get better" and, to be fair to him, handles the whole thing pretty well. There's one occasion where he gets some stick from a bloke who I know for a fact he doesn't like when things are in danger of kicking off, but luckily the bloke doesn't hang about long enough, staggering off to the toilet once he's exhausted his repertoire of cheap jokes.

'This is fuckin' unbelievable,' moans Volk after he's had his head patronisingly patted by some fat bird I recall him turning down a few years back.

I smile at him sympathetically. Amusing though it is, this whole incident must be one huge kick in the teeth. Having your sexual performance torn to pieces in a national newspaper is going to be hard for anyone to take, let alone someone as image-conscious as Volk.

'What was Michelle thinking?' he demands to know. 'Do I really deserve this?'

'Probably,' replies Gaz.

'What?' says Volk in disbelief. 'Whose side are you on?'

'I'm not on anyone's side, but I don't think this is a particularly unexpected outcome after what you did.'

'And what exactly did I do?'

'You dumped her for no real reason other than that you thought you could trade up to somebody better now that you're famous. Don't you think she's entitled to be a bit upset?'

'Maybe. But *this*? Telling the nation I'm the world's worst lover? Why did she do that?'

'Have you heard of the phrase, *a woman scorned*?' Yeti asks him.

'Yeah.'

'Well there's your reason. Revenge, pure and simple.'

'But what does she really expect to achieve out of all this?' gripes Volk.

'Well, let me see…' starts Gaz. 'Your humiliation for a start. I think it's fair to say she's been successful on that front. Money? I'm sure she would've got paid a fair bit for doing that interview. Pride would be another reason… make her feel better about herself. And exposure as well. Have you seen the pictures? I can't see her being short of offers now those have been released.'

'Thanks a lot, Gaz! That makes me feel *so* much better!' scoffs Volk. 'It's all bullshit anyway… she loved it.'

'Of course she did, mate. Look, it's all here in black and white….'

I've been waiting for the right time to air the offending article, whipping out my copy of the newspaper, which I've been sitting on all evening. And would you believe it? It's even open on the right page.

'Here we go… "Volkan has had his five minutes of fame. That's a good two minutes longer than he's ever lasted between the sheets". And what's this bit here? "There was no need for the Vulcan neck grip to send me to sleep; all he needed to do was take his clothes off". And check out the headline… "Sex With Volkan – It's Light-Speed". Tabloid journalism at its best!'

'Give it here!' snaps Volk, snatching it from my hand.

He aggressively rips up the pages in question, but not before gazing ruefully at the scantily clad beauty he so willingly gave up. He throws the newspaper confetti in my general direction.

'I've got another a copy at home,' I joke.

Yeti gathers up the mess and dumps it into one of the empty pint glasses.

'I'm considering legal action,' Volk announces.

'Yeah? And how the fuck are you supposed to prove it?'

'I dunno.'

'I can't see any of your exes leaping forward to say how great you were, mate,' Gaz tells him. 'Let it go. People will have forgotten about it in a couple of weeks.'

'And think about it,' I chip in. 'The next girl you shag might find herself pleasantly surprised.'

'*Will* be pleasantly surprised,' states Volk. 'There's no *might* about it. As if I'd only last three minutes. This is me we're talking about here. *Me*. Volkan.'

He lets out an arrogant scoff.

'Could've been worse,' is my closing statement on the matter. 'She could've said that you're hung like a Tic Tac.'

'At least she'd always have minty fresh breath though, right?'

Gaz shakes his head in disapproval.

'For fuck's sake… get off you high horse, Gaz. You know you love it. Anyway, you lot coming out the back?'

"Out the back" in this case means the converted barn behind the pub that doubles as the town's only dance floor. And the lack of competition doesn't exactly inspire the place to maintain a high standard of either music or clientele.

'Nah, I'm not really up for it to tell you the truth.' I think it's fair to say that my reply echoes the opinion of the others as well.

'Go on, you know you always love it once you're there,' grins Volk, digging me in the ribs with his elbow.

'It's a waste of money and you know it.'

'But you can't let those pints of Elaborate-Dance-Moves go to waste! Look, I'll even pay for you all to get in.'

'Oh, go on then.'

Volk is always well up for wiping his feet on the rhythm rug, and who am I to stand in his way?

Bundle Me Baby (One More Time)

Bertie is driving us back from a celebrity five-a-side charity football tournament in which we did ourselves no favours due to a general lack of fitness and an even greater lack of footballing ability. We were doomed from the start, really, since nobody was going to take us seriously with a name like Big D's Dynamos. You see, I hadn't thought of a proper one in advance as I'd been instructed to do, and Big D's Dynamos was the best I could come up with on the spur of the moment. This was met with disgruntled groans when announced to the others and made it difficult to hold our heads up high whenever the name was called out over the public announcement system.

However, the main problem was that, out of the five of us, Volk is the only one who plays football regularly. Bertie used to be quite good, but he had to give up due to the time pressures of his job. I'm not *too* bad, but my infrequent trips to the gym have yet to show any real benefits on the fitness front and I was thankful the matches only lasted ten minutes each. Yeti is pretty useful for a waif and he'd have done ok if only we'd come against Blazin' Squad, where his size would've been less of an issue. And as for Gaz, well, I'll be diplomatic for once and only say that some people are naturally good at sport, whereas others are not. We put him in goal.

Match 1: Big D's Dynamos 4-0 Page 3 Pin-Ups

It's often been said that football is a man's game, and it follows that a group of five blokes will generally be able to defeat a group of five girls. This match was no exception and the contest was more one-sided than a fat man on a seesaw. While there was little doubt in anyone's mind which was the more attractive side, good looks counted for nothing as the Dynamos cruised to a 4-0 victory.

Welcome to the Big Top of Fun, welcome to the circus! Volk took on the role of ringmaster, leading from the front and pulling the strings. Bertie was the strongman: sturdy, muscular, powerful in possession. Then there was the bag of tricks that is Big D, the magician. And let's not forget Yeti, the dancing horse, and Gaz, the acrobat.

Bring on the clowns.

The clowns in this case were the Page 3 Pin-Ups, and it took just thirty seconds for the Dynamos to take the lead, Volk latching on to a defence-splitting through ball from the Yeti and finishing with aplomb. Volk increased the lead less than a minute later, bursting through and slotting home coolly with the Pin-Ups' defence at sixes and sevens. Even at this early stage the goal was enough to put the game beyond doubt and no amount of whistling or whooping from the crowd was going to change that.

The third goal was a wonder to behold; some might claim it was worth the entrance fee alone. Captain marvel Big D broke devastatingly down the right and curled in a cross to the back post, where Bertie rose like a salmon to nod home from six yards. Two minutes later, Volk thumped home a twenty-yard rocket to complete his hat-trick, the ensuing bundle almost causing a pitch invasion, which the stewards did well to control.

Not wanting to inflict a humiliating rout on the Pin-Ups, the Dynamos took their feet off the pedal and were content with playing possession football for the remainder of the match. This show of respect was welcomed by the Pin-Ups, but it wasn't enough for them to take part in the much-anticipated shirt-swapping after the final whistle was blown.

Match 2: Big D's Dynamos 1-3 Blue

In contrast to the good-natured atmosphere of the previous round, this match was an ill-tempered affair and, had it not been for an exceptional level of leniency shown by the referee, neither team would have finished the match with a full complement of players.

The proceedings started off in a healthily competitive fashion, both teams trying to stamp their authority on the game early on through a combination of aggressive jockeying and full-blooded tackles. Most of the battling took place in the centre of the field and the game looked to be edging towards a stalemate, the number of chances so few and far between that Terry Nutkins could count them on the fingers of one hand. However, after four minutes of hacking and grunting, a fortunate double ricochet saw the ball fall kindly for Blue's Antony and he swept past a static Dynamos defence, lobbing the onrushing Gaz to make it 1-0.

The game's main talking point happened less than a minute later: Volk collapsing theatrically in the penalty area under a heavy challenge from Duncan. It was as clear a penalty as you're ever likely to see, but the boys from Blue took offence at Volk's dying swan, the accusations and finger-pointing that followed threatening to turn nasty. Fortunately they didn't and Volk was able to place the ball on the penalty spot unchallenged. With only four in the band, Blue had enlisted the help of Daniel Bedingfield between the sticks, and the signing looked to have paid off when Bedingfield dived athletically to his right to palm away Volk's spot kick. However, Dynamos equalised from the resulting corner, with Yeti scrambling in from close range.

That was to be the Dynamos' last taste of success, as from this point on the match was like the cloudless sky; it was all Blue. Simon took the game by the scruff of the neck, dictating play with intelligent movement and passes to which the Dynamos simply had no answer. Duncan and Antony locked up the defence and the Dynamos were reduced to occasional, speculative, long-range efforts that were easily dealt with by the cat-like Bedingfield. Meanwhile, the Dynamos became increasingly riled by Lee's continual backchat, and Volk had to be physically dragged away by his teammates on more than one occasion.

It looked to be only a matter of time before Blue scored and in the seventh minute they did just that, Antony running through to nutmeg Gaz, who was visibly distracted by the chants of "Ear we go, Ear we go" emanating from certain sections of the crowd. Blue added another after eight minutes, this time from the boot of the impressive Simon.

With victory sealed, the Blue boys decided it was time to start showboating. This led to the emergence of ludicrous flicks and elaborate trickery, which threatened to drag the game down into the realms of pantomime; so much so that nobody would have been surprised had shouts of "man on" been replaced with calls of "he's behind you". The final whistle couldn't come soon enough for Big D's Dynamos as they crashed out of the tournament.

As I said, we didn't really do ourselves any favours. People turned up wanting us to lose, and in the end we didn't disappoint. But I suppose I can handle a bit of public humiliation, seeing as it's for charity and all.

Gaz is a bit quiet in the car on the way back, mind you. I don't think he's too happy about being publicly heckled by strangers about his ear. One of the things about being famous is that you're expected to accept stuff like that, to grin and bear it. You shouldn't have to, but that's the way it is.

'Do we *have* to stop?' complains Volk. 'We're pretty much back home. Can't you wait?'

'No way,' replies Bertie. 'Everyone's starving and I could do with a chocolate milkshake.'

'But it's on the other side of the dual carriageway. We'd have to go all the way down to the traffic lights and turn around.'

'What difference does it make to you? It's *me* that's driving!' laughs Bertie, and Volk shuts up.

We do the loop and end up in the virtually empty car park of the Headington McDonalds.

'You can stay in the car if you don't want to go in,' Bertie tells Volk.

'No, no, I'll come with you. I just won't eat anything.'

'You're not vegetarian, are you?' asks Yeti.

'No. I just don't fancy eating any McShit.'

We enter Maccie D's. The interior is like that of any other branch: sterile and simplistic with beige and grey abounding to hide the dirt. You know how it is. As suggested by the barrenness of the car park, the place is pretty much empty, aside from a big black guy at one of the tables and a blonde girl in a baseball cap who is leaning with both elbows on the counter. It's the arse I recognise first, and everything else simply falls into place around it.

'Oh my god…' I whisper, the words lost in the shock of the moment.

And what an arse it is: perfectly rounded and firm, with a clearly distinct point where the leg ends and the bottom begins. I tell you, even though I'm about to die of starvation, the sight of it makes me salivate a great deal more than the line of Big Macs waiting to be served. It's funny, you know, given the amount of media coverage her breasts get and all that hoo-ha in the early days about whether they were real or not, that her arse never gets a mention. You'd think there was nothing special about it since it's so absent from the press. But you'd be wrong. When I see it before me now dressed in nothing but pink towelling trackie bottoms, I'm nothing short of astounded that the tabloids aren't questioning *its* authenticity; that journalists aren't speculating over the matter of butt implants (if such things exist), or whether she's had her buttocks sliced off and replaced with those of an Amazonian goddess. It's almost too good to be true; an arse born of a thousand squat thrusts. It is of vital importance that I act quickly.

'This one's on me, guys, what do you all want?'

The others exchange suspicious glances.

'What's the occasion?' queries Volk. 'You're usually a tight bastard.'

'No,' I counter, 'you're thinking of Gaz. What do you want?'

The opportunity of a free meal outweighs any concerns they may have about my motives and they happily relay their orders to me; even Volk, who seems to have left his standards in the car. And nobody asks for anything too complicated, either, so I don't have to waste time confirming their preferences.

'Ok, go and grab a table by the far window and I'll bring it over in a minute,' I instruct them.

'Do you want a hand carrying stuff?' offers Yeti.

'No, I'll manage. Cheers anyway.'

The lads traipse off and slide onto the benches of one of the tables around the corner that overlook the car park. It's hardly a view worth having, but it conveniently means they're out of sight and out of earshot. Now that I'm on my own I take a deep breath and stroll up to the counter, imitating the stance of the blonde girl with the agreeable arse. Ignoring the overwhelming urge to simultaneously dribble, stare and bow down at her feet, I play it cool instead, glancing across, making eye contact and then nonchalantly turning back to the member of staff who waits patiently before me.

'Good afternoon,' I greet the young man, whose mop-like hair looks almost as greasy as the food. 'Please could I have…?'

'Wait a minute,' he interrupts in a most unprofessional manner. 'I know you. Are you from TV?'

'I've been on TV, yes,' I reply vaguely.

'Thought so,' he beams excitedly. 'You're that bundling guy aren't you? Dom Carter, that's it. You're Dom Carter!'

'I am.' To this day, I still haven't thought of a sufficiently witty or interesting response to use when random people inform me that I am who I am.

'Wow!' he exclaims. 'Dom Carter and Britney Spears in *this* restaurant at the *same* time! Who would've believed it?'

'*Britney Spears*? Where?'

'Here,' says the girl standing next to me at the counter.

'Oh my god!' Now it's my turn to act all excited, "act" being the operative word. 'I can't believe I didn't recognise you! It must be your cunning disguise.'

She smiles, but doesn't answer. I guess she didn't really appreciate my joke, crap as it was. I curse myself for trying to be funny when a bit of old-fashioned British politeness would have sufficed. I'm close to blowing it already, so I turn back to the grimy youth to place my order, praying something incredibly charismatic to say will pop into my head. At least I actually spoke to her at all so it could be worse. If this had happened six months ago I would have stood here in silence and then regretted it for the rest of my life, torturing myself every single day with "what if?" scenarios based upon me charming the pants off her, in the literal sense. "If only I'd spoken to her we could be happily married by now," I would have told myself as I pounded my head against the wall of my padded cell.

However, one thing to come out of the celebrity bundling revolution has been reasonably frequent access to celebrities, so I've pretty much got over the gawping affliction that plagued me in the early days, when I was an amateur in the art of hobnobbing with the stars. These days I'm an older, stronger, more confident – and I'd like to think *sexier* – man, and I can schmooze with the best of them. You probably wouldn't think it by *this* performance, but let me assure you that media star and woman of your dreams are entirely different kettles of fish. Whereas I couldn't really give a shit whether Charlotte Church thought I was funny or if Andi Peters agreed with my political views, the current situation has got the whole pressure thing going on and I don't want to walk out of here today thinking that I didn't do myself justice because I had neglected to take my foot out of my mouth.

'Please could I have three Quarter Pounder meals, one with Coke, one with Diet Coke, one with Sprite… One Big Mac meal with Coke… er… Two lots of six chicken nuggets, an apple pie… er, one fillet of fish… One McChicken Sandwich meal with Coke. Er… is that it? Oh yeah, and one chocolate milkshake as well please, mate.'

'Please tell me that's not all for you,' says Britney.

'Pardon?'

'That's a lot of food. It's not all for you, is it?'

'Yeah, I'm trying to beef up a bit,' I say, patting my stomach. 'Of course it isn't all for me!'

'Well, you never can tell…'

'This is England, Britney. *Nobody* eats that much over here.'

'You calling us Americans *fat*?' she accuses, placing her hands on her slender hips and pushing her butt out to one side in mock confrontation.

'I suppose I am,' I admit. 'But I'm obviously excluding you from the generalisation. I hope that would go without saying, don't go getting a complex or anything. Although, I *have* heard you're something of a junk food queen, not that I'd ever have believed that until today.'

'*A junk food queen?*' she exclaims.

'Journalist's words, not mine,' I say, holding up my hands.

'Is that the sort of thing they write about me over here?'

'Yeah, that and your obsession with *Happy Days*.'

'My obsession with *Happy Days*?'

'I made that last bit up.'

'That's *soooooo* mean!' squeals Britney, drawing out the word "so" in that way Americans always seem to do.

Her food arrives and it looks to be far more than she could ever possibly fit in her trim stomach.

'You've ordered a fair amount of food yourself there, Britney. Where do you put it all? We've got more than one branch of McDonalds over here, you know, it isn't necessary to stock up.'

'It reminds me of home,' she sighs. 'Duh! What do you take me for? Most of this is for *him*.'

She nods in the direction of the huge black guy I spotted when I first came in, presumably her minder.

'Yeah, sure it is…'

'It *is*!'

Britney sounds so cute when she talks. I tell you, I could close my eyes and listen to her chatter all day.

'Just don't eat it all at once, yeah, take your time a bit,' I suggest.

'What*ever*! Tell you what, why don't you come and join me? You can make sure I don't make a pig of myself,' she smiles.

Get in! Britney Spears just asked me to dine with her. I know it's not exactly a romantic setting, but still.

'Sure, that would be great.' I try not to sound too keen, like I'm doing her a favour by allowing her ten minutes of my time.

Britney walks over to an empty table, delivering the vast majority of the food to her minder en route. Meanwhile, a heavily laden tray materialises in front of me and I hurriedly pay for its contents. I retrieve the items that belong to me and push the rest back towards the server.

'Can you do me a massive favour, mate, and take this lot over to the group of guys over there? Tell them I'll be over in a minute.'

'Sure.'

He grins a perverted grin that says "I know what you're up to" and takes the tray from me. It sickens me to think that he'll more than likely be wanking about this later.

I don't know whether you have ever sat opposite a stunningly beautiful person, but let me tell you that it's an experience quite unlike any other. Now, you could argue that beauty is in the eye of the beholder and that, because of this, you frequently sit opposite such a person in the shape of your present partner, but I'm talking about *real* beauty, genuine beauty. Because Britney has this by the bucketload. Lingering around her body like a perfume, following her about like a sweet-smelling fart, this level of exquisiteness means you can't help but stare, whatever she's doing. I ask you, how many people can still look gorgeous when they're wiping ketchup from the side of their mouths or picking the gherkins out of their cheeseburgers?

'Tell me how you made a name for yourself, Dom.'

'You mean you don't know who I *am*?' I answer, pretending to be all offended.

'I'm afraid not. *Obviously* you're a *massive* star over here. Maybe your reputation hasn't spread over to America yet.'

'That's something I'll have to work on, then. To be honest with you, I haven't done a great deal,' I say modestly. 'I'm one of those annoying people who became famous but nobody really knows why.'

'Oh yeah? What did that kid mean by "You're that bundling guy" then?'

'I have no idea.'

I'm reluctant to tell her, since I'm not sure how impressed she would be to find out that I had made it to where I am today by assaulting people like herself.

'What brings you to this part of the world, anyway?' I enquire as a means of steering the conversation away from my dubious past.

'What, you mean England?'

'No, Headington… Oxford.'

'Oh… um, I've been doing some promotional stuff in London and I had a spare day for once, so I thought I'd come and visit Oxford. It's a really beautiful city.'

'Cambridge is better.'

'Is it?'

'Yeah.'

My short, snappy answer backfires on me as the conversation flags, the silence becoming increasingly apparent with every second that passes. I panic as I struggle to think of something to say to fill the rapidly expanding gap.

'Who would you rather date? A man with no eyes or a man with no penis?'

The words sound even more ridiculous out loud than they did in my head.

'Excuse me?'

She'd heard precisely what I said and, like me, she can't quite believe it either. But it's too late now. I've said it, fallen into the hole and the only option now is to try and dig my way out.

'Who would you rather date?' I repeat. 'A man with no eyes or a man with no, er… penis.'

'Oh, a man with no eyes, definitely.'

She answered it. Thank fuck for that.

'Interesting. Why's that?'

'How would you have sex if the man had no penis?'

Interesting that her answer should be based around sex.

'He could use a strap-on. That would also mean he'd never be too tired or have problems getting it up. He could be as big as you wanted him to be. *And* he could last all night. All night, every night.'

'It's not really the same, though, is it?'

'I don't know. Isn't it?'

'Trust me, it isn't.'

'I'll take your word for it.'

'Plus,' Britney continues. 'If I was dating a blind man I wouldn't have to worry about putting my make-up on or looking bad first thing in the morning and stuff. And there would never be any arguments about which channel to watch. In fact, when you look at it that way, a blind man would make the perfect husband.'

'When you put it like that... I don't suppose you have a pen on you?'

'Why? Please don't tell me you want my autograph.'

'No, I want to go and poke my eyes out.'

'You're so funny!' she giggles. 'Here, use this straw.'

'Not right now,' I laugh. 'There are a couple of things I'd like to see before I give up my eyesight.'

The innuendo goes unnoticed, her decision to pull up her top a subconscious one. You know, it's the first time I look at her cleavage as she sits there tugging at her slipping collar, which in itself is something of a miracle on my part. Especially when you think about whose cleavage we're talking about here.

'Why are you asking me this, anyway? Is this your way of telling me you don't have a dick?'

'No!' I laugh, and Britney laughs too.

'Hey, Big D.' We're interrupted by an annoyed-looking Volk. 'You got me a Quarter Pounder. I asked for a Quarter Pounder with cheese.'

'For fuck's sake, man,' I protest in exasperation. 'Does it *really* matter?'

'Yes it does. If I'd wanted a Quarter Pounder I'd have asked for a Quarter Pounder. But I wanted a Quarter Pounder *with cheese*.'

'Jesus…' I sigh. There's no pleasing some people.

'Who's this?' asks Britney.

'Oh… sorry, this is my mate Volkan. Volkan Britney, Britney Volkan.'

'Pleased to meet you,' nods Volk, trying to look cool.

'*Volkan*? Is that a nickname?'

'No, that's my name,' Volk replies reluctantly. He's been down this path far too many times.

'You're kidding, right?'

'No, that's the name my parents gave me.'

'Wow. *Volkan*. That's really cool. They must have been huge *Star Trek* fans.'

'I think it has more to do with them being Turkish.'

'Oh.'

'Anyway, I'll see you guys later,' he says, and starts to walk away.

'Here!' Britney calls after him.

Volk turns around to see Britney waving a piece of cheese that she's taken from her own burger. It's half-melted, covered in ketchup and burger grease, and generally couldn't appear any less appetising without being dipped in an overflowing Glastonbury toilet. But Volk takes it, and he mopes off clutching his piece of cheese.

'Do you think I offended him?' asks a concerned Britney. She's such a sweet girl.

'I doubt it. He gets it all the time. I did exactly the same thing when I first met him. It's because he doesn't really look Turkish.'

'Yeah. And his ears are slightly pointy.'

'Are they?'

'No! Duh!'

Normally I wouldn't be able to take somebody saying "Duh!" to me in such a belittling tone, but since it's Britney Spears I let her off.

'Anyway,' she announces. 'I'm gonna go wash my hands. Don't go anywhere.'

Britney heads off in the direction of the toilets and no sooner has she vanished out of sight then Volk makes an unwelcome reappearance.

'What do you want *now*?' I moan.

Volk sniggers like a child and briskly rubs his hands together.

'Oooh, yes! This is it, Big D. This is the big one.'

'What are you wittering on about?'

'Forget Gary Barlow, forget Anne Robinson. *This* is the pinnacle.'

My heart sinks as I cotton on to what he's saying.

'No way. No fucking way, Volk.'

'Yes way. Come on, mate. This is a once-in-a-lifetime opportunity here!'

'Too right it's a once-in-a-lifetime opportunity. A once-in-a-lifetime opportunity *for me*! I'm doing alright here.'

'Don't kid yourself, mate,' he scoffs. 'She's just being friendly to maintain her image and stuff.'

'Trust me on this one. I think I might be in here.'

Volk bellows with laughter and slaps me hard on the back.

'You make me laugh sometimes, Big D.'

'What are the others doing?' I ask.

'Nothing much. Gaz can't talk because we challenged him to eat his Big Mac in three bites and his mouth is stuffed full of… Hey, don't try and change the subject. So how are we going to execute this bundle?'

'Please, mate,' I beg him. 'Let this one go.'

'No way! Dom, what is rule number five of celebrity bundling?'

'Oh, come on. Don't give me that shit.'

'Tell me, what is rule number five?'

'For fuck's sake. If a celebrity is sighted and an accomplice is present, an attempted bundle must take place,' I drone.

'Exactly.'

'Look, Volkan. All I'm asking is that just this once you let it go. Please, not this time.'

'Uh uh,' he shakes his head.

'What, do you want me to *beg* you? To *pay* you? Here…' I pull out my wallet and start counting out the twenties. 'How much do you want? A hundred? Two hundred? I can go to the cashpoint…'

'Put your money away, son,' he croons. 'No amount in the whole world would persuade me. This is too good an opportunity.'

'Come on, don't be a wanker,' I appeal.

There is the sound of a slamming door and we look up to see Britney coming back from the toilets. She stops briefly to examine the newspapers in the rack, and Volk turns back and stares me in the face.

'Listen, Big D, this is how it is. Britney Spears is going to get bundled here today. Whether you decide to be involved or not is up to you. I for one would be more than happy to be the one to lie on top of her if you aren't prepared to do it. The choice is yours.'

He gets up and walks back to the other table, raising his eyebrows at Britney as he passes her on the way. She gives him a close-lipped smile and strolls back over, pausing to give instructions to her bodyguard before returning to the table.

'What did he want *this* time?' she questions.

'Oh, nothing much. He wanted to double check I'd got him a Diet Coke instead of the regular stuff, that's all.'

'Really? He's a strange one that Volkan.'

'He certainly has his moments,' I say through gritted teeth.

Britney turns and gives her minder a nod. The man mountain gets up and leaves the restaurant and my heartbeat quickens as I find myself alone with the world's sexiest woman, as voted by the readers of *FHM*.

'You ok, Dom? You look a bit pale all of a sudden.'

'Do I? Must be the food.'

'You sure you're ok?'

'Yeah, I'm fine. Us Brits are often pale,' I smile.

Britney laughs shyly.

'Hey, listen Dom. I've got to go now, but it's been great chatting to you.'

'It's been great chatting to you too.'

It has. It's been fucking fantastic; the best ten minutes of my life by absolutely miles.

'I don't suppose that you…' She suddenly comes over all embarrassed.

'What?'

'I was going to ask you… it sounds stupid now.'

'What?'

'Would you walk me to my car?'

'Yeah, sure. I'd love to.'

She stands up and I drift immediately to her side. We are close, breathing the same air, standing on the same floor tile, the brushing together of our sleeves the first physical contact. I long to put my arm around her but can't bring myself to do it in case she rejects me, in case she pushes me away. We totter slowly towards the door, both trying to prolong the moment for as long as possible. Neither of us talks, overcome by an awkward timidity that wasn't there thirty seconds ago. My discomfort is worsened by the knowledge I'm sporting a semi, one that's about to break out into a full-blown erection at any second, and I thank my lucky stars I'm wearing a combination of tight underwear and thick jeans. I needn't have worried, though, as any feelings of libido are banished by the sight of the others loitering with intent, Volk pumping his fist at me and grinning like a man possessed.

I open the door and wave Britney through, her gratitude packaged up in a stupendously seductive smile that sends a shiver through my loins and makes the hairs on the back of my neck stand on end.

The traffic hammers past not more than twenty feet away, but we turn our backs to it and head towards the car park, which is still as empty as it was when we first arrived. I can see the giant watching us intently from behind the wheel of the car, hands on the steering wheel, engine already running. I expect he's wondering what the fuck Britney is doing wasting her time with the likes of a nobody like me when she could have any man on the planet. In a way I envy him, as his sole purpose in life is to protect something so precious, but part of me pities him as well. It must be hell spending so much time in the company of someone like Britney Spears but knowing you can never be with her. Personally, I think it would drive me insane.

'Well, this is it then,' says Britney, turning to face me, as transparent a come-on as you're ever likely to hear.

'Yeah, this is it.'

Volk, Gaz, Bertie and the Yeti have gathered in the corner of the car park. They try their best to look inconspicuous, but their heel-kicking and pacing about only serves to emit the opposite signal.

'You look after yourself, Britney.'

'Yeah, you too, Dom.'

I flick my eyes towards the others. It's only for a split second, but this is long enough to see them nodding their heads in encouragement.

'Goodbye, then,' she smiles, taking my hands in hers.

'Goodbye, Britney.'

She closes her eyes and tilts her head back, her lips slightly parted, pouting and shaking nervously, shimmering like a couple of pink slugs. It's now or never.

I wriggle my hands from hers and place them around her waist, squeezing gently, her flesh soft beneath my fingertips. And then we kiss; no tongues, just a tender stroking together of our lips. It blows me away. I manoeuvre my hands around to the small of her back and lean in towards her, our faces still held together at the mouth. I lean further and further, until we're twisted over like a couple of ballroom dancers, me bent over her arched back, pushing her to the floor, ready to spring back up and continue the dance.

Except I don't pull her back. I let her fall, lower her all the way down to the concrete where she opens her eyes, stunned, manic.

'Dom?'

But I'm not listening. I'm too busy climbing on top of her, stretching myself across that heavenly body that I've dreamt of being close to on so many occasions. This time is no different from any of the others. I'm running on autopilot, unable to stop myself. It's too late.

'BUUUNDLE!'

The shout reverberates around the car park, drowning out everything else, even the thundering traffic from the A40. I close my eyes and wait for the others to arrive, wait for the heavy impact of their bodies as they crash down on top of us, for the excited laughter as yet another celebrity bundle is carried out. But they don't appear. They are still standing over in the corner like before. Maybe they didn't hear the signal.

'BUUUUUUUUUNDLE!' This time I scream it louder, louder than I've ever screamed it before.

And this time they definitely hear me, and I smile to myself as I anticipate their arrival, the onset of four sprinting blokes all desperate to be the next on the pile. But they don't move. They're too busy laughing, Bertie turning away with his hand over his mouth, Yeti doubled over in pain and Gaz and Volk hugging each other in delight.

'What the…?'

I struggle to my feet, still staring at them laughing at me, watching their faces contort with hilarity at my expense.

'You fucking… Ow!'

Britney lashes out with her feet and catches me in the ankle. It doesn't particularly hurt, my exclamation more through surprise than pain.

'What's wrong with you?!' she screams as she staggers up off the floor. 'Are you some kind of *psycho*?!?'

I step towards her, palms open, pleading for forgiveness.

'I'm sorry, I…'

'Get the fuck away from her!' yells Goliath as he lumbers towards us. 'I ought to fuck you up, you sick motherfucker!'

'I'm sorry!' I declare as I back away. 'I don't know what came over me.'

'You're a fuckin' freak!' the minder asserts, pointing his finger at my face. And then, lowering his voice, 'Are you ok, Britney?'

'Yeah, I'm ok. He didn't hurt me, I'm just a bit shaken, that's all. Let's go.'

'Britney, I…'

'Talk to the hand, sicko.'

'I didn't mean…'

'Save it!'

They get into the car and screech away, Britney with her head in her hands and the behemoth shooting me a look that screams violent intent as they speed past. The shock is too much for me and I search for somewhere to sit down, a nearby concrete pillar providing a convenient stool. It's filthy and covered in bird crap, but I really couldn't give a toss after what just happened. I fold my arms across my knees and lean forward so that my head is resting on my forearms, staring down at the tarmac below; the same tarmac I had tried to bundle the princess of pop on just a moment ago. What the fuck was I *thinking*?

I'm telling you, I could sit here all day the way I feel. It would be worth it to avoid having to talk to anyone, to steer clear of being reminded how I had screwed up my one real chance of ever finding true happiness.

'I'm such a *tit*!' I shout out, the frustration suddenly becoming too much for me.

'You got that right,' agrees Gaz. 'Fucking funny, though.'

Raising my head, I see that the others have come over to revel in my self-inflicted misfortune.

'I can't believe you did that,' Volk laughs. 'Turned down Britney Spears for the sake of a bundle. You absolute monkey.'

'But you said…'

'I was winding you up,' he laughs. 'I still can't quite believe you actually went through with it. It's quite impressive, really.'

'You were winding me… you fucking bunch of cunts!' I'm angry now, livid in fact. 'Even if you *were* winding me up, you could've *at least* joined in once I went ahead with it!'

'With her bodyguard around? You've got to be joking!' hoots Gaz. 'I thought he was gonna kill you!'

'So did I, you fucking moron! I almost shat my fucking pants!'

'Ah well,' says Bertie the diplomat. 'No harm was done.'

'No *harm* was done?!' I erupt. 'That was Britney Spears! *Britney Spears*! Do you seriously think I'm going to get another chance like that again? Ever?'

I'm almost in tears now, the desperation welling up behind my eyes and threatening to break out all over my face at any moment. But I don't care. I've just blown it with the girl of my dreams and nothing else really matters any more.

'Just fuck off!' I yell at them.

'What?' asks Yeti.

'You heard me. Just fuck off, the lot of you. Piss off, get out of my sight. I don't want to look at you.'

'Come on, mate, don't be like that,' says Gaz, putting his hand on my shoulder.

'Don't touch me!' I bellow, sweeping his hand off me as if it were a fly. 'Just go, leave me alone!'

'Don't you want a lift back?' asks Bertie.

'I'll get the bus.'

I'm not even looking at them now, returning to my previous position of leaning forward and staring at the ground.

'If that's the way you want it,' sighs Bertie. 'Come on, boys.'

I hear them walking away, their footsteps fading out, followed by the opening and closing of car doors and the revving up of the engine. The gravel crunches as the Bertmobile pulls out of the car park, stopping briefly opposite where I'm sitting.

'You sure you don't want a…' His words are halted by the raising of my middle finger, and I hear the electric window winding back up and the car pulling away.

I sit there in the same hunched position for about half an hour, the earlier events playing through my mind on a continuous loop. With each passing I try only to remember the kiss, to hold on to that pleasant thought. But my mind won't let me. Instead it blurs over the good stuff, focusing instead on the forcing of her body to the floor, the look of fear and disappointment in her eyes, the others standing there laughing as the monster lumbers towards me with clenched fists. It's almost enough to drive me crazy.

The sound of a passing vehicle doesn't even cause me to look up, although I can tell by the noise it makes that it's a lot bigger than your average car. And the sound of the door being opened confirms this suspicion, a heavy metallic sliding rather than a silent swing. Many male voices can be heard from within, comments like, "Here we are then" and "I'm busting for a piss" and "I'm fucking starving" lost among one another, the exaggerated volume suggesting a widespread degree of drunkenness. I allow myself to glance up at the newly arrived rabble. They're all suited and booted, not to mention being fucking huge. They're probably a university sports team of some sort. Too big to be footballers. Too ugly as well, for that matter, and that can only mean one thing. Rugby lads. Fucking great. That's all I need right now, a minibus full of egg chasers. A couple of them run ahead, presumably the ones who were whinging about their bursting bladders, while the others come forward as a hulking, intimidating pack. I pull out my mobile phone and use it as a point of focus, a handy way of avoiding eye contact as they stomp towards me. And it seems to work as they clump past, oblivious to my existence. All except for one, that is, and unfortunately for me, one is all it takes.

'Hey, aren't you that guy, Dean, Dave… Dom? Dom! Aren't you Dom Carter?' he chirps.

'No.'

'Yeah you are. Hey, lads! Look who it is, it's that bundling guy!'

The rest of them stop and trudge back to join their mate, all peering at me and grinning with drunken fascination. I feel like a monkey in a zoo.

'Seriously, I'm not who you think I am. I just look like him. Honestly, I get it all the time.'

'Nah, it's definitely you. Anyway, I'm Matt. Pleased to meet you, Mr Carter.'

He holds out a hand for me to shake.

Ah, what the heck, I think to myself, and reach up to take it.

We Are the Champions

It's like I told you before: anybody can become a celebrity these days. I never really wanted it to happen, because a celebrity is a dangerous thing to be at the moment. The famous among us can't walk the streets in daylight anymore for fear of hearing the dreaded 'B-word'. Yet here I am, a good few notches above reality show contestants, but still a couple of rungs below the 'It girls'. I'd like to be able to quote Yazz here and say that "the only way is up", but I get the feeling Tara Palmer-Tomkinson's position is safe, at least for the time being.

'Hey, Big D.'

'Hey, Sarah. How's tricks?'

'Yeah, pretty good,' Sarah replies. 'How about you? What you been up to?'

'You know, same old shit,' I reply; "the same old shit" meaning nothing.

'Can I join you?' she asks.

'Sure,' I reply, shuffling over to make room.

Sarah kicks off her shoes and jumps into bed with me, giving me a peck on the cheek as she sits down, the skin on her face cold and smooth from the winter wind.

'Shift your legs over a bit, will you,' she requests, and pushes me over some more. 'Here, I got the stuff you wanted.'

'Wicked. Thanks babe. Leave it by the bed and I'll look at it later.'

'Sure.'

Sarah leans over and puts the bag on the floor.

'To what do I owe this unexpected visit?' I ask her.

'Nothing,' she smiles. 'Aren't I allowed to come and see my famous boyfriend?'

'Of course you are. I wish you could be here all the time.'

'So do I, but not everyone can afford to lie in bed all day. Some of us have to work, you know.'

'I guess. What time is it?'

'About twelve-thirty. Lunchtime,' she says, and starts to unbutton her top.

'My favourite time of the day,' I grin. 'Along with breakfast and dinner, of course.'

A brief fondling session later and Sarah is pulling her clothes back on and helping me with mine.

'I'm not full yet!' I protest. 'Where's my dessert?'

'I'll make sure I bring it later. I've got to get back to work… I'm late enough as it is.'

Sarah flings off the covers and hurriedly forces her shoes back on.

'I'll be back to see you around five. Bye, gorgeous!'

'Wait up,' I call out. 'I'll walk you to the door.'

'Very funny!' she laughs. 'See you later, Ironside.'

Sometimes, if only for a second, I forget that I can no longer feel my legs. I go to roll out of bed and suddenly find that I've got these two dead weights hanging from the base of my arse. I tell you, it shocks me nearly every time. One day I might get used to it, but right now I don't really want to.

The court case is still ongoing. I guess it's kind of hard to ascertain accountability in a bundle. I suppose you could blame the first person to get involved: that guy Matt, the instigator as it were. But if nobody else had joined in, this never would have happened. Besides, I almost wouldn't want all twelve people to get sent down for putting me in here. Most people would say I brought it upon myself anyway, that I had it coming to me.

'Think of all those poor children that got injured because of you,' they'll tell me. 'What goes around comes around.'

Well, they can all go fuck themselves.

Looking on the bright side though, if I'm confined to a wheelchair for the rest of my life, at least it won't happen again. It would take a twisted individual to drag a man from his chariot in order to jump on top of him. Then again, you could say it would take a pretty twisted individual to base his existence around the bundling of celebrities. But disabled bundling?

Me and my fucking ideas.

Anyway, I always said I would rather lose my legs than either my eyes or my knob. Now all I need are a blind man and a eunuch to debate with over who is in the worst position. We could televise it and everything.

You might not believe it, but I got a Get Well Soon card from Britney Spears. Yeah, seriously, she managed to find out where I was staying and everything, said that she understood why I did what I did. She even sent me a signed photo. Bless her. Get Well Soon. It would have been nice, except that I'm not actually ill, am I? I'm fucking crippled. I can't see a good night's sleep and a couple of paracetamol curing this little problem. Then again, I'm still pretty young, and that leaves plenty of time for the geeks of this world to come up with some miraculous surgical technique that will sort out this type of thing. Fingers crossed I can afford to pay for it when they do.

But you know what the worse thing is? I can't even get a job now because of the reputation I've gained. Who in their right mind would employ *me*? Even with the chair they still see me as a troublemaker. Look at me, I'm hardly an upstanding member (if you'll excuse the pun) of the disabled community, not with *my* background. A year spent bundling celebrities and trying to make a name for myself in the media world doesn't exactly look glowing on my CV. And it's not even like I can make any money out of the whole celebrity bundling thing; there are no opportunities for merchandise or TV spinoffs. At least, none that *I* can think of. Aside from a bit of advertising on mine and Yeti's website, the scheme is a bit dead as a money maker, although I'm sure somewhere down the line some shrewd bastard will make a mint out of what I've done while I'm left sitting here feeling even more bitter and twisted than I do now. I've shot myself in the foot a bit with this one, really. Well, both feet in fact.

I twist my body over and retrieve the plastic bag Sarah has left for me. In it I find a Mars bar, a can of Diet Coke and a copy of *Ok!* magazine. I laugh to myself as I lie there holding the items in my hands. Chocolate, sugar-free drink and a celebrity gossip mag. I'm such a fucking girl. If only the lads could see me now.

It doesn't take me long to flick through the pages of *Ok!* as I'm only really looking for one thing: stories about me. And sure enough, there I am in the celebrity news round-up section on page one-hundred-and-thirty-two, sandwiched between Christina Aguilera and Anouska Golebiewski from *Big Brother 4*. Now there's something to think about. The story itself tells of my recent discharge from hospital and everyone at *Ok!* wishes me well in my recovery. They also write that I'm seeing a shrink to help me come to terms with never being able to walk again. This is news to me; Sarah is all the therapy I need at the moment. To be honest, she was the last person I expected to visit me when I was in hospital, but she turned up with a bunch of flowers on my second day in there and since then she's never stopped coming. I'm certainly not complaining.

It turns out there's some other stuff in the plastic bag that I didn't ask for. She must have wanted to surprise me, I suppose. I shake the contents out onto the bed and examine the messy pile that lies before me. It consists of a couple of biros, an A4 pad of paper and a book entitled *An Idiot's Guide to Writing Novels*. Intrigued, I open it up and see that Sarah has scrawled a message on the inside cover. It reads:

> If you're determined to lie there in bed all day, then you can at least spend your time doing something constructive. Get writing!
>
> Love Sarah xxx

What was it I was saying about every goddamn celebrity writing a book these days? Well, it seems the fact hasn't been lost on my girlfriend, either. It's certainly not the worst idea I ever heard, but what the fuck do *I* know about writing? My highest literary accolade is a grade C in GCSE English Literature, and all that really proves is that I possessed average reading ability for a boy of sixteen. And I haven't read a single novel since. Then again, I guess that's the reason behind her buying me the book.

It doesn't take me very long to get bored of trying to plough through the writer's guide. I've never been very good at following instructions, even when they've been simplified to such an extent that monkeys can understand them. Besides, this is me we're talking about here. Me, Big D, the ideas man. I don't need someone telling me what to do. And anyway, how hard can it be to write an autobiography? I discard the book and pick up the pad and one of the pens instead.

'No time like the present,' I mutter to myself and put pen to paper.

> It all started in the summer of 2003 on a beautiful evening in the bustling market town of Thame, one of the many jewels in Oxfordshire's picturesque countryside. Dom Carter went to the local pub with his best friend Yeti, who is so-called because...

'For fuck's sake!' I exclaim and aggressively rip the sheet from the pad, hurling it in the direction of the bin but missing by a good few feet.

But if at first you don't succeed…

> Yeti, Volkan, Dirty Bertie, Gaz and Big D (that's me). An unlikely sounding group of young men if ever there was one, but nevertheless a group that would one day shake the world.

Swear, tear, scrunch, throw, miss. Start again. This is proving more difficult than I thought. I consider turning back to the *Idiot's Guide*, but it has managed to slide out of reaching distance and would probably be more trouble than it's worth to try and retrieve it. I'd only end up throwing it across the room again anyway, as the frustration is still very much brewing beneath the surface. It amazes me how wound up I'm getting about my inability to do something I already knew I was rubbish at, but the anger makes me more determined to succeed. It also makes it more difficult to think straight, and my mind has totally emptied itself of creative prose. Normally at a time like this I would go for a calming walk, but this option is no longer available to me, so I have to sit here and brood instead. Fucking useless, good-for-nothing legs. But these things take time, I suppose. Look at the whole celebrity bundling thing, for instance. That took *ages* to get off the ground. I look at the blank piece of paper in front of me and vow that this time I'll fill it. I will *not* be defeated.

'The personal approach. That's the key.' Talking to myself is something I've picked up over the last couple of months. Believe me, you would too if you spent as much time in your own company as I do. 'Don't try and be too clever, just tell it like it is, in your own words.'

That's it, in my own words, in the words of Big D…

An hour later and it's the television that chatters victoriously. I'm lying flat on my back like I've been knocked out and the pen and pad have joined the rest of the debris that already litters the floor. With all the will in the world, I ain't a writer.

Pain Sailing

I never imagined that waking up in hospital would be quite like this. Here's me, hauling myself out of the eternal darkness to a welcoming party of precisely zero people.

Without the looming heads to block out their glare, the sterile lights are too much for me and I close my eyes again. Upon reopening them a few minutes later, I find that I'm still on my own. I groggily glance to my left and see Dad pacing up and down the corridor outside, one hand clasped firmly to his chin, the other wrapped protectively around his waist. I can also see the backs of three heads, their scalps poking up above the windowsill like mountain peaks: Mount Volkan, Mount Gaz and Mount Yeti.

It's Mount Yeti that turns around first. Initially it's a lazy look, his head barely turning enough for his nose to appear from behind the curtains of hair, but as soon as eye contact is made he gets up and starts gesturing to the others, tugging at their arms, pointing, their heads turning one by one as they too look over at me. Their glances are quick; only long enough to confirm what Yeti is saying without having to acknowledge my existence. And then they're all standing, heading towards the door. But their progress is slow, disorganised, almost bordering on farcical. I've seen this type of delaying before; that night when Yeti summoned us to his house and none of us wanted to be the one to ring the bell. Something must be seriously wrong.

Dad enters first and the others follow close behind, huddled together for safety. Only a group of blokes can make walking into a room look so goddamn awkward, and they end up stretching into an unnaturally straight line at the foot of the bed, tall and rigid, like they're about to perform a choral rendition or something. I suspect they've already decided who is going to be the messenger – the one to be shot, so to speak – but whoever it is seems unwilling to step forward. I look at them all in turn, starting with Dad and then working my way across the rest of the group. Volkan's gaze is lowered to the floor, his head tilted forward in an attempt to disguise his expression. Gaz is biting his lip. And biting it hard, too. I can see the whiteness of the skin where the force of his teeth has expelled the blood. Yeti's eyes are visibly moist, tears on the verge of escaping his eyelids, his hands remaining clasped firmly behind him as he fights them back through willpower alone. But of most concern is Dad's reaction, or rather the lack of it. He looks blank, emotionless. I haven't seen him like this for ages, not since Mum's funeral.

'Tell me the bad news first,' I request.

As it happens, there is only bad news.

Dad does his best to beat around the bush and soften the blow, I'll give him that much. But there's no way of gift-wrapping the news that's his to deliver; no way of sprucing it up or presenting it in a positive light. I will never walk again.

'But hey, look on the bright side. We're going to Barbados next Wednesday.'

'Yeti won £17 million on the lottery.'

'You've been voted Britain's sexiest man.'

Like I said, you can't put an upbeat spin on this kind of information. And I can't deal with it right now. All I want is to go back to sleep and to wake up in a different place. To never wake up. I instruct them to leave and not come back until I tell them otherwise. They do as they're told, wearing expressions of disappointment as they shuffle out of the room, like they thought I might take the news better than this. But what did they fucking expect? Rather than go home, they take up the same positions as they had adopted before: three sitting, Dad pacing.

I look down at the shape of my legs underneath the blankets. They're still there, still attached. I don't see any reason why they shouldn't still work. But they don't. I can't even feel them. I close my eyes before the tears have a chance to flood out.

I will never walk again

I
will WILL
never NEVER
walk WALK
again AGAIN

N I A G A K L A W R E V E N L L I W I

It's fucking shit, whichever way you choose to look at it.

That was day one: the day I found out that because of some drunken, egg-chasing twats I would spend the rest of my life on my back or my arse but never on my feet; the same day that I had to consign myself to looking up at everyone for the next seventy years while they all looked *down* on me.

You'd think the first day would be the worst, but things never quite work like that in reality. I guess it's like breaking up in that respect. After the devastation of the initial news a period of numbness follows; a time when you're emotionless, an empty vessel. And relatively speaking, this period isn't really all that bad. Next comes the time for reflection, when you look to yourself for answers that don't exist. You question why you acted as you did, whether a different course of action might have saved you from your present situation, and you invariably reach the conclusion that any choices other than the ones you actually made would have resulted in a happier existence than the one you're currently living. That represents the low point, or so you'd think, the moment when it dawns on you that you have well and truly fucked your life up and may never be happy again. And then it's the supposed road to recovery; progress halted time and time again by sickening moments of realisation, usually in the dead of night, when all your psychological building blocks come tumbling down, as your world caves in around you for the eighth time in as many days.

But at least after a break-up you can take comfort in the knowledge that all is not lost. Although it may not seem like it at the time, the phrase about there being "plenty more fish in the sea" has a fair amount of truth to it. I couldn't see that before, but I can see it now. It's a real shame it doesn't apply in this case. It's not as if there's an abundance of fully functioning legs or spinal cords waiting for me to snap up. There are no false dawns, no glimmers of hope. I'm a lost cause and there's nothing anybody can say or do to change that. No size of insurance claim or award for damages could possibly compare to being able to walk. What fucking difference would it make?

I've had a fairly steady stream of visitors over the last week or so. It tends to be the same faces, the same motley crew that was there from the start. I guess you learn who your real friends are at times like these. It can't be easy being in the same room as a man who has hit rock bottom and isn't afraid to show it, and all the fair-weather friends suddenly seem to disappear into the shadows. They jump on for the ride but jump off again pretty damn sharpish at the first sign of queasiness. Bunch of shallow wankers. They'll regret it one day, when they finally realise they've built up an endless list of acquaintances but not one person they can truly rely on. If you spread yourself too thinly you eventually become invisible to the rest of the world.

This is not an accusation you can throw at Bertie, even though he has visited less frequently than the others. It's a busy time of year for people like him. Relatively speaking, that is. To the casual onlooker, his life is one long bout of busyness, working two weeks to our every one and sleeping only half as much. And right now things are even worse than usual for the Bertmeister and his social life has been forced to take a back seat once again. But as I've said before, we've become well used to this by now. Don't ask me to tell you what he does, because I couldn't. He's tried to explain it to me on a number of occasions, but all I can gather is that he's essentially getting paid a shitload for being an intelligent person doing a job that anyone could do if they were prepared to put the hours in. Nice work if you can get it.

On his first visit, he brought with him a DVD player and a selection of my favourite films. He apologised that he couldn't stay to watch any of them with me, but at least he managed to find the time to set the damn thing up, knowing that if he left it to me in my current frame of mind it would've ended up in pieces on the floor. On his second visit he brought a selection of new releases that he knew for a fact I hadn't seen. Where he found the time in his sixteen-hour working day to buy all this stuff I don't know. Maybe he sent one of his lackeys to get it. It's a thoughtful present either way. And all mine to keep, too; Bertie's no 'Indian giver'. It'll be interesting to see what he brings when he visits a third time. I'm hoping for a yacht.

My days and nights spent lying here have given me a fair amount of time for self-indulgent psychoanalysis as I struggle to find an excuse for my foul moods. It would be indescribably satisfying to be able to say that my utter lack of positive emotion is down to my genetic make-up and that there's nothing anybody can do about it, so they might as well get fucking used to it. And I think this is probably true. You see, I've come to the conclusion that there are two natural reactions to this kind of thing, depending on what kind of person you are. It's my theory that everyone in the world has an inherent belief that they're either lucky or unlucky. Faced with my situation, those that believe they are lucky people will say, "Well, at least I'm still alive". Those who believe they are unlucky people will say, "I can't walk anymore, how unlucky is that?" Right now, if somebody came in here and told me I was lucky to be alive I would punch them in the face. Crippled legs or not, I would stand up, march over to them and break their fucking teeth.

These are the thoughts that run through my mind as Sarah enters the room brandishing a bouquet of flowers. Judging by her attire I'd guess she's come straight from work. Black, boot-cut trousers hang over heels that make her a good three inches taller while her cardigan, also black, sits tightly over a sky blue blouse. They say women often wear black as a means of looking slimmer, but this isn't a tactic Sarah needs to employ. She's still looking as good as I remembered. Yet despite being the first pretty face I've seen since Britney (the nurses being disappointingly bland), I'm not in the slightest bit pleased to see her.

'Come to kick me when I'm down, have you? If that's the case make sure you do it in the legs so I won't be able to feel it,' I sneer.

'Nice to see you, too. I see you've lost none of your charm,' she replies, her voice carrying a friendly tone that throws me slightly.

'How did you find me?'

'Jesus, you sound like I've tracked you down to come and murder you! Kate told me you were here.'

'And how is Miss Melons?'

'Grow up, Dom.'

Sarah shakes her head and I feel more than slightly foolish.

'So why *are* you here, then, if it isn't to gloat?'

'*Gloat?* Do you *honestly* believe I'd do that?'

I shrug my shoulders dismissively, but the look of hurt on her face doesn't bring me any satisfaction.

'I heard you'd been injured, so I thought I'd come and see if you were alright,' says Sarah.

'How very thoughtful of you,' I respond sarcastically. 'Well, you will no doubt be pleased to see that I'm *not* alright!'

'Why would you say something like that? I've come to check up on a friend, that's all.'

'Friend? Is that what you think we are, *friends*? I barely know you, Sarah. You've come here out of curiosity to have a good gawp at me so you can go into work tomorrow and tell all your mates you went to visit somebody famous in hospital.'

'Get a life, Dom, it's nothing like that,' asserts Sarah.

'Isn't it? What is it like then? Sympathy? If that's why you've come you can forget it, because I don't need it.'

'Fine!' she snaps, tossing the flowers into my lap and heading towards the door. 'I'll come back tomorrow. Maybe by that time you'll have sorted your head out!'

'Doubt it,' I mutter, the statement applying both to her intention of coming back and to my stubborn head.

She doesn't hear me, though. My words are lost in the clacking of those high heels of hers as she marches away down the corridor.

She sticks to her word too, turning up the next day at exactly the same fucking time. I tell you, if she's going to make a habit of this I may have to move wards. Sarah enters the room without the smile on this occasion, but with no less purpose. And straight from work again, by the looks of it: same black trousers and same black cardie, but with a pink blouse replacing the blue.

She comes over and plonks herself on the end of my bed, as if stating her intentions to stay for the full duration this time around. And then she just stares at me, waiting for some form of apology, I'd imagine. Fair enough I guess, I certainly owe her one. More than one, in fact.

'I can't believe you came back after what I said.'

There's an apology in there somewhere if you look hard enough. It requires a fair amount of reading between the lines, mind you, but it's definitely there.

'I know you're bitter,' Sarah responds, seemingly accepting my gesture, 'but I also know that you're not the world-hating arsehole you like to make yourself out to be.'

'A world-hating arsehole,' I repeat. 'That's nice. I've been called a lot of things in my time, but that's a first.'

'Don't try to act like some big hero, Dom. It's not as if you're the first person who couldn't walk. People are born every year without the use of their legs, you know.'

'So? It's easier for them. They don't know what they're missing out on.'

'Yeah right. Don't you think they'd trade their first twenty-three years for yours?'

'Maybe.'

Sarah laughs. It's not the kind of laugh you make when something's funny, but a sarcastic scoff; a display of disbelief.

'What?' I say defensively.

'Nothing. Want to watch a DVD?'

It seems a strange request given the circumstances, but I'm grateful for any escape route out of the current line of questioning.

'Ok. Take your pick. As long as it's something funny.'

She stays and watches *The Goonies* with me, finding the bit where Chunk is forced into doing the truffle shuffle in order to gain access to the house almost as funny as I always do. Not a word is uttered by either of us during the course of the film, and when the final credits start rolling Sarah gets up and leaves me alone once more, promising to return again the next day. I don't even say goodbye, but I'm kind of hoping she does come back. It's good to have the company, even if it means having to take some stick.

I've soon had enough of the film's musical score and I start fiddling with the DVD remote, which is infuriatingly temperamental. It's one of those where you have to point the bastard at exactly the right angle, otherwise it won't work. The problem is I'm yet to find out exactly what this angle is and as a result I'm often left grappling with it for what seems like hours at a time as the words drift relentlessly up the screen. I'm beginning to lose patience with the whole thing when Dad walks in.

'You want this switched off?' he asks, gesturing towards the television.

'Yeah, please.'

I place the remote control down on my bedside table as Dad searches for the off button with the usual ineptitude of an old person confronted with modern technology.

'First one on the right,' I instruct him, struggling to disguise the impatience in my voice.

'Oh yeah,' he mutters, and the screen flicks off.

The DVD keeps whirring, but I choose to put up with it for the time being. The sound of the spinning disc is barely audible and the DVD player's off button is more difficult to locate than the TV's.

'Who was that girl I saw leaving?' asks Dad, signalling with his thumb towards the door and raising his eyebrows in approval.

'Who, that? Oh, that's just Sarah,' I answer with a lame attempt at nonchalance.

'Friend of yours?'

'Acquaintance.'

'Oh,' Dad nods. 'She's very pretty.'

'She's alright I suppose,' is my mumbled reply.

'How you feeling today?'

The question is always raised within the first two minutes of his arrival and its predictability never ceases to grate on me.

'Pretty much the same as yesterday,' I sigh. 'Which is the same as the day before that and identical to the way I felt five days ago and every other time you've asked.'

Dad doesn't answer, he just nods his head pensively and starts stroking his chin. I notice he's sporting more growth than I've ever seen him wear before. The stress must be getting to him; it's most unlike Dad to neglect shaving as he's not a great fan of facial hair. I remember him telling me once that "beards are for hippies and intellectuals", and he is clearly neither. Yet here he is running his fingertips through a good four days of growth. The look doesn't suit him.

'You need to start coming to terms with this,' he tells me after a prolonged period of stubble scratching.

'That's easy for you to say *standing* there. Did it ever occur to you that this kind of thing is kind of hard to accept?' I say, gesturing to my legs.

'Nobody's suggesting it's easy for you,' he reasons. 'Not for a second. But things could be a lot worse. You should count yourself lucky that you…'

'Don't say that!' I bellow. 'Don't you dare say that!'

'Is everything ok in here?'

A nurse appears in the doorway with her hands on her hips.

'Er… Yes thanks,' I answer awkwardly.

'Good. Well can you try and keep the noise down, please? You're disturbing the other patients.'

Her voice is stern, like a teacher's.

'Sure. Sorry.'

She reaches into the room and pulls the door closed before making herself scarce.

'Are the staff always this friendly?' jokes Dad.

'Don't change the subject, Dad. And don't give me that *you're lucky to be alive* bullshit either, because sometimes I wish I wasn't.'

'You're telling me you'd rather be dead,' he scoffs, shaking his head.

I can see my comment has angered him, but I don't really give a toss. If he wants to have a go then so be it. It's unlikely to make me feel any worse and will become yet another bullet point on my rapidly expanding list of things to be bitter about.

'Yeah,' I confirm defiantly. 'What have I got to live for? A shot at the Paralympics?'

'Don't be so melodramatic, Dom. What about all the people who care about you? We can help you through this.'

'This isn't fucking TV! Love and support and a bit of mind over matter isn't going to cure this fucking problem!'

Again I point to my legs. I've been doing a lot of that lately.

'Dom, your situation isn't unique. There are thousands of people like you who lead perfectly happy and fulfilling lives.'

'So everyone keeps telling me. To tell you the truth, I couldn't give a shit. If I had a decent job to go back to or a long-term girlfriend who might be willing to stay with me out of pity or something, things might be ok. But as it stands I'm an unemployed, single loser in a fucking wheelchair. And given that scenario, I *would* rather be dead.'

'Would you? Would you *really*?' Dad raises his voice for the first time since the accident. 'Well at least you can make that choice, unlike your mother. Wouldn't you rather she was still here in a wheelchair rather than not at all?'

I don't answer. What exactly am I supposed to say to that? Dad hasn't finished, though, as it always takes a long time for the kettle to cool down once it's boiled.

'But if you really feel that strongly about it, I can show you a big staircase you can throw yourself down. Listen to yourself, Dom. It's pathetic.'

Being called pathetic right to your face isn't an easy thing to take, but he's right and I know it. Of course I wouldn't rather be dead; it's just easier to act that way. The alternative is to start dealing with it and I know what a hard slog that will be, especially for somebody who has never been known for their fighting spirit or staying power. Planning my route to the nearest disabled toilet well in advance of actually needing it and the prospect of having to perform gymnastics once I get there is a scary thought. Plus I won't be able to get into some of the shops in Thame without the degradation of them dragging out a ramp for me. And we'll have to move to a bungalow, too. That or get one of those stairlifts old people use. It'll be one humiliation after another: people I used to know staring at me with pity as I wheel myself down the high street and strangers referring to me as "special".

Dad sees he isn't going to get anything constructive out of his visit, so he prepares to leave.

'I'm going now. I'll be back again in a few days to pick you up.'

'Ok.'

'Have a think about what I said, yeah?'

'Just go, Dad.'

He leaves frustrated and disappointed, head hung low in defeat; another visitor I've successfully managed to rub my foul mood onto. I lie back in bed and stare up at the ceiling, a fluttering sigh pushing its way through my lips and out into the sterile air. This is the point at which the terminally ill kid is supposed to walk in and show me the error of my ways. Fat chance.

Sarah is the only visitor during my last three days in hospital as she's the only one stubborn enough to ignore my request that nobody should come to see me until I move back home. I don't really know why I felt like I needed to indulge in this enforced solitude, but it didn't take long for me to get lonely and, were it not for my stubborn pride, I'd have texted everyone else to inform them I'd changed my mind.

Faced with seventy-two hours of nothing more than superficial pleasantries with the hospital nursing staff (who I sense think of me as a bit of an arrogant bastard, and who could blame them?), it was something of a relief to see Sarah again. I'm not always one to recognise a good thing when I see it and admittedly the continuation of my abrasive attitude cost me two days' worth of meaningful conversation, with Sarah departing as abruptly the second time round as she had done on the first occasion. It isn't until her third visit that I managed to swallow my pride and simultaneously rediscover my social skills, the relief at dropping the barrier so pronounced that I had to wonder why the hell I ever put it up in the first place.

'So what's been happening in the outside world, then?' I ask her.

Sarah correctly takes "the outside world" to mean the world consisting of my immediate gang of friends rather than the world as a whole and begins to fill me in on what has been happening. Apparently, Gaz has asked Kate out again. I knew the bugger would do it eventually. He's so goddamn obsessed with her, it was only a matter of time. It's funny, you know, how he spent so long waiting for the perfect moment and everything, but in the end it took the loss of his ear in a bundle to get things moving. And now here he is putting the moves on again. Sadly she turned him down, as I feared she might.

'It's a shame,' I say genuinely, 'but maybe it's for the best. Gaz should recognise he got lucky and accept that she's out of his league.'

'It has nothing to do with leagues, Dom. Nobody's out of anyone's league, even if they think they are.'

'Trust me, Sarah, Kate is out of Gaz's league. And I don't mean that as a criticism of Gaz, but Kate… well… look at her.'

'I don't see it like that,' argues Sarah. 'In my view leagues don't really exist, only people's personal taste. I accept that pop stars and movie stars might be unobtainable, but that's purely down to them living in a different world, one that people like you and I don't have access to. But in the case of Gaz and Kate, leagues have nothing to do with it. They go to the same places, they move in the same circles. Just because she doesn't want to go out with him doesn't mean she's too good for him.'

'But girls like Kate don't go out with blokes like Gaz,' I point out. 'It's a simple fact.'

'That may be,' Sarah replies. 'But as I said before, it's all down to personal taste. In my opinion, Kate could do a lot worse than Gaz. In fact, she *has* done a lot worse than Gaz. More than once. He's the first bloke she's been with in ages who truly cared about her and wasn't just in it for a shag or to have some arm candy to show off to his mates. He actually treated her with some respect.'

'Yeah, maybe. But that's probably because he knew deep down she was out of his league!' I laugh.

Sarah laughs too, realising that I'm not going to be convinced on this one.

'Look, Sarah, I hope you're right, really I do, because it would be nice to think that anybody can fall in love with anybody. But I think you're placing a little too much faith in personality as a means of attracting the opposite sex.'

'But what about Paul Daniels and Debbie McGee?' she asks.

'Hmm…' I muse, while thoughtfully scratching my chin. 'I can't begin to imagine what the lovely Debbie McGee ever saw in the millionaire Paul Daniels.'

'Ok, bad example,' giggles Sarah. 'Anyway, Gaz will find someone else. He's a nice guy.'

'Yeah, you're right,' I agree. 'He is a nice guy. One of the nicest. Don't tell him I said that, though.'

'Don't worry, I won't… Of course the *big* news is that Yeti's seeing someone.'

'*Yeti?* No way! What's her name?'

'David.'

If I'd had a drink I would have spat it out at this point.

'What the fu… *David?* Are you having me on?'

'Of course I am, you idiot! It's only been three days, Dom! What do you expect to have happened in that time? Oh yeah, and people are living on Mars now as well.'

'Very funny.'

'Sorry,' she smiles. 'And by the way, Yeti's not gay, you know. I can't believe you guys think he is.'

'You know that for a fact, do you?' I question.

'Look, trust me on this one,' she replies.

'What's that supposed to mean? What's he been up to? You two haven't…?'

'No!' Sarah exclaims. 'Jesus, Dom, are you sure they haven't operated on your brain as well while you've been here?'

'Well, funny you should say that… I've got this weird scar on the back of my…'

I playfully throw a cushion at her, but she catches it and throws it back. It hits me square in the face and then falls to the floor, much to our amusement. We sit there giggling like school children, and it brings me back to how I felt the first night I met her at the pub; before I asked her out and made a fool of myself, that is. I'm not about to make the same mistake again.

'So… How about you, Sarah? How's the engagement going?'

'Engagement?' comes her baffled reply.

'Yeah. Does your fiancé know about your daily hospital visits?'

'Pardon?!' Sarah frowns. 'I think they *have* operated on your brain. What on earth are you talking about?'

'You know what I'm talking about, Sarah. Show me your left hand,' I demand.

Still wearing an expression of total and utter bewilderment, Sarah holds aloft her hand, which I'm shocked to see is bereft of jewellery.

'Wow,' I declare. 'That didn't last long.'

'*What* didn't last long?'

'Your engagement.'

'What in the world gave you the idea I was engaged?' she asks in a state of disbelief.

'That night at the restaurant… I saw your boyfriend giving you a ring and you…'

'What, *this?*'

She lowers her left hand and then thrusts the right one into my face. Sitting on her index finger is a small gold ring, which doesn't play home to sparkly rocks of any description. If it had been an engagement ring it would have been the stingiest one ever. No woman in her right mind would have accepted it. I swallow hard as I realise I've got completely the wrong end of the stick.

'That's not an *engagement* ring…' asserts Sarah. 'What do you take me for?! If you'd bothered to stick around long enough to see what was really going on, you would have heard him say he was moving to Australia and that this was his parting gift. I didn't know myself until that day. We were beginning to drift apart anyway and a split was on the cards, but the whole Australia thing speeded things up.'

'You didn't have to accept it, though,' I say, trying to justify my jump to a completely wrong conclusion.

'What was the harm in accepting it? The chances are we're never going to see each other again, and imagine how he'd have felt if I'd rejected it. Besides, I still liked the guy… just not in the way I used to.'

'But what about the tears of happiness?'

'They weren't tears of *happiness*, you moron!'

I feel like a complete dickhead now, but something inside me keeps making me open my mouth and say stupid things.

'But you said you were going to split up anyway.'

'Yeah, but that doesn't make it any easier! I'd been going out with the guy for more than four years. When you've been through that much with a person and they tell you they're moving to the other side of the world, well… most people would find that upsetting. Wouldn't you agree?'

'But what about all that stuff outside the toilet?'

'I don't know. A moment of madness? You can't tell me you've never done something so out of character you can't explain it.'

The whole Britney Spears episode flashes through my mind.

'Er… maybe once or twice.'

'So you get my point, then?'

'I guess. So why have you come to visit, then, if all that was just a "moment of madness"?'

'Because I like you? You may find that difficult to believe, but I genuinely like you. Ever since that night we met in the pub, in fact. I didn't exactly make my feelings known in the most appropriate way at Don Luigi's, but at the time I thought that was what you wanted.'

'I did want it,' I admit.

'I know you did. It's good to know one of us had some morals that night. I think I left mine at the table.'

I laugh, partly because I find her remark funny, but mainly due to nerves. Something tells me I ought to say something, but I'm feeling a bit lost for words.

'So where do we go from here?' I often find that resorting to clichés is usually a good idea in these situations.

'I don't know. I've put my cards on the table, so it's up to you, really.'

It's up to me.

This is it. This is where I seal the deal. This is where I tell her how I feel, where I confess that I've thought of nobody else (Britney aside) since that night at Don Luigi's. I rack my brains for the right words to express my true feelings.

'You do realise that I can't walk' are the only words that come out.

'You can't walk? Well in that case… Of course I know that! Man, you're such a loser sometimes.'

'This isn't some sympathy thing going on here, is it?'

'Have you listened to anything I said?! Look, here's my number,' she scribbles down her digits on a piece of paper and plonks it down on the bedside table. 'If you want to make a go of it, call me. If not, I guess it's goodbye for the time being.'

And then she leaves. Now, normally in this situation I would wait a while, play it cool and make her sweat it out for a bit. After all, there's this thing called the "two-day rule" that stops you from appearing too desperate. But for once I choose to throw the rule book out the window, picking up the phone and punching in her number, frustrated by how long it takes for the call to connect. Eventually it does, the silence replaced by the sound of a ringtone that seems to go on forever before she picks up.

'What?' she snaps impatiently.

'Come back, Sarah. Please.'

'Good answer,' says Sarah, and she hangs up.

One for the Road

'You coming out later?' Sarah asks me.

'Doubt it.'

She doesn't even bother trying to talk me round, I ain't that fickle. Every persuasive argument that exists has been used on a previous occasion and neither of us can see the point in treading back across ground that has already been covered.

'I'll see you later, then. You know where we are in case you happen to change your mind.'

'Ok.'

I present my cheek, but she bypasses it and goes straight for the lips, giving me a lingering kiss followed by a departing peck on the tip of my nose. Something to remember her by.

That and her perfume.

'See ya, Dom.'

'Yeah, see you later,' I call after her, taking the opportunity to check out her bum as she leaves the room.

You know, it's kind of nice that her novelty has yet to wear off. I still find myself sneaking a peak at her when she's getting undressed, even though I've seen what's underneath about a hundred times before. And every now and then I notice something new about her that I haven't noticed before, like the way she sometimes nods or shakes her head in response to a conversation on a soap opera because she's so goddamn drawn into it, or the way she always brings her spare hand to her mouth when she's laughing on the phone. I tell you, she's pretty fucking special, and I know I've landed on my feet with this one. Or landed on my arse as the case may be.

'He's not coming out, then?' asks Bertie.

'No, sorry guys,' Sarah apologises. 'I'm sure he will eventually. Just give him time.'

The Bertmeister looks more gutted than the rest of them. I guess when your trips to the pub are as infrequent as his are, it's quite a big deal if one of the crew doesn't turn up.

'I'm worried about him,' says Gaz. 'He hasn't been out much since the accident and he hasn't once been to the pub. He used to pretty much live in here at the weekends.'

'Yeah,' agrees Yeti. 'Are you sure he's ok?'

'He seems ok in himself,' Sarah tells them. 'It's not like he's miserable all the time or anything. It's the chair. I don't think he wants people to see him in it, that's all.'

'But everybody's seen it already,' Volk points out. 'There were pictures in the paper and everything.'

Sarah sighs.

'I know. I've told him that, too. But it's not the same, is it? Put yourself in his position.'

'He's not exactly flying the flag for the disabled community,' says Volk, lighting up a cigarette.

'Why should he have to?' asks Gaz.

'With great power comes great responsibility.' Volk blows a perfectly formed smoke ring, which Gaz breaks up with his hand. 'You know who said that? Spiderman, that's who.'

'Spiderman's dad,' Yeti corrects him. 'Well, his uncle actually, but he was essentially his dad.'

'What difference does it make?' Sarah speaks up. 'This is Dom we're talking about here, not *Spiderman*.'

'All I'm saying is that people in his position should be raising awareness.'

'Why?'

'Because they can.'

'Because they can,' Sarah mimics. 'You do talk some bollocks sometimes, Volkan.'

Volk laughs heartily in a manner that says, "What do you know, you're only a woman", but he ceases the argument nonetheless.

'I'm only parked over the road. Why don't I nip by his house and pick him up?' suggests Bertie.

'He won't come,' Sarah assures him. 'He knows you're here... and besides, I already offered to give him a lift here and back. He'll only have a go at you for pressuring him.'

'Yeah,' laughs Volk. 'If Sarah can't persuade him with her womanly charms, what makes you think you can?'

'Why don't we take the pub to him, then?' is Bertie's alternative suggestion, which is met with blank looks.

'Stupid idea,' he concedes.

'It's not the same without him,' says Gaz, slowly spinning his pint glass back and forth as if he's shaping it on a potter's wheel. 'The conversation is lacking something.'

'Thanks a lot, mate!' blurts out an offended Volk.

'You know what I mean.'

'Yeah, unfortunately I do. You're right. It isn't the same.'

'Cheers for the lift, Dad. Sure you won't stay for one?'

I undo my seatbelt and wait for Dad to get the chair out of the boot.

'No, it'll make me feel old going in there,' says Dad as he parks my vehicle alongside the open passenger door.

'Hey, *I* feel old in there. Come in for one.' My words are strained from the effort of lifting myself out of the car and into the wheelchair. I'm getting better at this manoeuvre, but let me assure you it's still pretty goddamn difficult.

'No, you're alright. Have a good night. You sure you don't need a hand?' offers Dad.

'No, I need to do this on my own.'

He slams the doors shut and gets back in the car. He checks his mirrors then pulls out into the road, giving me a wave and a smile as he speeds away. Once he's out of sight I swivel myself towards the pub and wheel myself forward, trying to ignore the inquisitive stares of the group sitting at the front table as they peer through the window at me like they've never seen a man in a wheelchair before. It takes a little help from the bouncers to get up and over the step that marks the pub's entrance, and then I'm back inside my old stomping ground again. And it's still just as smoky as it always was, even at my lowly level. Everybody's eyes are a little red from the alcohol and the fumes.

As I glide past the bar it occurs to me that getting served is going to be a problem. My head doesn't even reach up to the bar and I can't see the staff thinking to look over the edge on the off-chance there might be a midget or someone in a wheelchair down there. I scan the pub for the others and am pleased to see that even in my absence they've gone for our usual table. They look deep in conversation, a serious one too by the looks of it. This is good, it means I can surprise them. I've been building up to this for weeks now, for this very moment; the moment I will announce my return in the only way I know how.

I reach up with my right hand and grab the handrail that traces the perimeter of the bar, its polished iron surface cold against my sweaty palm. After locking my wheels in their present position, I place my left hand on the chair's armrest. Tensing my upper body, I start to lift myself out of my seated position, my muscles straining hard against the weight that dangles below. For one horrible second it looks like I'm not going to make it, my strength deserting me as I begin to sink back into the chair, but then the adrenaline kicks in and I think back to all those days spent doing one-armed press-ups when there was nobody else in the house. *I can do this!* I tell myself, and I *can*, rising upright, pulling myself forward slightly, breaking free from my chariot.

And then I'm standing, back to my rightful position, propping up the bar, indistinguishable from the pissheads standing to my left and right. I look over to the table, but they still haven't seen me. They remain oblivious. Not to worry, it will make my entrance all the more spectacular. I put my left leg out in front of me, still clinging doggedly to the bar in case it can't take the weight. Little by little, I start to ease my grip, rocking forward slightly, testing the waters. But it holds firm, just as it did this morning in the house.

I let go of the rail, stepping out of my safety zone in the literal sense and take another step, more of a shuffle really, all the time feeling like Bambi on the frozen pond. I'm concentrating so hard on each step that I don't initially notice that the others have seen me, don't notice their eyes widening in disbelief as one by one they realise what is happening. Gaz is getting up out of his seat to help me, but Bertie puts a hand on his shoulder, pushing him down, and I can read his lips, 'Let him do it alone, Gaz, he needs to do it alone.'

Yeti has his hands over his mouth, rubbing his eyes every now and then to check that he isn't dreaming, sniffing the contents of his bottled beer in case it has been spiked with hallucinogenic drugs. Then there's Sarah, gazing at me like I've made a miraculous recovery from the latter stages of a terminal illness, a smile of love and encouragement painted across her angelic face, arms already open, ready to welcome me in on my arrival. And Volk, good old Volk, he's still trying his best to look cool and collected, but it's all too much for him, the tears streaming down his face as he nods proudly.

And then I'm there, the final couple of steps proving too much for me as my legs give way and I fall forward into their open arms, a grateful mass of limbs that cradle me, hold me, never wanting to let go.

'Welcome back,' they cry as they embrace me, their tears of joy wetting my face as they hold me close to them.

'You see!' I yell defiantly. 'What do those doctors know? I told you I could do it! It takes more than a severed spinal cord to keep me down!'

As if! This ain't fucking Hollywood, you know. I take a deep breath, then wheel my way over to them. The other punters that block my path edge back towards the wall when they realise there's a Dalek in their midst, their hands held high and out of the way, in case paralysis is some sort of contagious disease. I feel kind of like Moses as the crowds part before me, everyone shepherding each other out of the way to let the cripple pass through. But my progress is halted by the step that runs the length of the pub and separates the split levels. It's only a small step, although it's large enough for people to trip over (I've witnessed this with my own eyes, it's fucking funny), but for me it might as well be the size of a cliff.

'You could at least have chosen a table I can get to!' I bellow from my lowly position.

They all turn around wearing various expressions of shock.

'It's about fuckin' time you made an appearance,' is Volk's warm greeting. 'We thought you'd become a recluse.'

'Good to see you, too!' I grin back at him.

'Here, I'll try and get somebody to swap tables with us,' says Bertie.

He goes off to have a word with a group of guys at one of the lower tables and before we know it we're swapping seats. It's a good plan, except for the fact that it isn't a fair deal and Gaz is left without a chair.

'Don't mind me, guys,' he says, shrugging his shoulders. 'I suppose I might as well get the next round in. What's everybody drinking?'

Believe me, hearing those words after all this time is music to my ears.

'If I remember correctly… a pint of Social-Skills for Yeti. A pint of Elaborate-Dancefloor-Moves for the Bertmeister, and… how could I forget? A pint of Prolonged-Sexual-Performance for Volk.'

'What about me?' asks Sarah.

'Bacardi Breezer,' I guess correctly.

'And what about you?'

'Er, it's a bit early in the night for a pint of Make-A-Twat-Of-Myself, so better make it a pint of Social-Skills, same as Yeti.'

'So five lagers and a Bacardi Breezer, then?'

'Basically, yeah.'

Gaz goes off to join the queue at the bar and I find myself wondering whether his technique has improved at all in the last few months, otherwise we could be in for a long wait. Something tells me he's probably got worse. It's not that he has a pathetic physical presence or anything; his problem is that he doesn't use his politeness to his advantage.

Years of practice have shown me that by far the best tactic for getting served is to try and push your way as near to the front as possible, looking all the time for opportunities where fellow queuers are going to have to step aside to let people carry their already purchased drinks from the bar and nipping into the gap before it closes. Once you're there you must wait patiently for one of the staff to ask, 'Who's next?' this being your signal to point at one of the people either side of you and announce that 'I think this guy/girl is before me,' irrespective of whether the server is looking to serve you or not. The result of this is that said guy/girl will get served immediately (thanking you for your politeness in the process), and you will almost certainly be seen to next. Thus you get your drinks quicker than you deserve to and everybody is left thinking what a thoroughly nice person you are in the process. Waving a twenty pound note over the bar? Forget it. Contrived politeness is the only way to go. The reason Gaz always takes so fucking long is his mass overuse of the line, 'I think this guy/girl was here before me', especially if he's surrounded by women.

'At least you'll never have to worry about saving me a seat,' I joke. It looks increasingly likely that, true to form, Gaz will be taking his time.

The others look unsure as to how to react to this statement. I guess it's going to be a while before they feel comfortable laughing at my expense again. It's almost like the atmosphere when someone brings a friend along that nobody else has ever met before. You're always chatting away by the end of the night, but the early stages are hampered by not knowing what their sense of humour is like and you find yourself holding back a bit in case you offend them. You certainly can't take the piss out of them, not for the first hour or so at least. And that's what it's like now. These people I've known for about seventeen years (Sarah excluded) have no idea what to say to me. To be fair to them, it must be a bit of a shock to suddenly be sharing a table with Stephen Hawking. Well, a young Stephen Hawking. And one without the robotic voice. Or the intellectual ability. Nothing like Stephen Hawking, in fact. But the good thing is, when we're all sitting down, I almost feel normal again.

'Hey, guys. You don't have to worry about…'

My planned speech of reassurance is nipped in the bud by a large hand on my shoulder. We all turn around to see who it is and once again we're greeted by a familiar face, a previous bundling victim. It's Bummole.

'Alright lads?' he says, delivering a quick glance around our group to acknowledge us.

'Alright Bummole?' is our staggered reply.

I wonder what the hell he can possibly want, especially after what happened to him the last time he talked to us, but it appears all he's after is a no-hard-feelings handshake, offering me one of his big paws. I grasp it tentatively.

'Who's laughing now?' he chortles as he vigorously shakes my hand.

'Well, nobody I hope.'

I mean it, too. It would be nice to think that me being unable to walk isn't particularly funny. But they say that he who laughs last laughs the loudest, and Bummole is laughing pretty fucking loud. I don't think he means anything malicious by it but, as before, he looks as though he's had a few and I don't think he's going to stop in a hurry.

'Anyway, good to see you out and about again, Dom,' he snorts, patting me on the back so hard you'd think he was trying to save me from choking.

'Likewise,' I reply. 'See you, around Bummole.'

'Yeah, see ya.'

Bummole walks off, still happily chuckling away to himself.

'Shall we?' suggests Volk.

'Nah. We'd only get thrown out again.'

'What was that guy's name?' Sarah asks me.

'Who, that guy there?'

'Yeah.'

'Bummole.'

'Bummole?'

'Yeah, Bummole. As in bum *hole*. It's a long story, and not a particularly interesting one. I'll explain later.'

'Ok.'

Gaz arrives with our drinks. All of them, too. He's managed to swindle himself a tray to carry them on. If there was ever a man who shouldn't be entrusted with a tray of drinks it's Gaz, but he's done himself proud and the glasses aren't swimming in their own liquid, they're merely paddling.

'Before you sit down, Gaz… not that you can anyway,' says Volk, suddenly remembering the lack of a spare seat. 'But before you do… don't you think there's something missing?'

'What's that, then?' enquires a puzzled Gaz.

'To celebrate Big D's return to the pub, don't you think this deserves a toast?'

'No,' Gaz replies firmly, quickly cottoning on to what Volk is suggesting. 'Not again. I ended up losing it last time!'

'Which led to you getting it on with Kate,' I remind him, 'in a roundabout way at least.'

'The answer's still no.'

'Do it,' we tell him.

'Come on,' he whinges.

'Do it.'

'Come *on*.'

'Do it!'

'Ok, ok!' he caves in once again. 'But I promise you, this is definitely the last time.'

'I seem to recall you saying that before,' I tell him.

'I mean it this time. I'm getting a new one that doesn't come off and I'm getting it fitted next week.'

'You mean no more *ear's to…*?'

Gaz shakes his head.

'No way! Don't do it, Gaz!' I plead in melodramatic tones.

'You can beg all you like, but it's a small sacrifice compared with the benefits of a more realistic-looking ear. So you'd better make this one count,' Gaz tells us.

'Don't you get to keep the old one?' asks Yeti.

'Yeah, of course. But don't expect me to carry it round with me just so you guys can drink from it!'

'I'll get this round in,' offers Bertie. 'Six vodkas, is it?'

'Make it After Shock this time,' I instruct him, 'seeing as it's the final one and all.'

Gaz opens his mouth to remonstrate but then decides against it, the significance of the occasion outweighing his need for a clean ear.

'I'll give you a hand, Bertie,' says Sarah. 'After the length of time it took Gaz to get served I think you might need a woman's presence.'

She's right, you know, women always get served quicker at the bar. Sarah and Bertie leave their seats and Gaz wastes no time in slotting into one of the empty spaces. And so it's back to the four of us, the regular Friday night crew of old.

'So what you been up to, then?' Volk asks me. '*Besides* from shagging Sarah. You *are* still able to do...?'

'Yeah, yeah,' I butt in before he goes into any more detail. 'I've been writing a book. Well... *speaking* a book would be a better way of putting it.'

'How do you mean?' Gaz looks puzzled.

I pull the Dictaphone Sarah bought me a few weeks back out of my coat pocket and place it on the table. I always carry it around with me, on the off-chance I might get inspired. It hasn't happened yet, but that doesn't mean it won't.

'It didn't take me long to realise that I can't write for shit,' I say truthfully. 'But I can talk for England, so this seemed like the perfect solution. Oh yeah, and Bertie contributed a chapter about himself, because he thought he wouldn't feature enough otherwise.'

The three of them frown with incredulity.

'Let's hear a bit, then,' requests Volk.

'Nah,' I say, going all coy. 'I'd rather wait until the whole thing's finished.'

'But that's gonna take fucking years!' protests Volk. 'Go on, play us a little bit.'

'Yeah, go on Big D,' says Gaz.

'Fair enough. I'll play you the beginning… that's probably the best bit.'

It takes bloody ages to rewind the tape, way too long for my liking as it gives them time to build up their expectations.

'Ok,' I declare as the tape clicks back to the start of the side. 'I have to warn you, this is only the first draft and…'

'Just play the fucking thing!' Yeti blurts out.

We all turn around and stare at him, and he sinks quietly back into his chair, tilting his head forward so that his curtains draw over his face, which is red with embarrassment.

'Listen to this, guys.'

I press the play button. It's never nice listening to the sound of your own voice, but I know the others will only be hearing what they always hear.

"If we're going to go about this in the proper fashion, I suppose I ought to start by introducing myself. Although you probably already know me anyway, or know *of* me at least. You bloody well should do. Unless, that is, you've been so absorbed by your own self-importance for the last six months you've become blind to what's going on in the big wide world around you. If that's the case then it's time for a reality check; a big one at that. Because the thing is, most people seem to know me these days. For the life of me, I can't fucking help it.

It's like, normally, when you roll into a place, people try and suss you out, form that all-important first impression. But for me it's different. They don't need to form an impression, because they already have one. They've already made up their minds.

I guess that's one of the problems with being famous."

I'm faced by perplexed looks, all three expressing bafflement in their own familiar way. Gaz cocks his head at a funny angle,

Yeti looks for the answer in the wet patch beneath his pint glass and Volk peers down his nose at me like I'm some sort of cunt.

'Hey… don't worry lads,' I reassure them, pushing down on the air with my palms like I'm silencing an imaginary audience. 'I'll get one of those ghostwriters to make it sound better later.'

Acknowledgements

Thanks must go to Joy Tibbs for her editing services, and to Luke Westwood for the cover design. Thanks also to the usual people, who know who they are, and anybody else who thinks they deserve it.

Coming soon from Mark Fieldsend

Men of Few Words
Out of Mind

Lightning Source UK Ltd.
Milton Keynes UK
UKOW03f0909220814

237366UK00002B/18/P

9 781784 079109